It Takes Two

It Takes Two

a
novel

BY Elliott Mackle

alyson books
los angeles | new york

MANUFACTURED IN THE UNITED STATES OF AMERICA.

THIS TRADE PAPERBACK ORIGINAL IS PUBLISHED BY ALYSON PUBLICATIONS,
P.O. BOX 4371, LOS ANGELES, CALIFORNIA 90078-4371.
DISTRIBUTION IN THE UNITED KINGDOM BY TURNAROUND PUBLISHER SERVICES LTD.,
UNIT 3, OLYMPIA TRADING ESTATE, COBURG ROAD, WOOD GREEN,
LONDON N22 6TZ ENGLAND.

FIRST EDITION: FEBRUARY 2003

03 04 05 06 07 **a** 10 9 8 7 6 5 4 3 2 1

ISBN 1-55583-754-9

LIBRARY OF CONGRESS CATALOGING-IN-PUBLICATION DATA
MACKLE, ELLIOTT J. (ELLIOT JAMES), 1940–
IT TAKES TWO : A NOVEL / BY ELLIOTT MACKLE.—IST ED.
ISBN 1-55583-754-9
1. GAY MEN—FICTION. I.TITLE.
PS3613.A273 I8 2003
813'.6—DC21   2002042689

CREDITS
COVER PHOTOGRAPHY BY STONE.
COVER DESIGN BY MATT SAMS.

This

book is for
WiLLiam G. Thompson.

Author's Note

Friends to whom I am grateful for advice, encouragement and loving slaps upside the head during this book's long course of composition include Jerry Gross, Kathy Hogan Trocheck, Jim Duggins, Nathalie Dupree, Jack Bass, Bette Harrison, John Silbersack, David Loftis, Robert Daseler and George Mende. *It Takes Two* is a work of fiction. The characters and situations are imaginary and any resemblance to actual persons is accidental. I have played fast and loose with the physical geography and racial fault lines of Fort Myers and southwest Florida. The needless sinking of the USS *Indianapolis*, the resulting loss of almost 900 men and the disaster's subsequent cover-up by the U.S. Navy, however, are a matter of public record.

Dawn's Early Light

"WHY DID THE KLAN MARCH ON A SATURDAY NIGHT?" I asked my friend the Lee County detective. "And why the hell did you have to go watch the bastards do it—and leave me high and dry?"

I was trying to keep my voice down. But I was pissed. That February weekend in 1949 was my first real break since Christmas. I'd spent most of Saturday night by myself on a lumpy couch in the detective's rented room. He hadn't come home until long after I sank into shallow, jittery sleep. He'd tiptoed in, undressed quietly and slept noisily in his own bed 10 feet away. He was still snoring and mumbling when I woke up just after dawn. Deciding to let him sleep through whatever was on his mind, I'd pulled on one of his bathing suits, made a pot of coffee and collected the rolled-up Fort Myers *News-Press* off the front doorstep. After two cups and the front page, I dug a beach towel out of the closet, opened a bottle of warm beer, stepped outside and stretched out under a grapefruit tree in the rooming house backyard, alone again.

The second long-neck of the day now comforted my right hand. The bottle caps, church key and one empty bottle lay where I'd tossed them—beneath a spiky tangle of hibiscus, oleander and coral vine bunched up along the backyard's wood plank fence. The beer was a slightly bitter brew called Regal. Regal was once South Florida's standard lager. Today, 50 years later, the brand is extinct.

The detective had started the Ku Klux Klan story two minutes earlier. He was talking fast now, fast and low. He knew I didn't like him canceling our Saturday night date on zilch notice, and without even leaving a message. He knew I was unhappy. He just didn't know how unhappy. Not yet.

And the circumspect detective was just as pissed, having started the day with the discovery that an unexpected overnight guest, after drinking up most of the coffee, had paraded outside and flopped down in the landlady's chaise lounge to breakfast on beer and the Sunday paper.

The backyard had plank fence on two sides. The rooming house and a hardware store's back wall formed the other two borders of the unhealthy patch of grass. I hadn't given the possibility of somebody seeing me a thought.

And that's what pissed Bud Wright off. Loose behavior of any sort wasn't smart in conservative postwar America, even for unmarried heterosexual couples. And Bud set considerable store by appearances. This was a small town.

"Politics," he half growled. "Just politics was all it was, no marching to it. Sheriff got tipped off late yesterday that this organizer was in town from up north. A white man come to find out. Only the white man was set to speak at the youth meeting at the First African Methodist Episcopal Church. Fucking Klan didn't do nothing but walk over to Colored Town and stand around in their bed sheets. I got ordered to go keep an eye out, mainly because of other things that's been happening. That's what the boss said. Didn't want to leave a message at your hotel switchboard. Might of sounded funny."

I took another sip. "So how was it politics?" I'd been serving overseas the past six years. Still, I was vaguely aware that Florida politics meant more than always voting for the ruling Democratic Party. I knew the black-hating, Jew-baiting, Catholic-despising Ku Klux Klan had plenty to do with Southern voting patterns. And I knew that black folks didn't vote in any significant numbers.

But I was a pup then, a veteran fresh from duty in Occupied Japan. Six months earlier I'd finished my last assignment as manager of a Navy officers' billet in Tokyo. The place was little more than a glorified whorehouse. Now, at the age of 27, I—Tampa native Dan Ewing, University of Florida graduate, ex-lieutenant—was running the Caloosa, the third largest commercial hotel between Sarasota and Miami. I planned to make it a lot more than just a glorified whorehouse.

Cocky and well-paid, physically strong but prone to sunburn and before-noon drinking, I didn't feel I was much different from any other American war veteran.

Detective Bud Wright—Christian name Spencer, also a veteran—felt a hell of a lot different. But he wouldn't admit it, even to himself.

"Klan makes a bunch 'a the rules around here." Flexing a 60-pound barbell as he spoke, Bud moved to a sunny patch of dry grass 10 feet away. When he turned to set down the weights, his scalp seemed to flash and gleam beneath the flattop deck of his lightly salted dark brown hair. Slapping his hands together, ready to begin his workout, he grinned and added, "That church meeting last night was definitely politics. Klan ain't too fond of race mixing. Which is why the sheriff phoned me about it special."

"Too bad we didn't get together earlier," I said. "We could've slept at the hotel, in a room with no phone. Or gone out overnight on the fishing boat."

"I told you," Bud answered evenly. "We're going to quit all that. Fact is, we have quit. Last—was it Tuesday? What happened last Tuesday was a goddamn mistake. The End."

As if to punctuate his thought, Bud dropped into a series of pushups on the wiry St. Augustine grass. The bulky muscles of his shoulders and arms moved smoothly, without strain. Wrists and fingers clenched and relaxed, clenched and relaxed. Stocky legs tensed and tensed again, knees up and down, on and off the clipped lawn. His baggy, boxer-type swim trunks—olive drab with a yellow zigzag design—looked like the gear advertised in men's adventure magazines. An ex-Marine, Bud kept a stack of such reading matter under his bed.

To be honest, so did I, back in my room at the Caloosa. I also kept a couple of girlie magazines on hand, mostly for appearances. I was no fool. But I was also used to getting what I wanted.

Arguing about love with your partner is foolish, of course. And this wasn't the first time Bud had tried to butt out of whatever he thought we were doing. Like everybody else he'd been taught that men don't sleep two to a bed. He'd allowed me to stay with him at the rooming house exactly twice, both times when his landlady was out of town. We'd also used rooms at the hotel, the cabin of the Caloosa's fishing boat, even a blanket on an empty beach.

Later, he'd almost always swear that we'd made love for the last time. Actually, he didn't say "made love." He said "messed around" or "mixed it up." Aside from when the lights were off, he didn't use any such words for what he felt. He said, simply, that we were buddies. And tried letting it go at that.

I wasn't exactly in love with Bud that morning anyway. On the other hand, I wasn't taking his hands-off protestations too seriously. Life in the Navy taught me that words often short-circuit what some men are naturally inclined to do. In such cases, direct action beats Hollywood dialog all to hell.

After Bud completed 60 pushups, he rolled over onto his elbows. "Klan's been raising hell these past few months," he said. "That's their politics about any damn thing. They usually promise more violence than they deliver. All the parading is just to scare folks—and to work up a little intestinal fortitude of their own."

"Did they burn a cross at that church?"

"Naw. The kleagle gathered his troops out behind Ellery's truck garage—on Fowler Street, you know? And then they just ragtagged over to Colored Town and came back."

"All wearing sheets?"

"About half. Anybody ever tell you that a fat man in a Klan robe looks like a new Frigidaire with a cattle egret riding on top?" His laugh accentuated the rough-cut geography of his solid, Southern face. He had wide, practical eyes under hairy brows, bare-knuckle cheekbones, square teeth, a Marine sergeant's strong jaw and sandpaper cheeks no matter how often he shaved. A series of ragged bayonet scars began an inch below his left ear and stopped at his belt line. The scars and crew cut were what first attracted me.

"They wore masks?" I asked.

"Most of them," he answered. "Smart ones anyhow. There's courthouse talk about a demasking law being proposed. Think the legislature up in Tallahassee would pass such a thing?"

"Sure," I answered. "When the voters replace all the klegislators."

He laughed again. He was swinging his arms in circles. I asked if he'd seen anybody he knew.

"One from up the river," he answered. "Name of Davis. That I played baseball against. He's on somebody's grove-tending crew now. Was 4F in the war. Never amounted to much. Also a kid that pumps gas at the Texaco. And one old boy that clerks at the courthouse. Name of Leon Featherstone. Don't you figure he'd have better sense than to get himself involved in any such thing, being a public servant and all?"

"Sounds like a bunch of real civic leaders," I said. "Keeping the town safe from invasion by President Truman and Duke Ellington's band."

Bud started his sit-ups. "Preacher Pucklet was leading the women. He's pastor out at the La Belle Church of Apostolic Holiness, where my two aunts go. I recognized him right through his disguise. And I think maybe the reverend preacher-man recognized me. He looked kind of shamefaced-like."

Bud punctuated his commentary with a series of pauses and grunts. He spoke with the twangy backcountry accent of the Florida interior. Boss came out *beuss*, sheriff *shurf*, disguise *DIS-guys*.

"You going to draw patrol duty every time the Klan unfurls their sheets?"

Trim and dead fit, Bud wasn't yet out of breath. But the exercise had started tightening his voice. "Use my best judgment," he huffed. "Keep an eye peeled when need be. For instance, just a couple weeks ago they beat up a…a nice colored man. And somebody did burn a cross. In a schoolteacher's front yard. Teacher was white, but she was teaching evolution. Was how I heard it." Bud pulled a couple more sit-ups. "Preacher Pucklet calls evolution godless communism."

"What about the nice colored man?"

"Drank water out of the wrong fountain at Flossie Hill's department store."

"Jesus. That's a hell of a serious business. Damn serious."

"Myers cops wouldn't write up a report. Scared to."

The beer bottle in my hand was empty. I stood up. "You want a brew?"

He waved me off. "I'd rather we go out for some real breakfast," he said. "Wouldn't you?" When I shrugged agreement, he returned to the main subject. "Damn serious if the police, county commissioners and everybody else look the other way when a bunch of no-account crackers start beating up on respectable people."

I dropped down on one knee close beside him. "Cowboy Bud

gonna ride to the rescue? Save the downtrodden? Be a *hee-ro?*"

"Sure, Dan. All by my lonesome." The sit-ups continued, faster now. "Last night's march was probably a one-time thing. And I had my orders. To keep hands off. No interference. Not unless…unless a law got absolutely broke—the boss's law, you understand."

He got to his feet and began to run in place next to the barbell set. After he'd covered about a quarter of a mile, the pay phone inside the rooming house started ringing. I told him he ought to ignore it. Instead, he trotted to the back door and disappeared.

He was mopping his face with a towel when he returned. "There's a couple of bodies they want me to look at," he said, swabbing his big ears. "Street cop is already on the scene. But he's a rookie, the half-breed they hired in November. Sheriff left word that it's more than the boy can handle by himself. Switchboard operator says the neighbors called in about a regular shooting match at a tourist court down on Tamiami Trail early this morning. They need me to write up a report."

"Just a typical Sunday in Myers," I joked, trying to keep it light. "Only you've already worked a weekend shift." I didn't want Bud going anywhere—except maybe inside again, and with me. Still watching him towel off, I gathered up the newspaper. The day was already hot for February. "Did you know your nose is sunburned?" I asked, swiping my hand past his sweaty face.

He ignored the caretaking gesture. "I told my switchboard gal," he said, "how the coroner ought to go and look into it first. She said he's already on his way."

"Get hold of the sheriff on the phone," I said. "Tell him it's your day off. Tell him you've got a wrestling match to take care of."

Bud threw a couple of shadow punches my way. "Shut up, will you?" he said genially. "Right. Yes. Phone the boss up at the Police Benevolent and Protective Convention in Ocala. Tell him I'm gonna be busy taking a long afternoon nap—with a buddy. He'd like that—like to throw me in the holding tank, by the way. While his secretary types up a felony morals charge and a set of separation papers." He rubbed his eyes with his fists. "Shit, Dan," he said. "You got one thing on the brain all the time. You're like a kid."

"Two things," I answered. "You forgot the beer."

He looked down at the grass, serious. "Stow that, will you?"

"What about Matt Ramos?" I countered. "The switchboard gal couldn't track him?"

Ramos was the other half of the Lee County detective squad. He was the junior man, hired four months after Bud.

"Matt wanted to take off today," Bud answered. "Said he needed to carry Delores and the kids out to Buckingham, where she comes from, for some kind of picnic. In-laws and all. Church, maybe. I told him sure."

"What the hell?" I said. "Didn't I hear you tell me last Sunday this was gonna be your weekend off? That you were going off shift three days to spend time with me? Which is the reason why I'm not at the hotel counting bath mats."

His voice, when he answered, came out slightly high. "Sure, Dan. Sure, it's my weekend off. Today's Sunday. But Matt's a married man. A father. Have to give him the benefit. And the Klan deal came up sudden. And so did this shooting."

I tossed the empty bottle under the hedge. "Keeps slipping my mind," I said, pissed but resigned. "Every one of you Dick Tracy types can take off Saturdays and Sundays because there's positively no crime allowed on the Sabbath in Lee. No rape, no aggravated assault, no grand theft. But if some little situation does happen to turn up, it's always duty day for detective Spencer Wright."

Bud snapped the damp towel in my direction, grinning. "This is two bodies and a tourist court full of bullets, Dan. Not a shoplifting case. I've been called in because I'm available and highly trained. And I like making a decent living. Hell, I like this job. You know what I mean?"

I said sure, that my job at the Caloosa was all fine and dandy too. But I also wanted to spend time with my buddy when we both had days off.

He glanced at me hard. "This is time," he said. "And it oughtn't to take all day to write up a Sunday morning shooting."

I folded the towel I'd spread out on the chaise. Bud hefted the unused barbell. "You want me to drop you back at the hotel?" he asked. "Maybe phone you later?"

"I'd rather drive over with you," I answered. "Otherwise, I'll just work."

Scowling, he shook his head. Then, after a moment, he shrugged just as elaborately and said, "Guess it wouldn't be no harm in that. You figure you could stay out of the way while I check the slaughterhouse?"

When I said I thought I could, he winked and grinned. "We better shower and clean up, then. Slip into some decent clothes."

"You don't have any decent clothes," I answered. "Except that golf shirt of mine, the one you stole right off my back last Tuesday."

"Hate to break it to you," he replied, moving toward the house. "You remember that rain the other morning? Had to use your ratty rag to rub down the Jeep."

I swatted his scarred neck with the rolled newspaper. "Do you realize the emperor of Japan's former golf pro gave me that shirt? And you used it to wipe off your rust bucket?"

"We wiped Hirohito's yellow ass," he said, laughing. "Back when we was in uniform."

"The good old days, that right, Sarge?" I answered.

"Bull*shit*, Lieutenant," he replied.

"A shower, though," I said, knowing this sort of byplay lessened our competitive male-male tension. "That sounds like a hell of a good idea."

"Shut up, Dan. We don't have time for that kind of foolishness."

"Yeah, we do."

Once we got inside Bud's room, he stowed the weights under the bed and headed for the shower. When the hot water came on, he adjusted the flow, stripped off his trunks and stepped behind the canvas curtain.

When I dropped the borrowed trunks next to his sweaty

ones, my cock flipped up. Bud's naked ass drew me like a paper clip to a magnet. I stepped up behind him into the long, narrow tub.

"Soap your back?" I said, touching his neck and shoulders.

He stood a little taller. "We gotta hurry," he said. "My back's OK." He turned to face me, the shower spraying his neck and shoulders. His eyes were shut tight, his nipples erect, and his hard cock pointed up like a coat rack. He let me soap his chest and balls for a few moments, then turned slowly away.

"You got any shampoo?" I said, lathering up my underarms, gut and crotch.

"Bar soap's all I use." Bud reached back to touch my erection with both hands. "You're soapy enough, Lieutenant. Ready to rinse off?"

Moving sideways, he edged past me to the rear of the tub. I stepped forward under the spray. My stiff cock nuzzled his hard ass as we switched places. While I rinsed down and turned to face him again, he scraped water off his arms and chest with cupped hands. His dick looked like a stubby pipe left out in the rain. Stepping over the rim of the tub, he began to towel himself off.

We hadn't said anything else. Neither of us was willing to risk a definite refusal. And I couldn't think of any more jokes. By the time I was halfway dry, Bud had put on black socks and khaki boxer shorts and was buttoning the cuffs of a freshly ironed business shirt. A cotton pup tent rose between his open shirttails.

I stepped into my Navy-issue shorts. When they settled around my waist, my white tent matched his tan one. Pulling up my pants, I forced my tent pole toward the floor.

"That a Klan hood you're wearing down there, Sarge?" I said, pointing with my thumb. "Over your cattle egret?"

Already blushing, he grinned when he answered. "Could be a new-model Hotpoint stove, feels like to me. Might have to try it out sometime."

Flattening his tent as I had, he buttoned the front of his shirt, zipped up his pants and buckled his belt. "Good thing we got this situation on ice now. You ready?"

"Meaning we'll keep it for later?"

Touching my shoulder gently, he turned me toward the door. "I didn't say that."

"I like your cow bird better without the hood."

"I like you better in my Jeep," Bud said. "Let's go."

A^{mBu}sh

ROOKIE COP WALTER HURSTON WAS taking abuse from an angry
white woman when we arrived. Hurston was 20 years old, solidly built and just over five feet tall. The half Filipino grandson of
a pioneer Lee County family, he had shiny black hair,
weightlifter's arms and an olive complexion.

Hurston kept his chocolate-almond eyes on the woman's
flapping jaw until Bud moved in behind him. Though well past
the end of a long graveyard shift, the creases in the rookie's
white service shirt and fawn trousers remained sharply defined.
His spit-shined oxfords caught the mid-morning sun like
smoked mirrors.

The woman looked half a century older than the rookie.
Despite the early hour, she'd gotten herself up in high heels, a
chenille dressing gown—hot pink with lemon yellow lapels—
and enough rouge and lipstick to cover a fire truck. Her unnat-
urally blond hair was rolled into a half moon. Big doll's eyes—
bright as mirrors and rimmed by sooty lashes—clicked open
and shut behind oversize lenses. Too many years under the
rugged sun had blotched and creased her face and neck. She
was a native of Montreal.

Bud had parked the Jeep sideways under a water oak on the
cross street. Through the windshield, I had a clear view down the
long colonnade of the Royal Plaza Motor Lodge. The one-story
structure was built to resemble a Spanish monastery, hence its
red tile roof and yellow stucco walls. Every iron-hinged door,
except the one guarded by Hurston, was shut. Three cars were
parked on the tarmac out front: a dusty Dodge coupe, a prewar
Chevy and a new Ford sedan with the factory sticker still in
place. The shiny black Ford matched Hurston's shoes.

14

When Bud flashed his badge, the woman's attention shifted quickly. "I'm za manager," she announced in a heavy French accent. "And I muz inspect za damage to za room wisout no delay. Before I call za insurance and my owners. You don't believe me, you ask anybody. I have my duties here too. He can't keep me out." She gestured toward Hurston, raising both hands in frustration or polite fatigue. "A big officer on za beat, and always polite before zis. He say he doesn't even has a search warrant. I am Madame Claudette Marie Jenkins. I rent to respectable visitors only. No locals wisout luggage. No police—none, not once, of any color—were ever summoned here."

Like pretty much everything else in the Deep South in the late 1940s, Florida law enforcement was racially segregated. President Truman's integration of the armed forces in 1948 had been tepidly matched by a few progressive cities in the region. But Fort Myers wasn't one of them. Excepting three black maintenance men, two light-skinned officers of Cuban descent and the Amerasian Hurston, the Fort Myers and Lee County police forces were as lily-white as the most venomous Klansman could wish for.

Mrs. Jenkins' motor lodge, like her freckled skin and some of her clientele, was unofficially beige. Catering mostly to discreet Northern and Midwestern tourists who arrived with confirmed reservations, the Royal Plaza occupied a choice corner along the four-block stretch of South Tamiami Trail that divided the white section of Fort Myers from what was then called Colored Town.

After worried neighbors and one terrified guest phoned the police to report predawn gunshots, the police dispatcher sent Hurston to investigate. (Under the direction of a white sergeant, Hurston and the two Cubans were routinely assigned to Colored Town.) Hurston was no dummy. One glance at the bodies told him he needed to call for a backup. A *white* backup.

I heard Bud ask Mrs. Jenkins to either wait in her office or join the neighbors gathered across the street. He added that he'd consider it a personal favor if she kept the others from getting in

elliott mackle

the way until the coroner arrived to deal with the bodies.

"*Mon Dieu!*" she screamed. "So zair is not just one. Zat, zat…little officer over zair, he would not say to me. *Merde!*"

"I hadn't counted noses, yet, ma'am," Bud replied genially. "But I'll keep you posted."

Once Mrs. Jenkins retreated to her office, Bud returned to the Jeep, winked in my direction and unzipped an old briefcase he'd brought with him. The leather bag contained pens, pencils, clipboard, evidence bags, tweezers, magnifying glass, a war-surplus automatic pistol, cartridge magazines and an FBI-style shoulder holster.

"Got me some work to do," he said in a jaunty, pleased voice. "You sit tight. Don't look like it'll take all morning."

I'd already unfolded the borrowed newspaper. The sports page carried headlines about a long-shot winner in the previous day's stakes race at Hialeah over in Miami. "Better not," I murmured, careful not to look at him. "Somebody owes me breakfast."

By the time I'd read through the racetrack charts and started on the state high school basketball scores, the coroner arrived. Familiarly and maybe inevitably known as "Doc," Lemuel Shepherd Jr., MD, drove a battered battleship-gray Packard hearse with crimson crosses neatly stenciled on each door. The roof was fitted with a revolving red light and a siren that squealed like a terrified pig. Doc stopped the hearse in front of Mrs. Jenkins' office and shut off the siren. The rustle of palm fronds and oak leaves in the light morning breeze was suddenly audible. Doc set the noisy parking brake, then opened the cranky left door.

"Mr. E-e-wing!" he called in his honking, blurred baritone. "What a pleasure to see you in the daytime. Hope nobody's been—ha ha—shooting at e-e-you."

Doc and his wife were nighttime regulars at the Caloosa Hotel. He played poker a couple of evenings a week in the private club room hidden behind the dining room. The Mrs. held court among the ladies at the adjacent piano bar.

In a way I liked old Doc. But he wasn't easy to take. His

operatic voice veered from ear-splitting sharpness to velvety ground fog. His eyes—parrot blue, with feathery lashes and plucked looking brows—darted like a couple of caged finches. His head was thin, his hairline high, his brow habitually wet, his ears nailed tightly to his skull.

The rest of him was shapeless and jelly-like. He shrouded his 300 pounds in black broadcloth suits fitted with oversize, rubber-lined pockets for implements and specimens. His sweat-stained shirt collars and the strangulated knots of his wrinkled neckties stayed hidden beneath a cascade of jiggling turkey jowls.

Walking toward me, his attention shifted from my face to the Jeep's empty driver's seat, then quickly over his shoulder to the motel's colonnade and back to me.

He reached out to shake hands, his fingers looking as limp as empty gloves. His steely grip was always a surprise. Without releasing my hand, he drew me out of the Jeep, shifted his other hand to my side and turned me toward the rear of the hearse.

"Say hello to my assistants, Mose and Drackett," he said. "They've been serving time with me, off and on—ha ha—for quite a while." Doc had a nervous cackle he couldn't always rein in. "Boys," he called. "Boys—ha ha!"

Clicking open the coffin-sized rear door of the Packard, he stepped aside and cocked his head, a magician drawing rabbits out of a hat. Two black men, county prisoners in zebra uniforms, had been riding in the rear of the hearse, scrunched down out of sight. Now they unfolded, politely shuffled their feet and showed the expected bits of pink lip and brown teeth. Like most Southern men, they knew the parts they were expected to play in public, and had their step-'n'-fetch-it roles down pat.

"Yassah, Doc."

"Uh hum! As I do say."

"Boys," Shepherd said again. "Mr. E-e-wing is from Tampa. And he's just back from overseas. We got to treat our war heroes right. Smile nice and say hello."

I waved and bobbed my head in the old-time white-boy manner—as thoroughly embarrassed as the other men must have been. "Hey, fellas."

"Sah."

"Sah."

"Now, boys, we'll need both those stretchers," Shepherd continued, not missing a breath. "The Class A and the Class B. You-all can wait till I call you before getting them out. Because first, I'd better go get my hands wet, so to speak." He threw a wry grin in my direction. "Ha ha."

Mose and Drackett nodded carefully.

"Sah."

"Sah."

Collecting dead bodies can't have made for easy duty. But the two trusties' sentences on the blood-and-guts detail—if singularly unappetizing—must have beat the hell out of the hard-time alternatives. Breaking coral rock or chasing water moccasins out of roadside ditches on a chain gang are no pleasure trips either.

Reaching back into the hearse, Shepherd drew out rubber gloves, a physician's black valise and a Graflex box camera equipped with a flash. Then he turned toward the motel room where his duty, in the form of two corpses, lay.

I'd finished basketball scores and dived into the fishing column—red snapper and yellowfin tuna running nicely out in the Gulf of Mexico, snook closer in—when Bud returned to the Jeep. "Both of 'em shot real bad," he said, his voice low. "White gentleman in a business suit and a colored boy."

"The colored boy," I answered. "He's not wearing anything? His birthday suit, maybe?"

"Always got a joke ready, don't you?" Bud rifled through a box of printed Lee County forms stashed under the bucket seat. "Shot through the ear's no joke. There's blood and brains all over two walls of the room. Carpet looks like a Jap pillbox after Charlie Platoon got through with it."

"Which one's shot through the ear?"

it takes two

"The colored boy." Bud selected two forms and replaced the others. "He's got on khaki pants, an Ike jacket and a T-shirt. So get your mind out of the gutter."

"How many guns?"

"One, so far." Bud turned back toward the motel, then paused. "Funny, though. The white guy got hit at least twice. One shot blew his jaw off, and that would finish him. But there's also what looks like a bullet hole clean through his right wrist. So it's a real messy situation. But here's the catch: Walt Hurston found the pistol in his right hand."

"In the white guy's hand, you mean?"

"Yessiree, sir. Doc's taking photos now. Hurston says ain't nothin' been touched. So the thing don't add up."

"Jesus," I said. "I may not want breakfast after all."

"I'm now figuring this could take till 2 o'clock," Bud replied. "So you might want to try to catch a ride back."

I was about to say, "Nah, I'm fine," when the sudden squeal of tires took our minds off dead bodies and breakfast. A hundred feet away, out on Tamiami Trail, a red Ford convertible skidded out of a screeching turn and headed directly toward us. Zigzagging crazily and bouncing across the sidewalk, the soft-top slowed when it hit the soft grass border of the tourist court parking lot, then swerved to avoid the electrified VACANCY sign. The car slid to a shivering stop between Doc Shepherd's hearse and the black Ford sedan. We all ducked.

"Fucking crazy," Bud shouted.

"Who-ee!" Mose called out.

"Church bus be here," his sidekick echoed.

A round-faced white woman threw herself out of the car, hit the pavement running and rushed through the open door into the room where the two bodies lay. Her pink canvas jacket and canvas fishing pants seemed to blur as she moved. The image of an angry flamingo crossed with a stampeding dairy cow flashed through my mind.

Bud took off after her, dropping the printed forms and shouting, "Ma'am, Ma'am."

Claudette Jenkins threw open the door to the manager's office, stuck her head out, shouted "*merde!*" a second time and pulled the door shut.

I couldn't decide whether to stay put, follow Bud or dive behind the Jeep. Everything that happened next happened very fast. So I didn't get a chance to move.

A moment after the Ford-driving woman disappeared into the room, there was a shout—neither a helpless shriek nor a maiden's cry, but something more like a high-pitched bellow. The same voice quickly added, "Ah, you bastard! You swine!"

Something crashed against something else (box camera meeting stucco wall, I found out later) and Doc Shepherd yelled, "No, no, get back! Don't!"

Officer Hurston, instinctively more polite, called, "Ma'am, you don't want to—"

Bud's voice crossed his, "Ma'am, Ma'am, put that piece—"

Doc began to plead. "Please, ah, please put that down, Willene. You're disturbing my...ha ha!"

A shot and an immediate ricochet silenced the men's excited voices. Two seconds later, staggering wildly, the woman in pink burst back through the motel door, an Army officer's revolver held away from her body with both hands as if it was a small rabid animal. Eyes lost in wildness and surprise, she glanced down at the gun. She didn't seem to notice the running figures across the street—nosy neighbors and bystanders forced to seek cover. Instead, she spotted the Jeep and me in it. Her attention focused all too clearly. She raised the pistol and aimed.

Two years battling the Japanese in the Pacific taught me plenty. The first lesson was this: Never look a weapon in the face.

Twisting left and pushing myself down between dashboard and bucket seats, I curled my gut around the gearshift and clenched my ass tight.

As I headed south for safety, a crew-cut blur moved between my would-be assassin and her target.

Ka-thow! The first shot shattered the driver's-side windshield just above my head. The next bullet blew out the

Packard's massive front tire. After that, all I heard was the click-click of an empty weapon and the S-s-s of escaping air. Baritone yells, the sounds of a struggle and Willene's rising sobs followed in quick succession.

I reached up tentatively to check my neck and ear for serious damage. I found nothing beyond a few scratches.

Bud nailed the frantic troublemaker to the pavement within seconds. By the time I turned to see what was happening, she was kissing concrete, her hands pinned to her spine by Bud's right knee. "Cuffs, I need cuffs," he shouted. Beneath him, Willene tossed and gulped air like a gigged grouper.

Hurston snatched the handcuffs off his own belt, handed them to Bud and quickly stepped back.

"Don't you see I need help here?" Bud yelled hoarsely.

Hurston threw a questioning look at Doc. Doc caught it, moved forward and knelt before the prisoner without touching her. "Willene, Willene," he said. "Look at me, Willene."

"Get the bastard off me," Willene cried. "He's hurting my breasts. And get that nigger boy away from here."

"Willene," Doc repeated. "Look here."

All of which might have worked if she'd been ready to cool off. But when Bud lessened the knee-pressure on her hands, she sucked in a breath, rolled fast and aimed a leather hunting boot right at his privates.

Bud doubled over, both hands cradling his crotch. I felt my own balls contract in painful sympathy. I started toward him.

"Take hold of her feet," Doc shouted at Hurston. "But for God's sake be gentle about it." The coroner grabbed her shoulders and, using his substantial weight, forced her back down.

Like a rodeo cowboy securing a calf, Bud clicked the cuffs onto her wrists and then stepped away, one hand open, the other still gripping his nuts. Whirling, he hit the yellow wall of the building with the open hand. "Lady, you don't ever pick up a goddamn gun like that," he yelled.

"Shut up, you bastards," Willene screamed, her back arched in angry frustration. But when she dodged and rolled onto her elbow, she cried out in real pain. "It's too much. I won't have it," she sobbed. "I won't have it."

Doc was again kneeling beside her. "We'll get an ambulance and take you home, honey," he said. "Would you like that, Willene? And who's your family doctor? I'd like to call him for you."

Bud tried unsuccessfully to register an objection. "Doc, will you just hold it? What this lady needs is black coffee and a few hours in a holding cell. She's gotta be tight or doped up on some kind of pills. We need to take her in and book her. Have a matron look her over, draw some blood."

Doc ignored him. Ten years' seniority in the local bureaucracy—to Bud's 10 months—counted for plenty. And with dead bodies cooling where they'd presumably hit the rug, the medical officer's authority at least equaled that of a junior detective.

"Listen to me, Detective Wright," Doc answered pointedly. "What she needs is some rest."

By then, I was few feet behind Bud. Turning to face me, he took a step, halted, reached up and plucked a bloody sliver of glass out of my hair. His face, already pale, turned whiter. He shook his head, looked at me squarely, and asked, "The Jeep windshield?"

"And the tire on the hearse," I answered.

"Good thing it'll drive with the glass folded down." He tossed the glass shard away and shoved the heels of his hands together gently, over his crotch. "Jesus H. Christ," he said, looking me up and down. "You could of been hit. And then what?"

Clearly, neither the damage to the vehicle—nor to his nuts—was his main concern. He was controlling his emotions by force of will. "Jesus Christ, Dan," he whispered, his face going blue-white. "Goddamn, Jesus Christ."

"I'm a lucky guy," I answered, wanting to touch him. "Told you that already. And I ducked. So I'm OK."

Bud took a breath and whispered again, "Goddamn, goddamn, goddamn, Lieutenant. Goddamn fuck."

Doc appeared at my side, inspecting the scratches on my

neck. "E-e-you must have nine lives," he said, his voice for once as subdued as Bud's. "Otherwise, you'd have been—ha ha—my next customer, for sure, if your pal here hadn't moved so fast."

My throat went dry. He'd just confirmed what I thought I'd seen, that Bud had thrown himself between me and the gun. He'd saved my life.

Doc patted my shoulder almost absently and turned toward the hearse. "Mose? Drackett? Now where did you boys go? You safe?"

They were. The trusties had dived under the hearse and were unharmed. Clambering out, they dusted themselves off.

"Sah."

"Sah, we be fine."

"Fine as wine. But we got to get us a new whitewall."

Laughing glumly, Doc nodded and glanced down at the sobbing figure on the pavement.

Bud shook his head again, as if to clear it, then brushed his right hand across his eyes. "Doc," he called. "Who is this lady?"

Turning, Doc touched Bud's shoulder and gently propelled him toward the office door. "Can we talk inside for a minute?"

Mrs. Jenkins banged the door open after one rap and stuck her head outside. "I am packing my bags," she screamed. "It's like a war zone. With Russians! I call my owners from somewhere safe."

"Go comfort that there lady," Doc told her. "Pat her hand or something. She's a little bit upset too."

"Upset, hell," Bud countered, beginning to return to combative normal. "Let's talk fucking hell about upset—excuse my language, ma'am. I get upset when a goddamn bitch invades my crime scene, smashes up a county-owned camera, grabs the weapon we should of got prints off of and starts shooting up the street and just missing innocent people. And when I try to slow her down, she kicks me in the ding-dongs. What a fucking snafu."

Mrs. Jenkins shook her heavily ringed hands in Bud's face. "You watch the language when there's ladies present. Snafu, huh?"

Bud leaned forward. "You didn't hear what Doc said? Get

some smelling salts for the lady on the ground there. Or go finish your packing."

Bud turned his attention on the coroner. "Looks like you know this shooter pretty well, Doc. I got to wonder if she shot up this place earlier. And then drove back in case she hadn't finished the job."

"Sure I know her," replied. "Her people founded this town. Name's Willene Norris."

"Doesn't ring any bell."

"Her daddy was a county commissioner back in Franklin Roosevelt's first term. Ran for the State Legislature."

"So?"

"He owned the Ford agency. And left it to Willene and her husband when he died. Ha ha."

"Rich lady, huh? Used to gettin' her own way?"

Officer Hurston had sidled up behind Doc and Bud. He was nodding. "So you might want to go a little bit easy, Mr. Wright," he advised, keeping his voice low. "Unlatch those cuffs soon as she quiets down some. If you don't mind my saying so. Because Miss Willene and her mama, they know people. They know everybody."

"Unless I miss my guess," Doc added quietly, "that's her husband Hillard Norris in there with half his face shot off."

"Double fuck," Bud muttered. "Destroying evidence could just be the start."

Brushing his hand across his eyes again, Bud walked back to the Jeep and stopped beside me. In the distance, coming from downtown, I could hear sirens. Reports of more shots at the Royal Plaza Motor Lodge had been called in.

Carefully running a forefinger up the metal edge of the shattered windshield, Bud murmured, "Maybe you could just take a walk." His hand was shaking and he wasn't looking at me. "You could catch a ride if you get going pretty quick. Ain't gonna be no time for breakfast."

"Game's just begun," I answered. "Your old coach doesn't mind sticking around for all nine innings."

My argument went nowhere. He looked at me funny, as if

to say that private jokes and private names didn't belong here. "I shouldn't of brought you here in the first place, Dan, and come up on a crazy woman, gunfire and all." Blinking to emphasize the point, he added, "But from here on, you'd just be in the way."

When I started to say something else, he shook his head. "Fact is," he said, "you wasn't even here. Now take a walk." Cocking the thumb of his balled fist toward the highway, he murmured, "This is my job. I got to get statements. It's gonna be cats and rats for the rest of the afternoon."

Though his determined face seemed stuck in neutral, he suddenly brought his hand up, saluted me smartly and threw me a rough grin. "It ought to be routine from here on, Lieutenant. Some kind of crime of passion, looks like. So don't worry. Damned glad you didn't get hurt or nothin'. Now scoot."

Returning his salute, I turned and marched off down the side street.

I ate breakfast back at the hotel.

And
GRAb YOur SocKs

Emma Mae Bellweather, the hotel's big-bosomed boat driver, handed me two telegrams and a housekeeping problem before I'd half finished my delayed Sunday breakfast.

"These wires is marked urgent," she said, thrusting the envelopes forward with one plump hand while shading her tortoiseshell glasses with the other. "Been looking all over the goddamn base for you."

Light-headed and positively famished, I'd settled down at a table near the pool and told the waiter to bring whatever was quickest. Though I'd thought about telling Emma Mae this was my day off, I just smiled and stirred my coffee. We both knew it would be a waste of breath.

Emma Mae was a full-figured girl with a sweet, bovine face and a tongue that could etch glass. A former motor-pool mechanic, she swore more often and more colorfully than most chief petty officers. "Fucking fishing boat," she said, emphasizing the words by slapping bits of sea salt off her faded jacket. "Tub's been leaking like a pair of Cuban heels, boss. We caulked her again, though, so she's tighter than a nun's twat at Christmas time. Everything's under control. Strictly SOP."

SOP, or "Standard Operating Procedure" in military parlance, led directly to what I privately thought of as MSP—"Manager's Shit Patrol."

"But that's only part of my problem, boss," she continued, sinking into the chair opposite me. "Because I got another fuck-up situation that's beating me all to hell." Reaching into the basket of sweet rolls, she explained. "You know, we got two VIP guests, a Mr. and Mrs. Mayson."

"Yes, I've met the Maysons," I told her. "They're staying in a seventh-floor suite and paying top dollar."

Emma Mae explained that the Maysons had come to her a couple of days earlier to charter the boat for a late-afternoon fishing trip for two, for today.

"Now Mayson up and tells me he's invited four more folks to go along. That's six, including, if you please, that no-account weasel Lou Salmi."

Salmi, a wartime torpedo specialist, had served a long patrol under the officer who later became my boss, Bruce Asdeck. Now a swing-shift waiter at the Caloosa, Salmi had spilled coffee while filling my cup not five minutes earlier.

I knew Salmi and the Maysons about as well as I wanted to. Salmi, a George Raft stand-in with low-slung sideburns and pants too tight to ignore, had a smug, narrow face, sleek Mediterranean nose and honey-colored skin. I trusted him about as far as I could throw him.

Jamie Mayson, a pot-bellied machine-parts millionaire from Detroit, had approached me during an afternoon cocktail party in the club room. In a tone of voice he must have used for buying steel by the ton, he said he wanted to watch another man service his wife. The Mrs., a dark-haired Jane Russell type named Barbara, was more than game for it, he said. And he'd heard from his very close friend Bruce Asdeck that Dan Ewing had a real gentleman's touch and might help him out.

I'd have jumped at such a situation a year or two earlier in Tokyo. Performing for a powerful older man like Mayson would have seemed exotic, erotic and attractively risky. But now that I was committed to Bud, even loosely, it didn't tempt me at all.

Finding an acceptable actor for Mayson's little drama was a relative snap. Salmi, the onetime torpedo greaser, enjoyed a reputation as a stud who could fuck a hole in a phone book. As Mayson and I spoke, Salmi was standing four feet away, right behind the bar. So I called him over and made introductions. What else is a hotel manager for?

Salmi's midnight show had clearly been successful enough to take on tour.

"So what's the problem?" I asked Emma Mae. "Assuming you can keep the tub afloat long enough to ferry them out to the Gulf and bring them back?"

"Boat's going to hold together if we haul in fish from dawn to midnight, boss. Pump's working fine. But we ain't got Mae West jackets enough but for four, not counting the old coast guard inflatable you found for me. That leaves us one short, or two counting me, should we encounter"—here she took a bite out of an orange-pecan muffin—"some unforeseen emergency."

Is she worried about pirates? I wondered. *Out-of-season hurricanes? Unexploded mines?* It was true that we needed more life jackets. But it didn't seem like much of a problem, and I said so.

"That ain't all, Dan," Emma Mae replied. "My son-of-a-bitching advance order went in yesterday for picnic boxes. For three—namely the Mr. and Mrs. plus crew of one, plus ice, beverages and potato chips."

When I asked Emma Mae what the charter was worth, she answered that the Maysons were paying the going rate of $50 per half day plus tip. When I asked her what a box of war-surplus Mae Wests cost, she punched me on the shoulder, laughing. "No more than five goddamn smackeroos. But the marine supply store is closed, boss. So's the Army-Navy. This is Sunday, don't forget."

Behind me, Lou Salmi approached with the coffee pot.

"Hear you're going fishing," I said, catching his eye and throwing him a big-brotherly smile.

"Long as Mother Carmen lets me off," he answered, pouring carefully and wiping the lip of the pot with a napkin. "Already got my seasick pills packed."

"Mother Carmen" was our food and beverage manager, a South Texas transvestite who sometimes performed under the drag name Carmen Veranda.

"You think there's enough food in Carmen's kitchen to make up three or four more lunch boxes?" I asked.

Salmi bent closer. His jaw was freshly mowed, his aftershave lotion a blend of testosterone and gasoline.

"There's definitely no shortage of fried chicken, sliced ham for sandwiches, Cole slaw or deviled eggs, boss. I'll ask the good lady to pack the lunches herself. You want I should ask if she scare up a coconut icebox pie?"

I turned to Emma Mae. "Think you can find somebody from the marine supply to lend you a load of Mae Wests—and they could send me a bill tomorrow?"

Emma Mae looked shocked, as if I'd suggested robbing an orphanage. "Guess it can be done, boss," she allowed. "But I don't know that I'll find Cap'n Roy. He could be in church."

"You've got a couple of hours," I said. "He could be home watering the grass."

"Or out fishing," she said, mournfully, as if the whole thing was really a bad idea. "Or banging his sister-in-law, which I hear…"

"I could jimmy the rope shop door," Salmi suggested helpfully. "Probably take me 30 seconds, most of the locks I've seen around this burg."

"Let Emma Mae try first," I answered. "No use you going to jail on a nonmorals charge."

"Will do, Lieutenant," he said brightly. "Lemme go see Mother Carmen about pie and sandwiches."

I picked up the pair of Western Union envelopes and slit the flaps with a butter knife. "Bon voyage, sailor," I said. "Bring home some fresh fish for supper."

The first telegram was strictly routine. An obstetrician and his wife in Scranton, Pa. had a family emergency and were canceling their reservation. The second was anything but:

ARRIVE LATE MONDAY. DISCUSS IMPROVEMENTS TUESDAY.
DELAY RUFFLES AND FLOURISHES.
ASDECK

Bruce Asdeck, managing partner of the Caloosa's ownership syndicate, was headed south from New York. He was ready to talk about changes I'd proposed in hotel operations. The visit was strictly business.

"Ruffles and flourishes," according to our ship-to-shore-leave shorthand, was the code for whores. When I'd managed the New Victory Officers Club for then-Admiral Asdeck back in Occupied Japan, the two of us had worked out a system for identifying guests and the special services they required. "Overnight berth" meant one girl for at least six hours. "Hors d'oeuvres" was a fast-and-loose party that didn't necessarily turn into anything else. "Joe Palookas" were alcohol-abusing officers who threw furniture or roughed up civilian staff. "Kilroys" hung around gawking without spending a dime. A request for "full bath" at the club meant that the guest desired the in-room services of a compliant masseuse. "Shower privileges" substituted a muscular masseur. "Maid service" referred to girls under the age of 18. "Special arrangements" was a request for more than one girl at a time. "Share bath" meant that two grown men wanted connecting rooms. And so on.

The program Asdeck sold his investors in the Caloosa syndicate was considerably more radical than renting geisha girls and private rooms to horny, lonely officers. The Caloosa was conceived as both a year-round commercial establishment *and* as a top-dollar playground for winter visitors. Since my arrival as the new hotel manager that September, I'd busted my ass to make the right kind of changes, changes that would appeal to big spenders as well as to salesmen and manufacturers' agents who worked long hours and often saw clients at night. The improvements I planned to discuss with Asdeck included additional conference rooms on the mezzanine, heightening security and replacing most of the dining room waiters with good-looking waitresses, shapely Doris Day types.

Lou Salmi's return appearance at my elbow reminded me that the process wasn't finished yet.

"Gotta problem, Lieutenant," he growled, leaning down, his shaving lotion louder than his voice. "Got two gents ordering Haig Pinch on the rocks. Gents say they want the unopened bottle set right out here in front a God 'n' ever'body. Guess they don't trust us with their hooch." He leaned closer. "Can't do it," he added, his voice now a mosquito's whine. "You know what I mean?"

"Are they registered as club members?" I asked. "Did they just check in? What's the problem?"

Ordinarily, there was no questioning a reasonable request by a guest. Rules were made to be bent.

"It's Sunday, Lieutenant. Don't want no complaints."

I looked around. Salmi's two thirsty gents—prosperous dentists from Orlando—seemed unlikely to complain to the authorities about illicit bar service.

"Take care of them," I said. "Whatever they want."

Salmi looked shocked. "It's your call, Lieutenant. But I serve hooch out here and anybody can see it—passing by, like from a boat on the water. Could be our ass."

Interpreting the finer points of liquor service was clearly not Salmi's specialty. Just as Salmi closed his gaping mouth, Homer Meadows, one of the older, more experienced black waiters, emerged from the kitchen hefting a tray of lunch plates.

Staff-wise, Asdeck and his first two general managers had been heading the hotel in the right direction. Fighting Southern tradition, they'd replaced half of the property's elderly black waiters with younger white men. Losing the Pullman conductors was an improvement but no real solution. In any case, Homer was a gem, the crème de la crème of the old dining car tradition, his dignified unflappability honed by years of faithful service on the Louisville and Nashville line. I couldn't stand to fire him. And with waiters like Salmi on the loose and too many young women getting married and starting families, I couldn't afford to lose him.

I flagged Homer down, pointed to the pair of dentists and told him to fetch a bucket of ice and an unopened fifth of Haig and Haig. "Tie a linen napkin around the bottle," I said. "Tell the gentlemen it's on the house. Explain that we can't open their pinch bottle because it's Sunday."

Salmi's mouth opened and closed like a beached fish.

"Close out your patio tabs," I told him. "Homer's taking over out here. Go check on his four-top. Then go see if Carmen needs you to pick up any tables for him in the dining room. When you're through in there, get yourself a bath and fresh uniform. Report to the club room at 2. Shift lasts until midnight."

"Can't be done, Lieutenant. Supposed to go fishing."

"Throw a bucket of ice cubes in the tub to cool yourself off," I said. "You get paid to carry trays, not chase pussy."

He smirked. "Get paid for both, Lieutenant." He looked around, proud as a terrier puppy lifting its leg for the first time. "Anyhows, that was your call. You set me up with Barbara and Mr. Mayson last night. And it all went OK, have to say."

I was sick of looking at him, sick of his rancid smell and self-satisfied dodging. The guy thought with his dick—shoving the Mayson assignment in my face. "Get out of here," I said. "Report to the club room as soon as you get back."

I probably should have fired him on the spot. But, like I say, I was still short on decent help, including hotel security. One or two rooms had been broken into. Pilferage was higher than I liked. Brightening up the balance sheet with liquor and girls required countervailing muscle.

For that, I'd penciled in the name of Bud Wright. If Asdeck gave me the go-ahead, I intended to offer him the job of security chief at $10 a week more than I knew he was getting from Lee County. Loyal, trustworthy, honest and all the rest of the Boy Scout agenda—plus his wartime experience as a Marine—guaranteed he'd keep the property battened down, lined up and looking as close to legal as necessary.

And, if he worked in the hotel, maybe even slept in a spare room occasionally, I'd see a lot more of him. A connecting room next to mine probably wouldn't appeal to him right away. But I could wait.

Figuring first things first, I hadn't brought up the subject with Bud yet. Though I doubted Asdeck would balk at any part of my plan, I also figured the proposition would sit better with Bud if permission was already granted and the money budgeted. Asdeck and I would settle the matter on Tuesday.

The rest of the day went like breakfast—small problems to fix, guests to satisfy, staffers to cajole or discipline, account books to tally. Emma Mae's fishing trip took off on schedule, a new supply of inflatable life preservers stowed in the forward cabin. The party returned safely, beer chests empty and fish lockers full.

Following innkeeper's routine kept my mind off Bud, at least for a while. But by 11 P.M., after a room-service supper of broiled, freshly caught sea bass with lemon butter, mashed potatoes and Regal beer, I wanted to see the guy a lot. Though I knew it was cold shower time, I kept drinking. And thinking.

The events of the morning—two dead bodies, prisoners in uniform, a crazy woman with a gun, a man I cared about risking his life for me—all of it had gotten under my skin more than I wanted to admit. I needed to know the reasons behind what had happened. I'd been shot at before. But that was in wartime.

The night my ship was torpedoed in August of 1945, I'd counted dozens, maybe hundreds of men in the water, some dead, others dying. We stayed there, out in the empty Pacific Ocean, for nearly a week, ignored by the otherwise triumphant U.S. Navy. It wasn't long before the sharks arrived.

I'd dreamed of those cruising sharks ever since, dreamed of oily seawater and starry darkness, of watery graves and fire cutting through the war's familiar blackout zone. Worse, I'd dreamed of the temptation to quit fighting, suck salt water and turn shark bait. Though I was usually able to douse the night-time flames with beer, and in extremes with stronger stuff, I had-n't found a permanent cure. Grabbing on to someone in the dark was the only way I knew to shut down the nightmares.

That Sunday night in Fort Myers, I figured the nightmares were due. By the time I popped open a fourth long-neck, the drawling voice of Ensign Mike Rizzo was falling softly on my ears. Mike was goofing off, shucking his sweaty clothes after a long watch below decks, repeating words he'd said there in our stateroom on the USS *Indianapolis*. He was talking about luck, saying that I was his luck, that the gallant old ship was lucky, that he needed to be with me, that I gave him all the luck he'd ever need.

And then, as always, he disappeared. The night turned cold and black, as dark as the Pacific after our cruiser upended and sank. But I could hear Mike calling to me out across the water, calling, "Where's my lieutenant? Why aren't you aboard when you're needed? Who's going to fight the fire with us, ride the ship on down to hell? Ahoy, Lieutenant, ahoy."

Mike always called and called until I woke up, wet all over, my mouth as salty and rotten as a bay beach at low tide.

Setting the half-finished Regal on the room service tray, I pushed back from the table, stood up and pulled a clean shirt and a cotton windbreaker out of the closet. On the way out of the building, I let the desk clerk know I'd be taking a long walk. Then I headed for Bud's rooming house. After what I'd been through that Sunday, I was damned if I'd sleep alone.

THE UNIVERSITY OF FLORIDA AT GAINESVILLE was my hotel school and commissary college. As a Phi Delta Theta freshman, I bussed dishes, peeled spuds and swabbed toilets. Senior year I served as fraternity house manager and treasurer. In between I waited tables at the faculty club, lettered in swimming, joined the Navy cadet squadron and cracked books just often enough to keep the dean in charge of athletic scholarships happy. On graduation day, the Navy gave me a commission, a new set of uniforms and orders to report to the Navy Yard at San Francisco within two weeks. Fifteen months in the Pacific gave me a man's wartime experience. As junior supply officer aboard the *Indianapolis,* I managed the officers' wardroom, whipped slippery squads of stewards into shape, learned to keep the coffee flowing during battle and was promoted the expected couple of notches.

I was nothing special, in other words, except for one easily overlooked detail.

The detail was my relationship with Ensign Mike Rizzo. Mike was a dark, compact, slow-talking mechanical engineer from Baltimore. We began sleeping together three days after he carried his sea bag into my cabin. For almost a year, we were what is now called "lovers."

"Ship is goddamn noisy," Mike had called down from the upper berth the second time we sacked out on the same watch. "Too much racket up here. I got to get some shut-eye."

"That's just old Lieutenant Andrews," I called back over the ship's roaring din. "They say he departed for mid watch one night in 1938—and never reported back. He only comes out when there's kamikazes in the area."

Though I didn't expect Ensign Rizzo to take me seriously,

he did, at least at first. We were both kids, remember, and he was just out of college.

"You're fucking with me," Mike said. "My grandma had a ghost in her attic in Alexandria. Told me she saw it twice, both times on Christmas Eve. Fuck, now I'm scared too. It's like a boiler-plate factory up here."

"Andrews always preferred the upper," I called. "I couldn't sleep either, the first couple of months after I drew that rack. Quiet as the Waldorf-Astoria down here, though."

"We could switch," Mike said hopefully. "Since it doesn't bother you anymore."

"Junior man gets the upper. That's in Navy regs somewhere."

"What?"

"You're junior man. Andrews was the junior man."

"I'm the scared junior man. You mind if I come down there, Dan? That OK?"

Like a kid at a campfire, I was just telling ghost stories, so I didn't think much about it. Swinging his legs around, Mike lowered himself to the deck and turned to face me. He'd sacked out in a tan GI undershirt and nothing else. The dim light was behind him. I pulled my feet up to make room at the end of the bunk. He folded himself into the farthest corner. There wasn't much headroom and he had to lean over to fit. As he settled down on the mattress, his hand landed on my ankle but he jerked it away quickly. When I didn't protest, he put it back where it had been.

"Lot quieter down here," he whispered. "You're right."

After about 30 exhilarating seconds of feeling Mike's skin on mine, I slowly pushed my foot against his leg, as if stretching. Then I withdrew it, suddenly terrified. *Is he testing me?* I wondered. *Or are we both wanting to risk this?* Navy regulations may or may not have dictated that junior officers occupy upper bunks, but they had plenty to say on the subject of sodomy during wartime.

Mike squeezed my ankle gently. I'd never been touched this way, but I liked it and it made no sense to fight what was going on. So I slid my foot under his thigh, amazed at the welcoming, unfamiliar feel of his wiry hair on my naked skin.

"Kind of cramped at this end," he said eventually, his voice and his breath going heavy. "So maybe I'll come up there with you."

"Yeah," I whispered. "I mean…sure."

Taking a deep breath, he slowly slid his hand up the groove between the bulkhead and the mattress. I reached for him and pulled him in behind me. The cabin was hot. We were both drenched in ice cold sweat, the kind that starts in your armpits and between your legs and quickly soaks your sheets.

Curling his arm around my waist as if we'd settled everything, he patted my stomach and spooned himself up against my back and legs. "I was hopin' you wouldn't mind," he added. "Feels a lot safer this way."

"Think I'd better click the lock on the door," I said. "Don't want old Lieutenant Andrews busting in where he doesn't belong."

Men at war take their pleasures, and chances, as they find them. The locked door was a hell of a chance but this was the first trusting physical companionship either of us had found. We never speculated on what other men might be doing behind closed doors, or on what we would do if the war stopped. We didn't have words for what we meant to each other, or for what we did. We never used the word "love."

FEAR Itself

THE WALK TO BUD'S ROOMING HOUSE took less than 10 minutes. I tapped lightly on the door and Bud let me into his two-room efficiency without a word, checking the hallway in both directions before resetting the latch and stepping back. The morning's wing tips, black socks and cowhide belt were gone. His shirt was open. So was the fifth of Bacardi rum I'd brought over the night before. The bottle was half empty.

"Took me all day to mop up that motor lodge," he said, his voice going thick when I asked why he hadn't phoned. "Took twice as long as it ought to have—because of that danged woman rootin' around in the crime scene and all. Wanted to book her, but Doc sent her off in a ambulance. We'll have to haul her ass in yet, for general questioning. Was past 3 o'clock before we got back to the office. Then I had to write it all up in qua-druplicate. Doc was still slicing on old Hillard Norris when I checked the morgue right after 10. Didn't think I should call you at the Caloosa so late," he concluded, slurring the hotel's name, "Caloo-sha."

When he started to say something else, I shut him up by putting my right hand over his mouth and my left hand on his hard-muscled shoulder. He closed his eyes as I eased him down to the carpet.

After switching off all but one of the lights, I knelt down beside him. "Come here, Buddy," I said.

And he did. He stayed stony-faced and stiff-armed at first, but eventually put one hand on the back of my neck.

"Shouldn't of taken you with me this morning," he whispered, tentatively hugging me back. "I put you at a bad risk. Would of been my stupid ass in the cane grinder if you'd got hurt. Wouldn't of ever forgiven myself."

I should have told him right then that the bad dreams were coming on like Jap torpedoes. I should have said I needed him to hold me tight and not do anything else until the sun came up. I might have said I was starting to care for him. I might have asked him to tell me he felt the same way. Instead, trying to make sense of the crazy day, I asked him to tell me about the mop-up and what happened later at county headquarters.

"Thing don't add up, first of all," he said, leaning back a little so he could run his fingertips down the middle of my shirt front, as if counting buttons. "Colored boy and a white man right there in the same room, both of 'em shot to hell. First glance, it looks like the white man shot the other one. Plugged the poor colored boy right through the ear canal. Pretty much like a firing range and he scored a bull's eye."

"Doc knows the wife, doesn't he?" I said. "Wilma? Willie Jean?"

"Willene," Bud corrected. "Willene Norris. Dead man was her husband, Hillard. They got a daughter Hillary. Pretty cute, huh?"

"Rings a bell," I said. "His name does, Hillard Norris. Don't know which bell, though."

"You meet a lot of people," Bud agreed. "Hard to keep track sometimes." His rum-thickened tongue got in the way again: "Some-timesh."

"And he's from around here? What does he do—I mean, what *did* he do?"

"Car dealer," Bud answered. "Rich as grease. Came to the motel last night driving a new Ford and wearing a Hickey Freeman suit. Mrs. Claudette Marie Jenkins was making up stories when she denied lettin' in any guests with no luggage. When we got down to it, she admitted to rentin' to Norris two, three times before. And didn't ever didn't see any suitcases. Looks to me like he was tom-cattin'. His coat was hanging in the closet, along with his necktie. Had a box of rubbers in a drugstore bag right by the bed. One of 'em been used. Doc found it floatin' in the toilet."

"And you said the colored guy was wearing an Ike jacket?"

"Almost like he lived out of his B4 bag. Ike jacket and khaki service pants. Skivvies had a serial number stenciled on the back. I put a call in to Army records."

"No wallet? Driver's license?"

Bud lay back on the rug, his hand now loosely gripping my arm. "No ID at all. Hurston said he's local, and he's running the ID tonight. Weapon could belong to him, a take-home souvenir from the front. I'll go through all that tomorrow, far as I can."

I covered Bud's hand with mine. "So he shot Norris twice? Then shot himself through the ear and put the gun in Norris's hand before he hit the floor?"

"That don't make no sense," Bud replied, laughing and reaching for his glass. "And there's another thing."

"I bet," I said, leaning up on my elbow, putting my hand on Bud's hip to steady myself. "A commie-pinko angle?"

Our faces were close again. I could count the thick hairs of Bud's brows and lashes. He pushed back, sipped the Bacardi, replaced the glass on the rug and licked my ear slowly, up and down. I shivered when his cold tongue hit my earlobe.

"Found a woman's suit jacket in the room," he said. "Jacket

with a laundry mark. I figure to run that down too, soon as…"

"Sounds simple enough to me," I said. "One of the men was in the room with a chippie, hunting for doughnuts. The other man came in—maybe he was the pimp, and the other guy hadn't paid for what he'd ordered. The pimp shot the cheating customer; the chippie shot the pimp and took off. Case closed."

Bud put his hand on my hip, drawing us closer. "The woman's jacket was on the floor, not in the closet. Might as well of been a butcher's apron. Had blood all over it."

"So maybe the chippie got hit too?"

"Wasn't no bullet holes in the garment. We still got blood samples to test. Jacket looked to of been kicked almost under the bed. Doc was taking set-up photos when Mrs. Willene Norris hit the beach. I have to speculate that the chippie left there fast."

"Or the widow Willene leaving the first time." I was so tired I almost giggled. But the pressure of Bud's wandering hand, which had now found the inside of my leg, stifled that.

"Right, yes. Could be. Anyhow, Willene, she kicked up a storm and disturbed the original position of the lady's jacket when she grabbed the pistol. Haven't seen what Doc can save from his photo plates yet. Camera got broke, you know."

Bud's free hand had inched around to my spine, just above the belt, the tips of his fingers moving lazily. "Got to see Doc's autopsy report before I can do much else."

"And your boss," I said, moving as close. "He'll be back tomorrow wanting answers?"

"Guess so," Bud said. "He left Ocala well before the convention got through. Last seen in Tampa. But that was sometime yesterday evening. Be better if he gets back right away—to make a statement."

I made a questioning noise.

His hand was now under my belt, an inch or two inside the back of my pants, pulling up the tail of my shirt. "Reporter from the *News-Press* showed up just as I was climbing into the Jeep to drive home."

"Good thing it still drives," I said.

"Oh, it drives," he said. "Be taking it over to the shop tomorrow, see if they can locate a surplus windshield. Anyhow, this *News-Press* bastard wouldn't let up. Picking and picking, like a buzzard on a highway with a runover raccoon. Kept asking about 'foul play.' He said that a bunch of times. I had to tell him I wasn't at liberty to say nothin'."

"So don't," I said, reaching for his belt buckle, throwing a leg over his hip, wanting only to be held tight.

"We better not," he said. "The window's open."

The window was blocked by thick overgrown shrubbery. Still, I got up, lowered the sash, drew the curtains and returned to his side. I touched the scar on his neck. "The landlady still gone until tomorrow, Bud? That right? And nobody has rented the room next door, at least up through this afternoon?"

He put his hand on my hip lightly, keeping our bodies separated by about an inch. "Can't be too careful. Don't guess you noticed anybody around when you come in, did you?"

Bud wasn't much of a drinker. He said "no-tished."

Answering that except the two of us the whole town was asleep, I fetched a couple of pillows from the sofa, doused the remaining lamp, slid one of the pillows under his head and settled down beside him. "You don't have to do anything," I said. "Just hold me. Don't talk. Wake me up if I start the nightmares again."

And that's what he did for a while, until I dozed off and awoke to the touch of his lips on my ear and his hand on my trouser button.

I moved closer and resettled my arm around his waist. His pants and boxer shorts were gone. His cock was as hard as the bamboo handle of a fishing pole, and about the same stubby shape. Without thinking too much about it, I touched the tip, then explored a little lower. Though the head of his cock was soaking wet, his nuts still hung down in the sack, loose and unready. Moving back to his cock, using my thumb and index finger, I began working the moisture into the flange beneath his

it takes two

short hood of foreskin. Shaking his head, he pulled away.

"You sure you want to get into this?" he whispered.

Circling the corona with my thumb, I said, "You're the one poking me in the belly button, Sarge. I'm just following orders. But, hell, yes, I want to."

He got most of my clothes off, then turned, leaned back with his head on the pillow, and pulled me on top of him. By then I was as stiff as he was, and almost wet enough to get inside without hurting him. I spit in my hand, added that to what I'd produced down below, found the slot and tap-tapped at the opening. He pulled his legs wider. It felt as if he somehow grabbed my hips and cock and pulled me inside him. Saying only, "Uh, uh," he clenched and relaxed with short, rhythmic breaths.

"We ain't keepin' score, Coach," he muttered. "Hit me a home run with that bat you got. We can win…but get my jock off, my strap. Help me."

Leaning forward, I kissed his neck and ears and closed-tight eyes. Pulling out, I took his straining cock in both of my hands, slid the hood back, touched the flange and licked it. He twisted around, as if I'd pinched him hard and he was trying to ride the pain. I touched his nuts. They were drawn up almost tight enough to fire. I pulled on the sack gently, hoping to slow him down. His eyes popped open in surprise. "Could score," he whispered. "You, Coach?"

Easing down until I was nearly on top of him, I swabbed his chest with my tongue, mopping the track of hair that grew between his navel and his neck. When I touched the tough buttons on his chest with my mouth and teeth, he sucked in roughly. Thick sweat ran off his shoulders and gut and down his sides. He smelled like Lux Soap and salt spray and pine tar. I was steaming too, the sweat soaking my undershirt, running off my arms and down the crack of my ass as I plowed his gut with my cock. Rising up to meet me, our heads now side by side, he touched my cock and my nuts just as I had his. After a few seconds of push-pull handling, first tentative, then aggressive, I had to back away from what he was about to do. Understanding me, he slid both his hands around my hips to draw me forward and inside again.

The dark threads on his arms and the steaming carpet in his pits, the stiff crew cut, the fur on his thighs and calves, the dark mat on his ass—the hair on his body was the sexiest thing about him. That and the scar that ran from his neck down his side. I kneaded the scar with my open hand. It was wet now, like his chest, and heaving.

The hot, closed room seemed to move—yeah, I know, a cliché and a cheap one, but true all the same. I was half dreaming, out of my head. The ship rolled in stormy seas and I was with Mike and Bud both at once, riding the built-in lower bunk in officers' country, hitting wave after wave, timing my thrusts to the ship's movement. Both men were under me, both grunting out the kind of words men only grunt to each other. "Yeah, right there, Coach. You got just the spot. Keep on it, Dan. God, God help me. Yeah, yeah. Right in there. I'm dying. Aw, fuck."

The thing worked for a while longer, Bud still wearing his open shirt, me in just my undershirt and socks, the naked Mike Rizzo there with us and then suddenly gone.

Rocking under me, Bud moved faster and faster, taking five or six little breaths, then stopping. Then repeating the series. "Help me, Coach. Keep on it, Coach."

Just when I figured I ought to go for a home run and let the man on third either score on his own or take an out, Bud's movements slowed and then stopped. His prodding cock, hard as a stick between us minutes earlier, softened and retreated. Touching him there, I felt only his coursing, preliminary wet-ness. When I stroked him with my thumb, the pressure quickly returned. I knew what I was doing. Within 30 seconds he was stiff again. He shifted under me.

"Show me," he moaned. "Show me, Coach."

Bud suddenly shook his head and coughed. For an instant, his whole body hardened. Releasing his grip on me, his thick arms fell away, straight out from his shoulders. His palms rolled upward. Christ in a soiled white shirt.

I thought he was about to pop, or popping, and that I would soon follow. But I was wrong—on both counts.

Within seconds, his head turned slowly turned to one side and he passed out for good.

After a couple more thrusts just to make sure his eyes wouldn't blink open again, I rolled off gently, stood up and looked around for something to clean myself with. A discarded set of boxer shorts was the best I could do.

As I moved away, Bud seemed to shiver, so I detoured into the tiny sleeping alcove, pulled the gray Army blanket off the Hollywood cot, returned to his side, lay down beside him and settled the blanket over the two of us. His hand slipped into mine and he pulled me close. "Best goddamn coach in the world," he mumbled. "And don't you forget it."

"Sure, Buddy," I answered. "We'll hit us a coupl'a homers next time. Plenty more balls where that came from."

Feeling safe for the moment, lying skin-to-skin with another brave but sometimes frightened man, I closed my eyes and risked the Pacific's nightmare storms. The walls of the house were thin, and I could hear occasional trucks and cars passing on the street. The wind threw stray branches against the window time and again. After a while I dropped off into a dreamless, waterless sleep.

Perhaps an hour later, a jerky series of groans and splashes woke me. I guess I don't have to explain that I was an uneasy sleeper. Reacting as if fresh nightmares were blowing in off the Gulf, I got to my feet and started moving before I had time to think.

Yellow light, the thin outline of an oblong hole in the darkness, led me to the bathroom door. I tried the handle. Unlocked. Another groan came from inside. I flung the door open. Bud's face hung unsteadily over the toilet bowl. His wrinkled shirt was wadded up in his left hand.

He retched up a ribbon of bile. "Get out, Dan," he said between heaves. "Get out of here."

The sight of him kneeling on the cold tiles woke me up fast. Dropping down beside him, I stroked his naked shoulder. "Hey, Buddy," I began, hitching my voice somewhere between barroom camaraderie and locker-room concern. "What's a matter? Coach is here. Take your time. Go easy."

He steered his face toward me, evidently startled that I hadn't jumped to follow his order. His eyes had red cracks in them. Stray vomit coated his wrung-out mouth and chin and had drooled down the matted hair on his chest and belly. I tried not to think how recently I'd dragged my tongue across that fouled carpet.

Bud lunged heavily at the switch plate by the door, pawing out the light. "I mean it. Get on away. Don't fool with me any more tonight."

I sat on the bath mat, not touching him. "Is this because we didn't finish?"

The room stank of rum and bile. I flushed the toilet and it stunk a little less. He shook his head and shrugged, as if to say he didn't know the answer. After a while, he touched my knee and my arm and put his face on my chest and started heaving again—not vomit but sobs. "You could of gotten killed. It would of been my fault. What if we never…got to, you know, finish anything like what we were doing…again?"

I wanted to laugh. Instead, tears popped out and I half sobbed and half laughed with him. "We will. All you want, Buddy. Any time."

"We ain't supposed to be doing this." He swabbed his mouth with the soiled shirt. "We could go to jail, be charged with degenerate perversion and unnatural acts. I could lose my job, everything."

Bud was right. Florida in the late 1940s was a model of Old Testament intolerance in matters sexual, political and social. Laws on the books criminalized, without exactly specifying, the abominable and infamous crime against nature. Though the laws were selectively enforced, one misplaced hand or well-understood word, one step outside the patriarchal system, one thoughtless, drunken mistake could get a man arrested, his name printed in the papers, his family and career destroyed, his ruin practically assured.

"We just gotta keep our heads down," I answered. "No talking out of school. This is our personal locker room."

"You could of gotten killed," he said again. "Shot by a deeranged female—a crazy widow woman that's hysterical over nothing to do with you, me or the gatepost. Next time, it could be some rabbit-faced cracker wearing a bed sheet. We got to stop this. Got to be friends, is all. So nobody can't say nothing."

I might have told him about my plan to hire him as chief of hotel security. I might have said there's nothing more natural and less degenerate than sleeping next to the person you care about. But I was no crusader. I was just a man who'd run out of luck during the war, a guy who'd found out what he wanted the hard way, and who'd learned that he'd better go after it again when the going seemed right. And I figured Bud wouldn't remember much of this anyway. So I stuck to the original blueprint. I'd tell him my plan when I could back it up with a job offer, with the go-ahead from Admiral Asdeck.

As we rocked in the dark, he kept up his drunken protests that we ought to never mix it up again. Halfway through a confused statement on "manly friendship" and on what he still had "to learn" from me, Bud touched my cock. When I got hard, he obliged me with two or three strokes, but then began to nod off. Switching on a light, I pulled him to his feet, turned him around and guided him toward the cot. After getting him settled under the Army blanket, I found another blanket, returned to the rug and, after a while, heard the reassuring sound of his snoring.

A little before sunrise, I took a shower, dressed, put on a pot of coffee and dug through the medicine cabinet for a bottle of aspirin. The pay phone out in the hall started ringing at 6. I let it ring.

Bud's face, when I woke him, was the color of a bad day— gray to partly cloudy, with storm warnings. He managed to gag down a handful of aspirin with his coffee before demanding to know why I was still there.

"You were sick as a dog," I said. "Just wanted to be sure you were OK."

"Feel like bull crap. But you can't do anything about it." He swigged down more coffee, coughed, stood up, crossed to the bureau and began rummaging for clean socks and underwear. When he didn't find any, he gathered up his clothes from the night before. Moments later, I heard him swear: "God damn, Dan. Fucking son of a whore."

I felt my chest go tight, wondering what he'd found. What he'd found was my Navy-issue boxer shorts, the ones I'd used to wipe myself with after we'd mixed it up. "God damn, Dan. These got your laundry mark and serial number on them and you were going to leave them here? Suppose I sent them out with my stuff and the washwoman saw that? It'd be my ass, sure."

I spread my hands, laughing. "I found a clean pair in the middle drawer," I said. "Must've been your last set. Want to switch?"

He hurled the soiled shorts in my direction. "Weekend is finished," he said, pulling on yesterday's underwear. "You just march on back to your hotel. Maybe we'll get together for coffee next Saturday. Probably not before then. Could get to lookin' funny, two guys hanging around all the time. You know what I mean?"

His offhand, dismissive tone pissed me off more than what he said. Sure, in many ways, maybe in most ways, he was right. But I didn't like hearing him put so much emotional distance between who we were and what we'd been doing.

"Good thing we wear the same size skivvies," I said. "I'll get the ones I'm wearing back to you soon as I can. Light starch or regular?"

He looked uncertain. "You ain't going to send them out, are you, Dan? Those got my serial number on the back. And they're laundry marked too."

"Maybe I'll keep 'em," I answered, stuffing the other set of shorts into my back pocket. "Feel like I'm inside the Marine Corps every time I put 'em on."

"I'm dead serious," he said, smiling thinly. "All it takes is one little thing."

"The hotel laundress can't read her own name," I answered. "Nice lady, and she works hard. She does each load of laundry by hand, but she didn't finish second grade."

"Well, Jesus," Bud answered. "That's all right, then. We don't have to worry none."

"No," I said. "Not about that."

L⚭se Lips 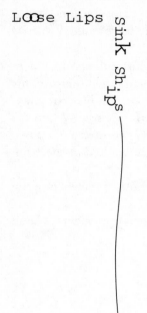 sink ships

SPENCER "BUD" WRIGHT MOVED TO Fort Myers eight months before I stepped off the troop ship in San Francisco. Both of us had been raised within driving distance of Myers—me in Tampa, four counties to the north, him in La Belle, in Hendry County, a few miles east. We joined the Lee County American Legion post independently during the autumn of 1948. We were thrown together by accident almost immediately.

As junior members of an ad-hoc Navy and Marine Corps committee, the post commander directed us to plan a nautical-themed menu for an upcoming Columbus Day barbecue. When the other vets on the committee failed to appear for an organizing meeting at the Legion Hall, Bud suggested I take charge. Nailing down the project's details took 10 minutes and one round of drinks at the bar. Then we ordered a second round and started talking.

The sharpshooter sergeant was surprisingly pleasant company. An attractively built if slightly over-muscled man, he seemed level-headed as a judge: straight thinking, law abiding and conventionally idealistic—in short, an ambitious young cop, and thus about as likely a man for me to get naked with as Harry Truman.

His brown suit, white businessman's shirt and sporty, black-and-white wing-tip shoes were clean and neat. He'd removed his green and peach floral necktie and wadded it up in his coat pocket. The tip peeked out like a pastel turtle's nose. When he reached across the bar to fill his paw with peanuts from a bowl, a leather holster and the handle of a pistol winked at me from under his arm.

After downing my own fistful of peanuts, I asked how he liked working in Myers.

"Better job over here—regular raises, good prospects. I send money back home."

"Home?"

"Mama and my sister."

"You're not married?"

"No," he said. "Not yet."

What a clangy little word—"yet." I asked if he'd also been a detective in La Belle.

"Didn't have none. Force is too small. Sheriff, couple of deputies is all."

"No place for advancement?"

"Right. Yes. Not much crime to speak of. One old lady who taught me sixth grade turns out to be a shoplifter. And Saturday nights there might be a cut-up colored girl lying out behind some juke joint. Domestic entanglements, fights, drunk Indians, that kind of thing."

"No cattle rustling?"

"Some. Pretty easy, with land unfenced and all." He coughed, then added a bit of judicious, apolitical ass covering. "Not that the open-range law necessarily needs changing, you understand."

This servant of the public trust didn't know me well either, of course.

"Doesn't sound like Tom Mix and Jesse James," I said.

He shook his head. "The Lee County job turned up, I came over and took a couple of tests, got me some books and I'm set."

"Enough serious law-breaking to keep you busy in Lee?" I asked, wondering whether he might show up to investigate my club room one unlucky day.

Hunching his neck down and glancing around, he drew his hands up into machine-gun position. "Ack, ack, ack, ack, ah, ah, ah," he whispered, grinning like a maniac and fanning the crowd with flaming lead. "Pow!"

Damn, Dan, I thought. This guy's got surprises up his sleeve. He may be a jarhead, but he's no humorless grunt. Probably brave as hell. Probably earned a chestful of decorations on some stinking beach. Took out a pillbox, won the goddamn war single-handedly.

Quit that, Lieutenant.

Nothing here for you, nothing beyond another vet to say hello to. It could get in the way, you hanging around with some law-enforcing stiff who works for the sheriff. Some yo-yo who's gonna get married in a year or two and have a baby the next month and need a pay raise. He'll be looking for some way to fill his book, and into his empty mind will pop... Just quit it.

"On downriver from La Belle..."

Wright's shift in topics had passed me by. But the strand became apparent soon enough.

"We might stay out on the river all night, running dead slow," he said, his voice softening. "There'd be gators out there. We'd see their red eyeballs in the lantern light. And we hauled over to Lake Okeechobee a fair amount of times too."

He was talking about fishing trips before the war, being out on the water with his hometown buddies on the Caloosahatchee River and out on the vast shallow lake that feeds the Everglades basin.

But his memories triggered my own—the dark water of the

empty Pacific, floating dead men and circling sharks, loneliness and loss.

Bud noticed, and made the right noises, inviting me to lay
out the details of my particular hell if I wanted to, or to keep
silent. "You was in the Pacific the whole war?" he said.

I said I'd spent some time at Peleliu, been in and out of
Guam and Oahu and a few other islands, but was mostly aboard
a heavy cruiser. I didn't go into details.

"Fishing was great in the bay, though," he continued, picking right up on my reticence. "Nice mangrove snapper, so thick
they'd practically jump into your hand. And we caught mullet
and striped bass. Been a long time since I was out there, though.
But, to make a long story short, I never did get out in the Gulf."

"We fished out in deep water a lot when I was a kid," I said,
catching the conversational ball and tossing it back. "My uncle
had a Chris Craft he docked in St. Petersburg. Now I've got one
of my own, or the hotel does. Did I tell you I manage a hotel?
The Caloosa? Our boat driver's taken me out a couple of times,
showed me some fish holes. You want to go out to open water
one day?"

"When?" he answered. And I saw from his eyes and the set
of his jaw that he wasn't kidding or just being polite.

I suggested the following Sunday morning. "Unless you got
to be in church," I added. "Course the boat leaks and the motor's
cranky, but we'll be all right if we stay in sight of shore."

He said Sunday morning sounded fine, adding that he had-
n't been to church much since the Japs quit shooting at him. And
so the date was fixed.

The hotel's boat was a classic 38-footer built by the Wheeler
Brothers in Brooklyn, New York, in the decade before the war.
Low and wide-beamed, she had a flying bridge for spotting game
fish and an open afterdeck with outriggers and fighting chairs.
The original owners were well-to-do Germans who wintered in
Palm Beach. After Pearl Harbor, the Coast Guard comman-

deered the vessel, used her as a submarine hunter around the Florida Keys, and declared her surplus when the absent owners failed to immediately reclaim her at war's end.

Casting off from the hotel dock right after breakfast the next Sunday morning, Bud and I were rolling through moderate Gulf chop an hour later. We rode on the fly bridge up top, and from there the view of the tree-lined shore and the open horizon was great. I steered. Bud grinned like a boy, flattening his hand in the wind and flying it like a dive bomber as the boat pitched up and over the swells.

When the wind from the northwest dropped, I headed the boat into it, set the throttle to trolling speed, fixed the rope yoke Emma Mae had rigged for the wheel—the devices together formed a primitive autopilot—and led Bud down to the afterdeck.

After years of turning raw sailors into messmen and supply clerks, I knew better than to merely bait a hook for him, drop the line overboard and let him jiggle the pole until a fish wandered by. Instead, I walked him though as much as I could remember of what my Uncle Bob taught me. I explained when to use an outrigger and how to rig it, how to let a fighting chair and a sturdy reel wear down a big tuna, and the subtle nip-and-bob signals ocean fish inadvertently display when going after bait. We talked about gaffs, nets, wire leaders and weights, not to mention how to kill the motor if the captain should accidentally fall overboard.

At the end of the short seminar, after he'd asked about a dozen questions, Bud went inside the cabin, stripped off his shoes and socks, and exchanged his creased denim jeans for a pair of cutoff khakis. When he returned and settled down in the port side fighting chair, the cuffs of his white boxers formed a border around the inside of his loose cotton shorts. I have to admit the sight was hard to ignore.

I'd already stripped to T-shirt and bathing trunks. Once Bud got a fishing pole in his hands and carefully swung the baited lure overboard, I stepped behind him, raised the heavy metal and wood lid of the ice chest and pulled out three long-necked Regal beers. Popping them open, I handed one to Bud, slid another into a cutout groove in the arm of the starboard chair and poured the contents of the third into the roiling wake behind us.

"Lures fish," I explained. "Draws 'em just like blood draws…sharks. They can smell it a mile away."

"Who taught you that?" Bud wrinkled his eyebrows.

I flipped the empty away from the boat. It skipped lightly from wave top to wave top, then dug in, splashed and bobbed to a stop. "My uncle in Tampa says this is the secret to catching big-ass fish."

"God damn!" Bud replied. He stood, carefully balancing the rod and reel in one hand. "Let me try it. I'm learning something now." Tipping the bottle up with his other hand, he swigged deeply, then emptied the remaining brew into the wake. Deftly side-handing the empty bottle overboard, he sat back down—and a hungry, sizeable dolphin immediately struck his hook, snapping the tip of the pole and ripping out line.

"Fuck me to kingdom come!" he shouted. "Your uncle must be the best goddamn fisherman on the coast."

Bud jerked the rod up to set the hook and began to reel in line, pulling and relaxing like a natural. I quickly set my rod in the holding cup and got behind him to offer suggestions, few of which he actually needed.

Within 10 minutes, his eight-pound fish was gaffed and iced down. We trolled north along the coast for another hour but didn't get a second bite. At Boca Grande, I headed the boat back to the southeast, keeping the wind behind us. Three more Regals offered to the waves helped only a little. Bud landed a kingfish and I took two small but eating-size black sea bass at the fish hole Emma Mae had noted on the charts. And that was it—not a washout, but no big haul either.

Still, it was clear I'd made a convert. After I put the captured bass to bed, Bud leaned back and said, "This is better than I expected. Fucking better. And not only because we got us a fish or two."

Nodding, I sucked on my beer and let him talk.

"Because you know," he said, "you remind me of a man back home, my baseball coach at La Belle High School. He looked kind of like you—that light red hair you got, and you're both on the weedy side, like runners."

"Swimmer," I corrected him. "Medium to long distance."

"No shit," Bud said, sounding impressed. "Who'd you swim for? You set any records?"

I admitted that I'd swum one dual-meet record in high school but won nothing except letters after moving to varsity level. My pair of wartime state records hardly seemed worth mentioning.

"Coach Andy led us to the league championship in 1942," Bud replied, being careful not to top me. "That was my senior year. He always found the gasoline to get us to games in Myers and Bradenton. I probably wouldn't of graduated at all except he tutored me some in chemistry and math."

"He sounds like a good coach."

"He was. And you been coaching me good too. You explained how the equipment works, what to expect. You're telling me about things I don't know. And that's what Coach Andy did. Shit, I couldn't catch a fly ball with a butterfly net until he showed me how to lead it with my eye and the top of the mitt. Leading—that was a big chunk of what I learned from him."

"Nobody expects swimmers to catch anything except the guys in front of you," I answered. "You're out in front at the end, and you touch concrete before the other skin-fish does, or you lose."

White mounds of cumulus were welling up over the main-land. The noon sun was high overhead. Our shirts and shorts were sweat-stained and sodden. Stepping inside, I fetched a couple of towels.

I was mopping my face when Bud pulled off his golf shirt. The long, leather-edged scars that ran from his neck down his side hit me first, even before the understated USMC tattoo on his upper arm, and the dark, curly thicket of hair that ran from his throat to his waist. I didn't say anything, but my mouth must've been hanging open, because he glanced over at me and grinned.

"Ran into a door," he said, touching his side with the towel. "Happened to be a Nip sergeant behind it. His troopers and a bayonet got involved too. Nips came out of it worse than I did, by the way."

I rubbed my face. "Worse would be some pretty cut-up Nipponese."

Bud dabbed the scars again. "Thought about taking the Nip sarge's ear as a keepsake, but the medics were on top of me by then. I put up a fuss, so one of 'em got me the bulls-eye flag out of the sergeant's pocket. Must be at home in a trunk somewhere."

I whistled. "Sounds like you didn't spend the war on a parade ground."

He shrugged. "You go where they tell you to go." Then he slapped his knee and grinned. "Have to say this boat is a helluva lot better than any landing craft your fucking Navy ever provided. Your captain that delivered us to Tarawa didn't put no beer aboard either."

We were nearing the shallows west of Redfish Pass. Returning to the fly bridge, I cut the motor, moved forward, tossed out the anchor and set it.

"Too hot for fish to bite," I explained. "I'm gonna get in the water and cool off." The sight of the nearly naked, scarred-up ex-Marine was raising my temperature. And it seemed like a complication the day didn't need.

Bud said he thought he'd skip the swim this time. So I turned my back, dropped my shorts, pulled off my T-shirt and dove overboard.

Twenty minutes later, back on board, as I started toweling off, Bud seemed to stare at me; then he brought up his old coach again. "Can't get over it," he said. "You even walk like him a little. Voice ain't the same. He talked loud, and I don't hear you doing that. And your ears is kind of different. But you got his red-haired chest and green eyes and long cock."

"Hey, thanks," I said, still determined to keep the conversation locker-room light. "Don't remember what any of my old coaches' ears or hairy cocks even looked like. Guess they had 'em. Swim coaches don't necessarily shower with the team."

"Course he was older," Bud continued, his voice gone low, clearly not caring about my old coaches. "So I guess he looked bigger and hairier to me. I was just a kid."

The grown kid, I saw when I glanced over at him, was blushing. He was also throwing a first-class boner. His erection, stiff and unmistakable, strained against the thin cotton cloth of his shorts and raised a pup tent along the open right cuff.

"He must've been quite a guy," I said. "For you to remember him this long."

"Guess I thought of him as my best friend at the time," Bud explained. "He got me through to graduation. So I kind of hero-worshiped old Coach Andy. Course I see now he probably never even noticed me—as anything more than just one more of his junior Shoeless Joes."

Then Bud did something that really surprised me. He stood up, looked me straight in the eye, shucked his shorts and skivvies, stood there a moment with his stubby hard-on bobbing well above horizontal, and said, "Yeah, what the fuck, I guess I had a thing for him."

Then he jumped into the water feet first, came up shouting at the chill and swam away.

Bud's hard-on had considerably lessened when he hauled back into the boat. Toweling off fast, he pulled on his pants and shirt while I hoisted the anchor. Though he rode home seated beside me, he refused another beer and kept his mouth shut. When I tried to lighten the situation with a joke about his earlier display—"Glad there weren't any weasel-eating barracudas out in the Gulf today"—he gave me a sour look.

I was probably out of line there. Then as now, grown men seldom referred to each other's equipment, much less aimed jokes in that direction—not regular guys, anyway.

And, at that moment, Detective Spencer "Bud" Wright looked like one helluva regular guy. The bone he'd thrown had nothing to do with me, I figured, except that I'd served as some kind of trigger for memories of his boyhood crush.

That was his privilege. Heterosexual men were allowed to remember getting hot and sticky with their high school teammates and coaches. All they had to do was laugh it off as a phase, then mention the bitches they planned to fuck.

At least I hadn't made any jokes about Coach Andy—or mentioned the checkered history of my own Mr. Slugger.

Back at the dock, Bud thanked me and said he'd had a pleasant day. But he refused to take any fish. "Got a rented room," he said, staring down at the wooden planks under his feet. "And I ain't going to try cooking fish fillets in a coffee percolator. Anyhow, you can probably use 'em at the hotel."

He also didn't say anything about wanting a second lesson in the fine art of fishing. So I didn't offer.

But five days later, I picked up the phone in my office and there he was, sounding friendly and a little out of breath.

"Hey, Coach," he said. "That boat of yours didn't sink yet, did it? You got any more fishing trips planned? I probably still got a lot to learn. And I could buy the beer this time. We could waste a whole case of Regal. Catch every dolphin in the fucking Gulf."

We did catch six or seven fish. The day was even hotter and when I suggested another swim to cool off, Bud agreed with a quick nod. After we anchored, he followed my lead when I started pulling off my clothes. When he dropped his shorts, his cock popped up just like the first time, hard as oak.

He tried to shield himself with his hands. "Can't help it," he said. "Don't know what's got into me."

He stepped to the gunwale of the boat, ready to jump in.

The sight of him, all of him—not just the muscled frame, snappy crew cut and eager cock, but those badly mended wounds of his—was getting to me. A familiar, icy electricity danced dangerously around my midsection, and a little lower.

Though my pulse was pumping lightly, Mr. Slugger stayed remarkably calm. So this time I felt safe enough to venture a joke I hoped would also be taken as a compliment.

"Some men need wine, women and song to get revved up," I called. "Looks like fishing does a pretty good job for you."

Turning, he looked me up and down. "Let's get in the water, Coach," he said. "Come on, OK?"

I followed him in and we swam away from the boat. Bud was a surprisingly strong, if ungraceful, swimmer. He took off fast and stayed out front. Stopping after perhaps a hundred yards, he turned, grinned, splashed me in the face, then dived under. Within seconds, I saw and then felt him dart between my legs, pushing my knees apart quickly but hardly touching me further as he passed. He turned, came up behind me and splashed me again.

I went after him, getting an arm around his neck and quickly ducking him. As I pushed him under, he curled back on his shoulders, his knees rising, the water pasting his body hair to the tan skin above his beltline. From the milk-white skin below his waist, Bud's phallus rose out of the water like a mast.

He came up laughing and spitting water. Diving again, he got me around the waist and pulled us both down. I slipped out of his grip. As he lost his hold, his hand grazed Mr. Slugger, who was now definitely getting interested.

What the hell, I thought. *If this cop wants to play, he's found his man.* I dove deep, came up beneath Bud slowly and slid the tips of my fingers along the insides of his knees and thighs. When he clamped his legs shut on me and attempted to paddle backward with his arms, I stayed with him, coming up for a breath and then pulling myself on top of him.

He gulped air. His grin turned scared and angry. I pushed him down again, then wrapped my arms around his chest and waist. Our two hard bats brushed. He shook his head. Then he pulled himself against me, tried to thrust once or twice, and turned away, gulping air.

"Submarine attack," I said.

He let it pass.

Reaching around, I touched him gently—the hair on his chest, his belly button, both nipples. His nipples, surrounded by curls, were hard as thimbles. My bat was lodged up behind him, feeling wonderfully uncomfortable. I reached down and tried to reposition it under his ass and between his legs.

He elbowed me away, misinterpreting the shift. "You ain't. Uh-uh, no. Let's keep that area off-limits, Coach."

"Hey, Buddy," I answered, reaching for him again. "Are you OK?" I touched him lower down, slipping the thin hood of his hard cock behind the groove and squeezing gently.

Turning to face me, he put his forehead on my shoulder and began to play with me the same way, fumbling a little, maybe because I'm minus a foreskin and therefore built differently. It didn't take long for him to learn the ropes. In a few seconds, my forehead was on his shoulder, and I said, "Yeah, Buddy, right there, right there, right there." And we were pulling on each other slowly—and then faster, and then slowing down—and then sinking like harpooned seals because it got to feeling so good we forgot to kick our feet.

Breaking apart, we came up laughing. "Let's get in the boat," I said. "Before we drown."

He shook his head. "We ain't finished with this, Coach. Do you think?" Drifting back and steadying himself, he held my waist with his feet. His hard cock, the hood still retracted, rose and fell like a red-topped periscope breaking the surface.

Touching his knees, I said we might end up as floaters if we tried to finish things where we were. He reached for me. "We ain't stopping," he said, sounding determined. "Show me how else you want to do. Boat's fine. Race you back."

Later, side by side in on a sweat-soaked narrow bunk, I touched the rows of milk pearls lining his belly. "Definitely two colors," I said, running a finger into the wetness, spreading it and drawing a circle. "Your cream's thicker than mine."

He looked down, a neutral, tired expression on his face. "I'm thicker all the way 'round. When I get my steam up, anyhow."

"Out of steam for now," I answered, touching the curves of his relaxed shaft and sack. "Want me to see if I can get your pressure back?"

Bud pushed my hand away. Then, suddenly hearing something, he stood up, moved quickly to the open door of the cabin and peered outside, sweeping the ocean. Looking at him, I could hardly breathe. In the 1940s, sex between males went hand in hand with fear.

"God damn," he said as he stepped back inside the cabin, rubbing his belly with one towel and throwing me another. "There's a boat out there, coming up from Estero Island. Anybody could have chugged right by and seen us, seen what we was doing."

I'd shifted to the middle of the mattress. The sensation of mixing his sweat with mine made the whole thing seem a little more real. "We'd have heard a motor if somebody got within half a mile of us." I replied. "Relax, Buddy."

"Could have been a sailboat come up." Bud pulled his shirt over his head. "Fucking acting like a bunch of snot-nosed kids, we was. Draining our nuts. Forgetting there's other people around."

"Your old coach says it felt pretty good too," I answered, trying to get back in the game. "Your coach says his Buddy has a good set of hands and a bat that sure shoots a helluva home run."

"Lay off," Bud said. "Why don't you put on some clothes?"

"Because they're on deck," I said. "Because I'm going to splash the cream off before I get dressed."

"Man," he said. "You're not getting me in the water again. So forget that idea."

I stood up, suddenly pissed and disappointed and feeling thoroughly naked. "Not my intention, Sarge," I said. "But then what was yours, throwing that woody in my face if you didn't want to roll around?"

He pulled his shorts up, zipped and buttoned them. "Like I

said last week. You remind me of my old coach. I must of had a thing for him, wanted to be his little jerk-off buddy. Must of wanted to do what we just did, with him, in the shower room. Big fucking deal."

Men are apt to turn either sad or angry soon after they shoot off. But they can be humored. So I tried another joke. "Everybody's got a school-kid jerk-off fantasy," I said. "Only this was kind of a daytime wet dream. Wet, huh? You get it?"

He smiled. "I get it," he answered. "Now why don't you go rinse off, so we can head back."

He picked up the towel he'd brought me and handed it over. "Anybody ever tell you, you look a lot like Van Johnson," he said. "Only not half so good looking?"

This sounded like a battlefield promotion to me, from hometown coach to redheaded movie star. "I've heard it once or twice," I answered, slapping my butt. "But my ass isn't as wide as his. And I've got better legs."

Bud shrugged. "Your toes point in when you walk. At least you got two legs and two feet, though, instead of just one and a stump like that ruptured-duck flyer he played in the movies. What I mean is, you and Coach Andy, you both got cheeks like Irish lumberjacks. You both got Van Johnson's orange hair and washed-out eyebrows."

"Swim coaches look for pigeon-toed kids," I answered, stung and yet elated that he'd noticed so much about me. "Kids with small, strong hips. We just glide through the water like baby porpoises."

"Your shoulders is OK too," Bud allowed. "And arms about as long as your legs. And Johnson's white teeth—like searchlights."

"Remember in *Thirty Seconds over Tokyo*?" I said. "When the Army Air Force pilots go aboard the Navy carrier? And one of them sacks out in the admiral's cabin? There's a double bed and curtains. And the wardroom's big enough to hold the Goodyear Blimp. Pure Hollywood. And Johnson's teeth probably come from MGM."

"I never saw no admiral's cabin," Bud said. "Marine grunts get carried as baggage."

"I was in charge of one," I said. "Flag officer's cabin is about twice the size of a B4 bag opened up. You couldn't swing a cat."

"Didn't know you kept pussy on Navy ships," Bud joked, now definitely loosened up. "They sure didn't let the Marines have none."

"It was strictly one-handed sea pussy," I lied. "Officers had to show their blue movies inside their eyeballs. We figured you Marines played group-grope in the showers."

"You didn't provide us no showers, Lieutenant." He paused two beats, then added, "Just buckets of salt water." He threw his towel onto the bunk and glanced around the cabin. "This ain't gonna happen again. My mistake. Don't take it personal."

There wasn't any answer to make. So I went back on deck, dipped one end of the towel in seawater, washed the semen and sweat off my chest and stomach and crotch, rubbed myself dry and pulled on my shorts. "No worries as far as I'm concerned," I said, looking back at him. "This goes no farther than the boat. Loose lips sink ships."

"I appreciate that," Bud said. "But I ain't worrying much. See, I got a girl I been dating. And she don't let me build up too many wet dreams. Don't need nor want nothin' else."

"Sure glad I could help you out," I said. "That's what friends are for."

"No they ain't," he replied. "Though I have to say I've had a lot worse—from experienced Philippine whores, by the way."

I laughed. But I gave myself a good talking-to before bed that night while I was brushing my teeth:

You're still looking for another Mike Rizzo, Dan.

You know how that goes, Lieutenant.

So quit looking, Dan. And quit mourning. Mike is dead as President Roosevelt. He ain't gonna show up stateside any more than he did in Japan or Guam or Peleliu—when you wouldn't quit checking the daily survivor lists. Don't get crazy on me now. You've just gotta keep moving.

All
clear

IN JAPAN AFTER THE WAR, I'D GOTTEN NAKED with dozens of sun-tanned, physically fit younger men with drawls. Even so, it didn't always help.

Waking up in a dark room, shivering and soaked with sweat, I'd shout and kick as if swimming desperately toward a disappearing life raft. One surprised officer, himself the survivor of a submarine sinking, held a pillow over my face to shut me up. A few months later, an Australian colonel with a shot-up knee and bad dreams similar to mine asked me to be his mate and live with him on a cattle station in Queensland. I thought about it—until the dreams hit again.

Men with battle scars were my drug. Healed-over bullet holes got my cock stiffer than a barracks full of flexing peckers. A fighter jock with burns on his arms and two rows of medals on his chest could park his boots under my rack any time. Shrapnel marks were better than pornographic pillow books for getting my attention.

I was swimming laps in the Caloosa pool four mornings after the fishing trip when it hit me: Mixing it up with this latest Mike Rizzo stand-in seemed to have stopped the nightmares. No shipwreck, no lifeboats and sharks, no crying out in the night and waking in a cold, feverish sweat. Nope, the encounter had resulted in calm, unremembered seas and starry nights, hour after hour of pure rest and the relaxed air of a vessel in peacetime going about its business.

I thought about him off and on until just before noon and then picked up the phone and asked him over for lunch. He said he had a busy schedule and that it wasn't a good idea, but to let him think on it.

So we said goodbye, and I figured that was that. He called back a couple of hours later. What about him taking me to lunch? He claimed to know a diner over on Fowler Street, a place that fried up pretty good shrimp and snapper. The lieutenant had been the host twice, he said. Now he'd buy. I said that sounded fine and we agreed to meet at the diner early the next week.

After that lunch, over coffee, we talked for a couple of hours—soldier talk, where we'd been during the war, whether we might have crossed paths somewhere in the Pacific, making no reference to the fishing trip of the previous Sunday. Sure, that was what would now be called subtext. But we were mostly seeing if the two of us clicked mentally, not just as players in a coach-student script.

We talked about work; men usually do. He wanted to do a good, honest job for the sheriff, wanted to make something of himself, build a career, move up. I said less, but enough: that I'd been a club officer in Japan, and that my old boss had retired, invested in the Caloosa and asked me to come aboard. Bud asked if I'd ever had a girl and I said that I'd dated in high school but hadn't had much time for women in college, being on an athletic scholarship and having to work part-time.

He invited me over to see his rented room the following Saturday afternoon. His landlady was out of town, and it wasn't long before we were down on the rug, wrestling half-naked. He ended up getting angry and silent again at the end of the session, after we'd both shot off.

Two weeks later, we used my room at the Caloosa Hotel. We started with a swim in the pool, then went upstairs to shower and change before dinner. Toweling each other down after a preliminary round of stand-up hand-pussy, he asked if I was ready for a little serious action. I said I'd taught him a trick or two and what did he have in mind?

What he had in mind was getting inside me. We took it slow. I knew how to protect myself when he started losing his mental bearings. He never seemed to turn angry that afternoon. He even thanked me afterward, blushing like a kid on a first date. Later, we ate dinner together at the diner on Fowler Street.

My nightmares stayed on leave.

We arranged to hit the Legion hall the next Tuesday for spaghetti night. Only he had to work an arson case unexpectedly. The following week a group of VIPs arrived and I had to cancel. Figuring that the Legion wouldn't run out of spaghetti, we settled on the third week to get together. I walked over to the rooming house a little after sunset to pick him up. The landlady let me in. Bud's door was unlocked and I went inside. He called to me that he was still in the shower.

Keep in mind that was almost three weeks since our last get-together. Being horny as hell, and thus a little crazy, I figured I'd try a quick poke at Bud's fantasies. Rifling through his closet and chest of drawers, I came up with a faded La Belle High School baseball jersey and a jockstrap. Stripping quickly, leaving on only my white gym socks, I redressed in the modified coach's outfit.

When Bud came out of the bathroom, he stopped short, laughed, then scowled and told me to quit messing with his stuff. But when his bat lengthened out we both started giggling and playing grab-ass.

"Your coach has got another thing or two to teach you," I explained after I'd wrestled him down on his cot. "It might hurt at first but you're gonna like it," I said, touching him in places I knew rang his bells.

He stirred under me, twisting and bouncing as if to escape. "I ain't ready for nothing like that," he muttered. "Lemme get inside you again."

And so we split the difference, and the relationship became more complicated and reciprocal. I taught him some of the Asian tricks I'd learned—how to warm a man up so he's ready to be entered, how to massage the prostate, when to pause and reassure a man, when to charge forward, how to hold fire.

"You're turning me queer," he whispered late one night a few weeks later, sounding sad. We were stretched out on an old blanket on a deserted beach on Sanibel Island. "I like you a lot. I like being with you," he confessed. "And I like it with Slim"—Slim being Slim Nichols, a waitress at the Arcade Café on First Street. "You teach me more," he said, "but—"

At that point I put my hand over his mouth. "But she poaches eggs better," I murmured in his ear. "And probably darns your socks. I got four cooks working for me. I'll buy you socks if you need them. So what do you want for breakfast? I wouldn't mind waking up with you day after day."

That was more than I intended to say. His admission had gotten to me. Still, he didn't exactly take my words as a proposal of marriage. Reaching out past the edge of the blanket, he grabbed a handful of sand and forced it into my mouth, gripping my neck with his other hand. "How about I have me a redheaded ex-lieutenant for midnight chow. And then the hungry lieutenant can have a slice of tough old jarhead for dessert."

I spit the sand onto his chest and rubbed it in hard, the grains catching the black curly hairs. "If I didn't rate my Buddy pretty high," I answered, trying to talk around the sand in my mouth, "I'd tell him queer was too good for an ex-marine. I'd tell him to forget using words like that. And I'd say lemme go wash the sand out—so Coach don't scratch his Buddy's piece of barracuda bait when he swallows it later."

Hiking on Estero Island one stormy November afternoon, I asked if he and Coach Andy ever touched each other.

"Course not," he answered without hesitation, not even looking up.

"But you wanted to. You knew what his hard cock looked like."

Bud took a breath but didn't break stride. "Like I say, I hero-worshiped him. And he always slapped me on the butt after I hit a good one. And he rubbed my shoulders before I went up to bat. He hugged us when we scored. And I guess I got ideas."

"And what happened?"

"We was in the showers late, after a big game my junior year. I got a hard-on and he got one too. Nobody else there. Hell, I'd seen players shoot off together in the showers, even pull each other off. But I'd never done nothin' like that. Coach was lookin' at me, soapin' himself hard and staring at my bone. So I reached for him."

"And he reached back?"

"He slapped my hand away. And then he just grabbed his towel and got out of there. Took me aside the next day and told me I needed to learn to keep my hands to myself. And he never patted my butt or massaged my shoulders again. But we didn't stop being friends. And he kept to the tutoring schedule."

"Look but don't touch," I said. "Even though he must've wanted to mix it up as much as you did. Probably more."

"You think so? Course I wondered. Felt real guilty and embarrassed at the time. Scared I was turning queer. Did I tell you he was a married man? I went to my granny—only because she was who I talked to the most. Told her I liked one of my teachers real much. And she said that was natural. So I said, 'No, I mean I really like him. But I don't think he likes me.' And she hugged me and said it was good I knew my feelings, and that I'd always been a loving grandson to her and there'd be plenty of time to find somebody who loved me as much as she and all my family did."

"Nice. And your old coach didn't sit you down and explain that he couldn't risk touching a student without risking his job? No matter how close you two were, or how he felt? Didn't mention the words 'jail bait'?"

"No, I guess he didn't."

I stopped walking. Bud took a couple more steps, then turned back, looking quizzical. We'd halted near a deserted stretch of beach bordered by sea oats and oak scrub.

"So what Coach Andy taught you," I said, "is that being forward doesn't get you what you want. And that looking without touching doesn't get you off either."

"Hadn't never thought of it like that."

"He taught you not to make the first move—unless you want to risk getting your hand slapped. Boy, he was some molder of young male minds. I'm sure glad he didn't coach me."

And then I thought, *Hell, Dan, Mike Rizzo made the first move on you. And you never even saw anybody jerking in a shower, much less tried to help out, until after the war. You're a big one to talk.*

Bud's fists were suddenly up close to his chest. He had an angry, confused expression on his face. Then he blinked and almost immediately he opened his hands, palms facing outward. "Don't talk about my coach," he said, an edge to his voice.

"What do you want, Buddy?"

"What do you mean?" he answered, his strong hands still hovering.

"You can make the first move with me any time," I said. "There's no way Coach Dan is gonna slap his Buddy down."

"Fucking Coach," Bud answered, glancing around. Far out on the Gulf, a lone sailboat pointed north. "You don't mean right out here on the beach in broad daylight!"

"We can get in the water and make like we're in the shower. We just won the big game. Slugger Buddy Wright hit two home runs. And Coach Andy is swinging his soapy bat. His bases are loaded. He wants it as much as his Buddy does."

"I want to touch you, Coach. Can I touch you?" Bud had lowered his hands to his sides.

I reached out and slapped his butt. "Let's get wet," I said. "Don't let my trunks float away when you pull them off me."

"Fucking pervert," Bud said, grinning.

"Only for jail bait. You know I'll do anything for the team."

We used the bunk of the fishing boat another time that fall and once, when we'd both had too much to drink, Bud's war-surplus Lee County Jeep, parked in a palm grove 10 miles out of town. Romance? Hell, yes. Can't get any more romantic than sucking off your buddy in a Jeep by moonlight.

Love? I didn't know what real love was. But, as things turned out, I gave myself another good talking-to that Saturday in February—the night I spent alone in Bud's room, the night the detective broke a date to shadow the Klan march through Colored Town.

Lieutenant, you got to admit horsing around with this cop is great. He's nothing like Mike. He's not as pushy. But the feelings go deeper—when he can put them into words. The nightmares are gone. Maybe he's the one...

Hold on, Dan. You're not even close to tied down. And vice versa. He's still seeing the waitress. Who makes the first move there?

Horse shit, Lieutenant. He'll forget the bitch once we're together every day, after he quits his Dick Tracy job and comes to work for me.

Then ask him. Make the first fucking move. You've still got nothing to lose.

And so on, until I fell fast asleep.

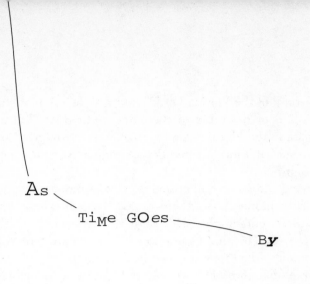

As

Ti_Me GOes

B**y**

SMALL-TOWN PAPERS USE EXTRA INK to distance themselves from
sensational local events, especially local events involving powerful advertisers. Hillard Norris's three-column obituary topped
the front page of the Monday morning *News-Press*. Continued
inside on page 6, the extensive coverage included an appreciative
editorial, an oversize photo of Norris's late father-in-law, William
Rufus "Big Bill" Turnipblossom, and two portraits of the dead
man himself. The story might as well have been written by a
press agent.

"Ford Dealer Mourned," ran the headline. Sub-heads supplied context but few details: "Shot Dead on South Side" and
"Civic Leader's Passing a Tragic Loss to Myers."

Sarasota native Hillard Albert Norris Jr., born in 1908, was
fulsomely praised as the highly successful managing partner of
the largest car dealership in Southwest Florida, a company
founded by his dynamic and forward-looking father-in-law.
Norris was recalled fondly by several of his employees and associates, cited as a generous contributor to the Community Chest
and lauded as a leading Mason, past president of the Chamber

of Commerce and of the Florida Ford Dealers Association, member of the Board of Stewards of the First Methodist Church, former delegate to the Florida Democratic Convention, graduate of the University of Florida, member of Sigma Nu, an Eagle Scout and so on.

The grieving widow was identified as a civic-minded descendant of Florida pioneers on both sides. Her genealogy was detailed in three paragraphs. Her activities—Women's Club, wartime Gray Lady, Hospital Committee Chairwoman, PTA volunteer and so on—filled four succeeding paragraphs.

The couple's daughter, Hillary, said to be presently at school in Mount Dora, earned two paragraphs.

Although paragraph 16 did mention that Norris's body had been found Sunday morning in a tourist court on the south side of town, the establishment itself was not named. Nor was a name attached to second victim, described only as "a colored man" who was "also found dead on the scene."

Post-mortem gunplay was ignored altogether.

Beyond general remarks concerning an ongoing investigation, the anonymous law enforcement officer mentioned in the uncredited story refused to speculate on what may have happened. Funeral arrangements were said to be incomplete.

When I saw the dead man's picture, I remembered him right away. An outwardly likeable small-town mogul with thinning hair and heavy-duty ego, Norris had been one of the Caloosa Club's regular poker players. Norris was never a big winner or a notable loser. And he was always a guest of his pal, an equally well-connected real estate broker and lawyer named H. (Hugh) Ridley Boldt. Norris had let me know right away that neither cards, liquor nor offbeat personalities (the club room's principal attractions) interested him much. But I never gave him a thought until his widow took a shot at me.

Ridley Boldt, a paid-up member who always picked up drink tabs when he won, gambled with us once or twice a week, often accompanied by his wife. The little woman, who also happened to be Willene Norris's first cousin, was mentioned toward the bottom of Norris's obituary.

I clipped out the story and stashed it in a desk drawer in my office at the Caloosa. The office wasn't much: a Mission Oak desk, a couple of metal filing cabinets, a bookshelf lined with hotel-school manuals, stacks of old menus and equipment catalogs, a flourishing philodendron vine in a blue and white Japanese pot. The drawers of the desk were mostly empty. I kept a framed photo of Mike Rizzo and the *Indianapolis* in the top drawer. For some reason I tucked the obituary clipping right under it.

Having worked all day Monday I was sipping coffee in the office just before dusk and sternly telling myself I ought to go swim half a mile before dinner, when a bellhop ushered in an apologetic Detective Wright.

"Mind if I shut the door?" Bud said after the bellboy departed. "Got my nuts busted all fucking day long. And they was already in bad shape."

He looked rumpled and definitely hung over: dark aviator glasses, a brown herringbone jacket, blue trousers with no belt and a tan necktie that didn't match the coat or the pants. When I switched off the overhead light, he removed the shades. His eyes resembled a brown and red jigsaw puzzle. Looking into them was enough to make me wince.

"Aspirin didn't help?" I asked, leaning back in my swivel chair, comfy as hell.

"Fucking yes, they helped. Else I'd of put the gun to my head"—he patted the holster inside his coat—"by noon. Been chewing them pills like candy."

"Have you eaten?"

"Shut up. Thought of food makes me gag. Ought to blame you anyhow for leaving that rot-gut Bacardi at my place. You better take it with you next time."

I knew exactly how he felt, having overdosed on Bacardi a time or two myself. So I was sympathetic up to a point. But we were both moderately aggressive males and he was pushing me a little too hard. "You left me with a case of blue-balls this morning," I said. "Do you hear me complaining? No, I took a cold shower like a man."

He glanced at the door to be sure it was closed, then touched the front of his trousers. "I'm hurtin' too, down here where the goddamn Norris woman kicked me. But I'll make it up to you," he muttered. "Some way."

His unexpected answer took me up short. He'd gone from aggression to submission in two sentences. Smiling, I said, "Couple of ways come to mind, Sarge."

He nodded, meaning we'd discuss my needs later.

"Got roughed up the minute I hit the office," he said. "Number 1, the boss come back from Ocala and wherever else the fuck he'd been. He chewed up my report on the Royal Plaza Motor Lodge incident first thing. Had me rewrite the sucker two times, said the first couple of passes was too long. You ever hear somebody complain about too much detail on a homicide report? Don't make no sense. Then come to find out he didn't like me naming any names in the Klan write-up. Said the citizens I reported as present was merely alleged and rumored, and I ought not to put them down."

When I suggested that the Klanners were probably the sheriff's relatives and political allies, Bud laughed quietly and continued his tired tirade.

"What's more, County Commissioner Frates called up and reamed the boss's ass out, said he ought to control his troops better and not let them manhandle a lady, especially when the lady is the wife and daughter of powerful constituents. Especially when the lady and her mama own a third of downtown. Especially when the lady is a personal friend and political supporter of the honorable fart and double-fart, you get the picture. So then I had to go all through what I'd written down in the first report and been ordered to take out, about Mrs. Norris sliding her car near about into the crime scene, busting up Doc Shepherd's camera and picking up the gun and cutting loose and all. Took another hour to turn all that into a letter over the boss's John Hancock. For Commissioner Fart-sees."

"If you want me to give a statement," I offered.

He waved me off. "Been trying to keep your mug out of this. I'll let you know if I need anything. I'm just blowing off steam."

I wanted to hug him and roll him in a blanket and carry him up to my room on the second floor. But I figured we could find time for that later. So I said, "Sounds like you hit a mine field. Hell of a day all around. Sorry if I made it worse yesterday—or last night."

He pounded the arm of his chair with a fist. "Bad day didn't stop there." Suddenly looking up, he said, "I appreciate that, Dan. You didn't make anything worse. It was that goddamn cunt Willene Norris. Was my mistake carrying you along with me."

"I wanted us to have the day together," I answered. "Anyway, close calls, my sore nuts—none of that matters."

"Right. Yes. Same here. Anyhow, the sheriff released the two bodies back to the families at 3 o'clock this afternoon, for burial. Doc wasn't half finished cutting on the colored guy—who he didn't start slicing into till this morning, and I'm not criticizing him for that, yesterday being Sunday. Was still some tests to run on Norris's organs, or that's what he told me later. We both complained down the hall. But it didn't do no good. Doc was told to wrap 'em up for the undertakers, and do it now. The undertakers was already on the scene, come to find out."

I remarked that this all sounded pretty irregular.

"Oh, Doc kept samples," Bud answered. "Don't know what of yet. He's doing his own tests. But he told me there's enough to check out whoever's scum was in the used rubber and he has blood samples from both men, the carpet and the lady's jacket."

I asked Bud if he'd seen the story in the newspaper. When he said no, I dug out the clipping. Bud whistled a couple of times as he read through it.

"She must be tight as ticks on a deer with everybody who's got strings to be pulled," he said finally. "From the mayor right on down to the newspaper publisher's wife."

"You see what they left out?"

He nodded. "Story this long, must be intentional. Not a word about Willene's shooting spree or her fucking up any possible prints on the pistol. The reporter on this—name of Ralph Nype, don't know why it don't say so here—tracked me down at the office yesterday. I didn't tell him nothing about any of that, just that we was looking into it. But he was already on to the widow lady getting involved. And he damn well knew the name of that motor lodge."

Somebody was running a railroad, no doubt about it. And it sounded like Bud might get tied to the tracks if he wasn't careful. I stood up, crossed around behind the desk, pulled him to his feet and put my arms around him. His hands stayed at his sides, stiffly, until I kissed the scar on his neck. Then he loosened up a little.

"I got sloppy last night," he admitted. "No excuse for it. You gettin' in the Norris woman's line of fire got to me. I'm sorry about, well, about leaving you high and dry when we mixed it up. Don't remember that part all too clear."

Patting his sides, I stepped back. "You know the joke about the horny sailor and the pogy marine?"

He cocked his head. "Could that be the one about the 18-button salute?"

"No, it's the one about the lieutenant buying the jarhead sarge some hair of the dog and a sandwich. You up for that?"

"Hot to go," he answered. "Where you have in mind?"

What I had in mind, pretty much on the spur of the moment, was giving him his first look at the Caloosa Club. On a Monday night the action would be slow. I'd be at his side to handle anything that spooked him. And if he did somehow spring a law-enforcement bone, well, that would answer a lot of questions too and pose a few more.

So I invited him to follow me. We might have used the camouflaged door that opened directly into the club from my office. (It looked like a closet from my side, a dry fountain from the other.) But I wanted to show him the members' set-up first.

elliott mackle

So we detoured through the lobby, crossed the dining room and entered what looked like a waiters' station, complete with swinging outer doors, utility sink, ice machine, bulletin board, flatware drawers, dirty-linen hamper and shelves loaded with dishes and glassware. Around a corner, a steel desk partly blocked the way to a second set of doors. The desk, two phones and the club room entrance itself were presided over by Brian Rooney, a muscular man of about 50 who doubled as a masseur in the hotel locker room. The club room doors were made of bulletproof steel and fitted with combination locks. Nobody got in uninvited.

Brittle piano music and faint laughter echoed beyond the speakeasy's entrance. Rooney rose to his feet and I introduced him to Bud. "He's my personal guest," I explained. "Local. We're a little dry and need to wet our whistles."

Bud flinched at Rooney's handshake, then grinned and squeezed back. The contest ended in a draw. "One temporary membership coming up," Rooney said, his South Boston Irish accent softened by a touch of merchant marine. "Little slow tonight. You gents can liven things up."

"We're not *that* dry," I replied, printing Bud's name on the card Rooney produced. "But you never can tell."

Having said that, I pushed Bud ahead of me through the unlocked doors. Glancing right, he immediately spotted the six-stool, mirrored cocktail bar, complete with silver cocktail shaker, martini glasses and bartender in a monkey suit.

The club room, formerly a banquet hall, had been expensively redone to match what passed for modernity in after-dark Miami. Besides a white baby grand, the fittings included cobalt rugs with a pattern of silver stars and moons, brushed metal tables and cocktail chairs with silver cushions and a grove of artificial palm trees. A froufrou decorator from New York had painted the trees white, sprinkled them with silver glitter, cut them in half and applied the pieces to the walls as what he called "Greek pee-lasters."

The mirrored bar, white ceiling, metal doors and base of the central dais were outlined in blue and white neon. A pair of plaster fountains were accented with spotlights.

To our left a light-skinned black man with waved, pomaded hair picked out "Moon Over Miami" on the albino Steinway. His spotlighted piano was raised on a round dais at the far end of the bar.

Looking up from his keys and smiling, Tommy Carpenter nodded in my direction and shifted into a Richard Rogers–style version of "Anchors Aweigh." After four or five bars of nautical rolling and pitching, he bridged back through "Popeye the Sailor Man" and a reprise of "Moon Over Miami," ending up in "Laura."

"And she's only a dream," he crooned.

Surprise washed over Bud's face. "You running a mixed-race club?"

"Not officially," I answered. "My boss hired the best people he could find. Tommy's a pretty good saloon singer. He's worked in New York clubs."

"Don't bother me none," Bud replied to my unvoiced question. "Bunked next to a mulatto guy on the troopship out of 'Frisco. He was from Indiana. We got to be pretty close friends out there."

"How close?" I said, verbally leering and thus missing the subtle, sad note in Bud's tone. "You dig any foxholes together?"

Bud looked away. "He made it over one fucking reef at Tarawa. Him and his buddy, another colored kid, they got their foxholes dug for them. With white crosses for decoration."

As if to emphasize that the dead are always with us, Doc Shepherd looked up from a felt-topped poker table, waved and put down his cards. "Mr. E-e-wing," he called, his voice honking and his many chins wobbling. "Are we safe here? Last time I saw you two boys together, the shooting had already started."

Doc and two other men, each seated behind stacks of cardboard chips and half-full glasses, appeared ready for a long night.

Bud stiffened but followed me over to the group.

"I'm buying this hero a lemonade," I answered, raising my

voice a little, "as a thank you for jumping in front of a pistol-packing widow." Tapping the table next to Shepherd's glass, I added, "It'd probably be unethical for a public servant such as Detective Wright to accept free beer. But can I offer you and your friends another round of iced tea?"

Doc introduced his pals—a pathologist and an obstetrician from the county hospital—and said they'd have whatever Bud was having, as long as it was bourbon and water.

From experience, I knew that what sounds like unwelcome innuendo is often no more than idle conversation. But when the innuendo has to do with two single men being viewed as a pair, I also knew that defusing the potential bombshell is better than letting it tick.

"Detective Wright and I were in the same convoy during the war," I fibbed. "Turns out his lieutenant ate in my ward-room from Pearl Harbor to Kolombangara. And my mess chief and Marine Sergeant Spencer 'Bud' Wright here got to be pretty close friends in the CPO's mess over on the USS *Missoula,* which was our sister cruiser. So we've had some catching up to do."

"Hell of a coincidence," one of the physicians observed.

"Whose deal is it?" the other asked. "You two young whip-persnappers want to jump in and lose some money?"

"Take a rain check," I said. "Three sweet teas, coming up."

"Was a major, not a lieutenant, led us over there," Bud whispered, following me to the bar. "And you know I didn't ride any cruiser to Kolombangara."

"They don't know that," I answered. "Maybe I got it wrong. Could have been a fishing boat I was thinking of."

Grunting, Bud poked me in the back. "Smart guy, huh?"

Two women sat together at the bar. The older one, a small, sporty type with a white streak in her short dark hair, was Lucille Shepherd—the coroner Doc Shepherd's wife. The other woman, Wanda Limber, was a Navy flier's widow who paid her rent by turning tricks for the club's best customers. The unlikely pair were the female version of drinking buddies.

Both women were very attractive. Lucille Shepherd was a Fort Myers fashion plate. A trim woman who wouldn't see 40 again, she'd gotten herself up in a tailored black-and-white check dress, matching spectator pumps, cherry-red lipstick and over-size eyeglasses. Wanda was a bottle blond with Ann Miller legs, Kathryn Grayson tits and subtle Elizabeth Arden makeup.

We joined them as they put down their drinks. I got in on the last words of the conversation: "holed out with her 9 iron." The two women were discussing golf.

"I was telling Mrs. Shepherd about the 1939 Southern Collegiate Ladies Championships at Pinehurst," Wanda said, winking at me. (She was about my age and had even fewer illusions.) "Actually, I was telling her about how I didn't win."

"She came in 3 under par," Lucille said. "So by all rights, Mrs. Limber ought to have been inside the clubhouse polishing up the trophy."

"Well, I was," Wanda laughed. "And then somebody waltzed in and told me about Judy Rogers's chip shot. It was my last big tournament. Butch and I married the next month, the day after he finished advanced flight training. And we were transferred, first to Mayport and then to San Diego. And then the war…"

A bottle of Regal appeared on the counter.

"Same thing," Bud said, glancing at me. "Unless you got hot coffee."

"Cream? Sugar?"

"Black."

I wasn't minding my manners. Lucille stuck her hand out in Bud's direction. "We met at…?"

"The sheriff's Christmas party, ma'am," Bud answered. "Down at the Legion Hall."

"Which is where Bud and I first crossed paths," I explained, adding, "Down at the Legion Hall, I mean. Never met the sheriff." A decent cover story never hurts anybody. Especially when it's true.

"But we figure we was probably in the same boat during the

Pacific war," Bud put in, grinning and shaking hands with both women.

Lucille hooted. "All in the same boat for sure, if the Japs were shooting at you." Then she glanced at Wanda, whispered, "Oh, my," and covered her mouth. But Wanda just smiled.

The bartender set down Bud's coffee. "Anything else for the pretty ladies? Or for you two handsome gentlemens? You wish is my *commandante*."

Cabildo Morales was only filling in as bartender until we found someone suitable. His formal title was Club and Restaurant Manager. "Mother Carmen," his backstage nickname, derived from Carmen Veranda, a drag character he'd created while touring with the USO. Carmen had spent the war as an Army entertainer, singing and dancing in soldier shows. After discharge, he auditioned for transvestite nightclubs in New York and Miami and got a few bookings. But competition was tough. He had to make a living between engagements. So he started waiting tables at the Roney Plaza Hotel in Miami Beach. A natural, he moved up to host and then floor manager within a year.

Even wearing a tuxedo, he used mascara, light eye shadow and lip rouge. No more than five feet tall—he was from South Texas, and three quarters Mexican—he wore lifts in his boots to appear taller.

Lucille thought he was cute, up to a point. Wanda was his confidante and partner in practical jokes. I found his sissy voice and girlish vapors a little hard to take.

Bud Wright couldn't stand him right from the start.

And Carmen must have sensed this. So he gave Bud the full treatment. "The *Legion* Hall," he whispered, mincing the words slightly. "You must be another one of those brave boys"—and here he cocked his hip and switched his voice back to B-picture cowboy twang—"brave boys in uniform I sang and danced for in the beaches and the trenches and the hills and the sand dunes."

When Bud didn't say anything, Carmen turned to me, pulling his voice down into a Joan Crawford growl. "He doesn't know I'm a star—a star in temporary eclipse. The sand dunes were my downfall."

"Bigger than Garland," Wanda said. "Bigger than Olivia de Havilland."

"Sand dunes and spike heels are a tough combination," Lucille said sympathetically.

"I can do Olivia doing Melanie Wilkes," Carmen replied, still using the south-Texas drawl. "I can do Judy. But Carmen Veranda is bigger."

Conveniently—or maybe he overheard some of this—Tommy Carpenter swung into a torch version of "Somewhere Over the Rainbow."

Framing his face with his hands, gazing soulfully at imaginary spotlights, Carmen sang along with the piano for a couple of bars.

Grinning appreciatively, the women pantomimed applause. The men at the card table didn't seem to notice. "Why, oh, why," Lucille sang back, fumbling the rhythm in a good-natured way, "can't I have a refill on this scotch and soda?"

Catching the next tune in Tommy's Broadway medley—or maybe he knew what was coming—Carmen danced a couple of shuffle steps, then picked up "I'm Just a Boy Who Can't Say No."

Bud wasn't smiling. He hadn't touched the coffee and was standing with his arms at his sides, obviously uncomfortable at the impromptu drag act.

Carmen moved to fill the drink order, pouring with one hand and, with the other, snapping his fingers in time to "Doing What Comes Nat'churly."

Nudging Bud and pointing across the room, I suggested that he carry our drinks to a table while I ordered sandwiches. Bud nodded, said goodbye to the women, picked up the coffee cup and beer and moved away.

I motioned Carmen down to the far end of the bar. "Do me a favor," I said. "Ask the kitchen to put together a couple of clubhouse triple-deckers and maybe a relish tray. On the double."

"Excellent," Carmen replied, now all business, pulling an

order pad and pencil from under the bar. "With chips and slaw?"

"Whatever you think will be quickest," I said.

"What I think," Carmen said, the breathless Conchita accent gone, "is that your friend is wearing a G-man's brassiere under his coat. He also knows the, how you say, corpse-cutter. Is he a cop?"

When I answered that Bud was just a friend of mine, Carmen wouldn't let it rest. "Are we in trouble, Danny? Break it to me gently. You know I can't stand shocks."

"They put us on a committee," I explained, saying more than I needed to. "Over at the Legion Hall. I took him fishing a couple of times. I don't know anybody in this town, except people I work with."

"People who work for you," Carmen corrected primly. "So J. Edgar's not going to arrest anybody? Or take down names? You sure there's nothing I can do to help?"

"Not tonight. He's my guest. He's definitely off duty. He needs a sandwich."

"I'll tell you what he needs: a couple of sessions with Wanda's sandwich—hold the lettuce and tomato. He looks like he swallowed a set of handcuffs."

"He's hung over, which is why I need you to run back to the kitchen and put in the order. On the double, like I said."

"He must have been quite a T-bone before his neck got branded and his hair went to seed. Maybe one of Hirohito's rancheros got to him?"

"Carmen, why aren't you on Broadway?"

"Hope that scar doesn't run too far south."

"No idea," I said. "The sandwiches?"

"I'm practically there, Danny." Carmen batted his eyelashes and twirled away.

"He's a freak," Bud said as I sat down. "A fruitcake. Makes my skin crawl."

"Carmen's OK," I said, aware that Bud lacked backstage

experience. Bud hadn't had an older friend to show him the ropes at Boy Scout camp. Nor even a helpful uncle with a YMCA membership. He still needed considerable man-to-man education. It looked like I was going to have to be his counselor as well as his coach.

"He works hard," I said. "Manages all my food and drink business. He used to be a singer, that's all."

"He acts like a girl," Bud protested. "How do you put up with it?"

I emptied my beer before answering. "He puts in a 10-hour day," I finally said. "His books balance. He never runs short on supplies. Personally, he doesn't appeal to me any more than Wanda does. I'd just as soon go to bed with Brian Rooney out there, if I was forced to pick one of the three. But people seem to think he's funny. Most of the guests do. There's been exactly one complaint about his behavior, and that was from a bullying asshole who insulted him, said he ought to get casts for those limp wrists and asked if he'd had his balls removed when his foreskin was cut, creepy shit like that. Carmen told the sucker to go fuck his hat."

"Up to me," Bud answered, "I think we both ought to get outta here, go to the Fowler Street Diner. Can't talk in this place, not with that fairy flitting around like some kind of ballerina, and Doc and his wife sitting right there wondering what the fuck I'm doing here."

"Why do you think they're wondering anything?"

"Well, it's natural, ain't it? Wondering what two guys is doing together on a Sunday morning and then again on Monday night? Two guys that don't work together, that ain't related and that didn't serve together or go to school the same place."

I looked over at Doc and the card players, then at the two women drinking at the bar, then at Tommy Carpenter who was artfully weaving a set of slow, jazzy notes into a shimmering pattern of variations on "I'll be Seeing You." Every one of the six other people in the room seemed to have forgotten that Bud and I existed. We might as well have been a hundred miles away.

"What we're trying to do," I said, "is make this club the one place in town where anybody is free to say or do exactly what he wants. The only real rules are that you don't talk about what goes on to outsiders. The members and guests have to be screened. Within reason, though, anything goes."

Bud's eyes followed mine around the room. "Anything? Bull puppies."

"Within reason, like I said, and as long as there's no shouting or fighting or insults."

My words sounded stiffer than a wire brush. But I wanted to get the meaning right. "Drinks and card tables are just the means, Bud, not the ends. 'We all risked our skins to save democracy,' the boss once told me, 'not only from Hitler and Tojo but also from the Mrs. Grundys, Cardinal Spellmans and Bible-thumping Senator Bilbos of the world.' That's why he and his syndicate bought the hotel and founded the club—that and to make a profit."

Bud sipped his coffee thoughtfully. When he spoke again his voice stayed low. "All these people are breaking the law—playing cards for money, buying mixed drinks, and that's just to start. And you're telling me that you and the fruit bartender are selling them the drinks and providing the card table? You're keeping what the statutes would call a disorderly house? And I'm supposed to say, 'Well, pin a medal on you, Lieutenant, and welcome to Lee County'?"

Turning in my chair so I could look straight into Bud's eyes, I said, "This is where I work. Running this place is what I do— what I know how to do and what I was hired to do."

"And maybe I don't want to know nothing about it," he answered. "Why'd you bring me in here anyhow? You gonna ask me to dance in front of Doc and his wife? That what you mean by anything?"

I shook my head. "Like I said, it's because this is what I do seven days a week. And because of what you and I do off duty. The thing between us is getting complicated. It's getting to be a lot more than just a good fuck. When the Norris woman almost

it takes two

shot me, you protected me with your body, and then went home and got plastered. Only just before you passed out, you threatened to cut me off for good, said we just ought to be pals. Bull puppies on that, Sarge."

And did Bud take all this as it was intended—as a declaration of, well, not love exactly, but of some kind of commitment and trust, of letting him know who and what I was? Hell, no. Not at first, anyway. He took it as the preface to a brush-off.

He cut his eyes down, then back, shooting arrows in my direction. The red tracks on his eyeballs were gone. "Sounds to me like all you want is a regular ass to plug. Maybe you better head back to the Legion Hall and pick up somebody else. Like I told you, only you won't listen, I'm going with this girl. And maybe the whole thing between you and me does need to stop once and for all. No bull."

I wondered if it had been a mistake to bring him into the club, tonight anyway, when he was hurting and embarrassed. But we were into it now, and there was nothing to do but keep going.

"We're starting to care about each other," I said. "That's why I wanted to go with you yesterday morning. That's why you shielded me when the Norris woman pointed the murder weapon at me—and why you're so scared of something happening to me you want to run away."

At this point Carmen arrived with our triple-decker club sandwiches—the turkey and bacon freshly cooked, the mayonnaise cool and lush, the toast warm, the lettuce crisp, the sliced tomatoes cold and tart. Each sandwich was cut into quarters, the wedges held upright with frilled toothpicks. Around each sandwich platter, Carmen arranged smaller dishes of French fries, Cole slaw, dill pickles, ketchup and sliced onions. After setting down napkin-wrapped silverware and a set of salt and pepper shakers, he stepped back. "Anything else, gentlemens?"

"Another beer," I said.

"And a refill on that coffee?" Carmen said, lifting the lid of the pot.

"Better not," Bud said. "Gotta get some shut-eye sometime. One of those beers maybe."

"A pleasure," Carmen said, turning away.

"The beer's not particularly illegal," I said, picking up a sandwich wedge and biting into it.

Bud gathered up a handful of French fries and fed them into his mouth one by one between sentences. "The bourbon and water and the martini cocktails are definitely covered by the local-option statute. The card game in a place that sells booze— whatever kind of license you have, and I'm assuming you have one—that's a misdemeanor for sure, or maybe a felony. Running a mixed-race staff, much less employing that fairy queen bartender you've got, you're asking for the governor and the whole state supreme court to blast in here and cart you off to the poky. And me? Just being seen in a place like this could cost me my county job. Good fries, though."

I laughed, maybe a little too loud. Hell, I was nervous. A lot was riding on this conversation.

Doc must have heard me because he looked over, tossed a handful of poker chips onto the table and threw me a thumbs-up. I waved back, a two-fingered V-for-Victory salute.

Bud got the point right away. "Doc's got 10 years' seniority on me," he growled. "And with his professional rank he can do what he wants to."

"And that's what the club room is for," I said, wondering how the hell the argument had tied itself up in such a neat bow. "Just harmless fun. We're not doing coat-hanger abortions. Meyer Lansky and his mafioso pals don't have a dime in the place. I resigned my commission to come work here because I know Bruce Asdeck is an up-and-up kind of guy. Come on, Bud. I don't want to have any secrets from you."

Reaching under the table, his action shielded by the table-cloth, he squeezed my knee, then ran his hand up and down my thigh a couple of times before withdrawing it. "Here's my secret," he said quietly. "Fact is, aside from my girl, you're the only, ah, person I been with in two years. Course I'll take my share of responsibility for what we been doing. Only you're throwing a lot at me at one time. I'm a cop and a jarhead and I'm trained to think in a straight line. You run in pretty fast company—admirals and all, college scholarship, commissioned officer. And you're telling me some of the laws don't matter."

"They matter," I said, "because they get in our way—in Doc's way, when he wants to play cards; in Mrs. Doc's way if she wants a mixed drink in public."

"And I'm sworn to uphold the law," Bud said. "And not to pick and choose between straight and crooked."

"Only you do," I said. "Every time you get naked with me, it's some kind of felony in this state, and you're risking a trip to Raiford Penitentiary."

Bud glanced at me, then up at Carmen, who had silently arrived with two beers. Without a suggestion that he'd heard what I'd said, Carmen opened the bottles, set them on the table and went away.

"Don't think I haven't thought about it," Bud answered. "Haven't you?"

I squeezed him back under the table. "Guess you're worth it," I said. "Anyway, when they start racking up charges on me, sodomy's gonna be way down the list."

He cocked his head back and looked at me quizzically.

"You just added them up, Sarge. Mixed drinks, card games, racial integration—and that's probably not the half of it."

He shook his head, picked up a fork and went to work on his bowl of slaw. "Didn't see a thing," he said, throwing me a smile and a wink. "Never been here, in fact. Don't even know how to spell the word *sod-o-my-whatcha-callit*."

Brian had admitted several more people to the club room. Tommy took a break and then started playing dance music. Bud finished his slaw, fries and sandwich and started on what was left of mine.

Betty Harris, Wanda Limber's housemate, entered the club and came over to the table to say hello. Also a war widow, she was a good-time girl and a part-time whore, and worked as a secretary in a broker's office. I introduced her to Bud and when he stood up to shake hands she asked him to dance. He accepted and away they went.

He fox-trotted better than Betty. When Tommy shifted into a tango medley, Bud picked up the beat. The man kept pulling surprises out of his pocket.

A bank vice-president named Herndon Milledge cut in on Bud and Betty. Getting into the game, Bud led Wanda onto the dance floor.

I watched him move, knowing the feeling of his hands on my sides. His elbows pumped in time to the music. Just for a moment, I imagined cutting in on Wanda, dancing away with Bud and licking his ear to the tune of "Some Enchanted Evening."

But I figured that could wait for a much looser party in a private room upstairs. Instead, I asked Lucille Shepherd to dance. She was always quite a card.

"Hold me just a little closer," she said, her off hand pressing against my back. "So I know you're a man."

"If we get too close," I said, "you may not like the way I tell you."

She wiggled her hips suggestively but moved back an inch or two. "I'll let you know if I have any complaints in that department."

"Geisha girls don't dance," I said. "So I'm out of practice."

"Shouldn't be a problem for you to *get your game back* around here," she said, with triple emphasis on the phrase "get your game back."

"Have to wait till I have some free time," I answered. "Bruce didn't hire me to dance. Only game I play is reading accounts and riding herd on staff."

"Lem won't dance," she said, referring to her husband. "Won't play golf either. Says any kind of exercise robs him of the energy he needs for his work."

I replied that that must be a trial for her.

"Not at all," she said. "He gives me a good allowance. I employ a maid who cooks his breakfast and dinner. He never complains if

I play 36 holes with the girls. I don't complain if he plays cards with the boys. I enjoy a little drink and a little music."

The tune ended and the dancers applauded. As the clapping died, everybody in the club became aware of angry shouts just outside the metal doors. "You go to hell," a man yelled. "Get out of my way."

Brian's voice, softer but equally determined, cut him off. "If you'll just step out here, sir. Here! Sir!"

Tommy swung into the gallop theme from the "William Tell Overture."

I asked Lucille to excuse me and went to investigate.

A stranger had tried to talk his way inside. Brian had checked the members list, the investors list, the VIP and temporary guests lists for a name similar to his. No dice. The man had then offered a $10 bribe. He became abusive when Brian asked him to leave.

After I introduced myself as the general manager, the man lowered his voice, shook my hand and gave me his business card. He explained that he lived in St. Petersburg and was engaged in the wholesale plumbing trade. A friend named Joe Smith, he said, had told him about the Caloosa Club. He asked me to make an exception and admit him—because he was in Myers on business and "just felt like having a little toot."

I explained that the toot-toot-tootsie was for hotel guests and paid-up club members only. No exceptions could be made. "But," I said, turning him around and heading him toward the dining room, "there's no reason why you can't apply for a membership, and no reason why you can't fill out your application while you enjoy a steak dinner as our guest."

He brightened up a bit, so I asked Brian to find him a good table, one over by the window, and to bring him a membership form and a pen.

A few days later, Carmen and I vetoed the application. People who don't know how to be polite are not good club material.

Bud was standing outside the club when I finished with the

troublemaker. "Time to head home for a little shut-eye," he said.

So I walked him outside, expecting to find the Jeep parked near the door. But the Jeep was already in the shop for new glass. Bud would be walking back to the rooming house.

We shook hands and he turned away. Then we heard—and saw and felt at the same instant—a *puff-ha-ha!* and an eruption of flames rising from far end of the riverside parking lot east of the hotel. Two or three white-robed men standing in shadows beyond the explosion began to cheer and clap. At the river's edge, a fiery cross lit up the night. Dancing and shifting in the soft winter air, the flames caught the light chop of the river and revealed a second clot of robed figures farther away.

"What the fuck?" I said. "Thought they only went after uppity colored people and school teachers."

"Probably just some good citizen happened to tell some other good citizen about you and your race-mixing piano player in there," Bud answered. "What was it you said about harmless fun?"

My teeth suddenly started to chatter. "Th-th-thanks, Sarge," I said. "Maybe I'd better go call the fire department now."

The cross, two planks wrapped in oil-soaked rags, burned brighter and hotter, lighting the parked cars, the yard and the brick and masonry side of the hotel. Upstairs, I could see guests at their windows, peering out from behind curtains and shades. A rough, hissing purr and a ribbon of smoke rose from the flames. I could feel my ass clench and unclench. I took a breath. Suddenly, I wanted to vomit. For the first time since leaving the Navy I was scared.

Bud laughed darkly. He sounded tired but not alarmed. His voice was steady. "You tell the fire chief you got a cross burning over here," he said. "And he'll get right on it. He'll ring the fire bell, saddle up his troops and tell 'em to go out for coffee. Might take all night to get a fire truck here."

The Klansmen started moving toward the street. The robed man at the front of the line was carrying a rifle. Bud lifted his hand, held it flat out but close to his chest and pointed toward the robed men. "See that little fella taking up the rear? That's the county clerk I mentioned, Leon Featherstone. Recognized him at that march on Saturday night. I think I ought to have a talk with him right soon. See what his thinkin' is."

"Sounds like an idea," I said. "If he'll give you the time of day."

"Oh, what with him bein' a public servant and all, I think he'll snitch to me."

"You're not worried about the Klan knowing you were here?"

Bud leaned close. "The enemy's the one I always figure is pissing down his own trouser leg. My shorts is dry, even if they really ain't." He touched my shoulder. "What you shaking for? You OK?"

Brian, Doc Shepherd and one of the card-playing physicians came up behind us in the dark. "Mine eyes have seen the glory of the coming of the Lord," Brian declaimed, giving full rein to his Boston Irish accent. "He has loosed the crazy crackers with His terrible swift sword."

"Ba-ba-bastards," Doc cackled, "hadn't quit their—ha ha!—monkey business after all."

"Thought somebody in that shit-ass crowd would have had better sense," the obstetrician said. "Especially during tourist season."

Bud stepped back to give them room. The shadows and the crackling flames momentarily highlighted the rough scar below his ear. I shut my eyes. *A Jap sergeant's bayonet rips through Bud's neck and throat.*

"Go get buckets and an axe," I said, opening my eyes and turning to Brian. "Douse that goddamn fire. Throw the fucking cross in the river."

ShApe Him Up or Ship H im Out

After the Jap torpedo ripped my ship's heart out, I floated and dog-paddled through oil fires, blanketing smoke, limp bodies, ungodly debris, torn flesh and circling sharks.

The night the Klan torched an oil-soaked cross on the bank of the Caloosahatchee, I pitched and bobbed on another endless, evil sea. Fleeing into dreams, I found what I least sought, and was in the Pacific again, attacked by wrenching stomach cramps, vomiting up alcoholic guilt and sadness, kicking and backstroking through oily water, always on the verge of giving up and going under, and never quite doing it.

Toward dawn, bells and terrified cries signaled all hope lost, abandon ship, run, dive, swim, hurry, Lieutenant, get out of the whirlpool, get clear of the whirlpool, the pool, the pool, the pool.

Tuesday morning arrived right on schedule, and in the usual way, through the cracked-open window of my second floor single. The steady splash of somebody swimming laps, the buzz-growl-pop of a lawn mower eating grass and pebbles, the rustle of palm fronds in the wind, and the aroma of hot coffee and bacon grease from the kitchen constituted a welcome sort of reveille.

Surfacing, holding my breath, I shoved back the damp covers, crossed to the window, sucked in humid river air, stretched stiff muscles, yawned and looked down.

A thin woman in a yellow bathing suit was kicking wakes up and down the sparking surface of the pool. A groundskeeper, sweaty-wet before 8 in the morning, was trimming a green-velvet strip of St. Augustine grass.

Pulling on trunks, I unfurled my rubber exercise mat, spread it out on the polished oak floor and started with 50 slow sit-ups. After 40 push-ups and 40 pull-ups on a metal rod I'd installed in the bathroom doorway, I ran in place for 10 minutes, then showered, shaved and put on my everyday manager's uniform: starched khaki pants, webbed belt, white camp shirt, dark blazer and spit-shined black oxfords.

I was transiting—going from mindset to mindset, using a jockstrapper's trick that dated from shore-leave days, running my brain in neutral and my body in high gear, consciously shifting my thoughts away from Ku Klux Klanner clerks and fiery crosses and half-baked sex with a drunken detective, and back to the game of managing a hotel.

Dropping down the service stairs, I cut through the kitchen, waved to the cooks, entered the dining room and settled onto a banquette near the glass doors facing the water. Outside, a man was practicing swan dives off the low board. The yellow-suited woman had finished her swim and was sipping coffee at a poolside table.

Homer Meadows, the experienced black waiter on the morning shift, almost immediately appeared bearing a pot of coffee, a pitcher of cream, a basket of rolls and a menu.

The menu was dog-eared and stained. I handed it back, asking him to check every menu in the bins, toss out the soiled ones and find a fresh set.

Emma Mae Bellweather crossed from the dock and came inside five minutes later. Pouring coffee for herself and buttering a honey-pecan roll, she scattered a handful of crumbs down the front of her bleached-out fishing jacket before she said a word. After she shook the crumbs onto the deck and removed the Washington Senators baseball cap she'd shoved far back on her Dutchboy bob, she asked how I'd slept and if I'd enjoyed the fish the Maysons caught on Sunday.

When I tepidly praised the sea bass and inquired, "Was it, by any chance, caught by Lou Salmi?" she got the joke right away.

"You mean oily and bony," she said, putting her hand to her mouth and giggling. "You ought to've gone out with us yourself. Ought to seen that rascal rubbing his nasty self up against Mrs. Mayson, just like a tom cat lickin' ripe pussy. And Mr. Mayson— get this, please. He rubbed suntan oil on both of their backs."

"So maybe it was Coppertone I was tasting, instead of Lou's hair pomade."

"I didn't say it," she squealed. "I sure didn't say it."

Her Caloosahatchee accent and quirky vocabulary were much like Bud's. Hearing her laugh, I might have been eaves-dropping on a less-inhibited Bud the High School Baseball Player or Cowboy Bud the Rancher. I shook my head and poured more coffee. I had to work.

"Anything unusual happening in your department?"

"Well," she drawled, fingering a donut. "Nothing too much. Except I talked to your boss, the admiral."

Pasting a pleased smile across my uncertain face, I said, "Oh, good. He's coming in tonight, right?"

Emma Mae patted my hand sympathetically. "Got here last night, real late. Was looking around after he got here. Wandered by the dock. Said he hoped to get in a little fishing. Desk clerk fixed him up with one of the keeper suites on 7. Surprised some-body didn't tell you already."

Not only had I failed to welcome the boss, I'd forgotten what night he was due to arrive. "Goddamn son-of-a-bitch," I mut-tered. "Piss up a rope."

it takes two

"Don't you worry about a fucking thing, Dan. The admiral was informed that our Caloosa bossman had put in a full day of work and was taking his well-deserved rest. Nobody told him you was fox-trotting up a storm in the club room earlier."

"Presume nobody told him about the visit by the Klan either?"

"Desk clerks and me, we agreed you'd want to brief him on that particular matter. Presuming you think the visit by those human turds had anything to do with the Caloosa. Is worth his notice, I mean."

Homer returned with a tray of food. Emma Mae began rearranging napkins and plates. "Hope you didn't mind me ordering for both of us, Dan."

"How could I forget a thing like the boss coming in?" I said. "Must be some kind of delayed shell shock. Wonder if there's a pill I could take, or something I could eat, like how carrots help your eyes. What vegetable improves memory?"

"This here is bacon and eggs and grits," she countered, charitably ignoring my run-on embarrassment. "They always give me strength. Desk clerk told me the admiral sent word he wants you to stop by his quarters first thing."

"No loose lips around this hotel," I replied, digging a fork into the steaming grits. "It was maybe two dances."

"Find me a operation where they don't gossip about the boss," Emma Mae answered, "and I'll show you a out-of-business cemetery."

I was smiling when I knocked smartly on Admiral Asdeck's door a few minutes past 10, after I'd had a chance to pick up the accounts ledger.

"Enter!"

He was seated at a room service table, his naked back to the view of the river, with papers, pencils, coffee cup, slide rule and humidor neatly squared before him. No doubt about it: The admiral stayed in shape. His shoulders, furry chest and flat belly seemed to have never known a hint of fat. Each strong arm bore a discreet tattoo. He was wearing bifocal glasses and white Brooks Brothers skivvies, the kind with buttons in front and strings on the side.

He stood up, and we greeted each other with an eye-to-eye handshake, the way military men often do. Slipping off his specs, he pointed me toward the sofa with one hand, meanwhile bringing his straight chair forward with the other. Every gesture revealed unconscious power combined with conscious care and grace.

He'd caught a flight from Miami to McDill Air Force Base the previous day, he said. And hired a car for the run down from Tampa to Fort Myers.

Nervous and ready to get started, I stepped right up to last night's lapse. "Look, Admiral, I apologize for not being awake when you got in."

"You aren't on probation, Dan," he answered, smiling now. "A man's got to sleep some time."

I opened my mouth to offer amiable thanks, then closed it when he kept on talking.

"You getting to know this detective pretty well?"

My mouth opened again, involuntarily. I hadn't planned on starting with a discussion of Bud.

"We...we had a good talk last night," I said. "Some of it was connected to a homicide investigation Detective Wright is running. And I showed him around the club. He'd been inside the hotel a time or two before but..."

Asdeck shot me a tolerant, fatherly glance. His balding head was close cropped on the sides and smoothly shaved around the neck and ears. "They tell me you two boys got caught in somebody else's shoot-'em-up Sunday over on the Tamiami Trail."

I tried to downplay what happened. "Felt like cowboys and Indians, that's right, sir."

"Don't guess they locked Mrs. Norris up in the loony ward? Good thing her aim was off."

I answered straight. But I wondered right off how Asdeck knew Willene Norris's name, what she'd done and where she'd done it. None of this had been in the newspaper. "Detective Wright slapped the cuffs on her," I said. "But, no, the coroner advised against taking her into custody. Mrs. Norris and her family own half the town, apparently."

I was aware that the boss always had more than one source of good information. But today's discussion was beginning to feel like a test, not a conversation.

Asdeck nodded, as if what I'd said explained everything. To me, of course, it really hadn't. So I went ahead and detailed the connections between Hillard Norris, Willene Norris, her card-playing brother-in-law Ridley Boldt and the Caloosa Club.

"Damn glad nobody on our side got hurt," Asdeck said when I finished. "Now what about the incident last night? Your buddy was here with you when the yokels torched the cross? What did he do? What, exactly, did he say to you?"

It sounded as if Asdeck was trying to find fault with Bud. Again, there was nothing to do but answer truthfully. So I did, explaining that Detective Wright had recognized one of the cross burners and planned to quiz him on the reasons behind the Klan's visit. Other than that, he'd seemed as surprised as I was and had said nothing out of the ordinary.

"He's looking into it," I added. "But his first thought is Tommy Carpenter, our pianist. Detective Wright figures the Klan sees us and our colored musician as some kind of Northern integrationist plot."

"The hotel as Harry Truman? With the segregated city of Fort Myers as the armed forces, huh?"

"Something like that."

Asdeck went to the window and looked out at the wide, blue-green Caloosahatchee. After a moment, he turned, shot me another glance and said, "I'll sleep better knowing the connection between the shooting and the burning last night."

That hadn't crossed my mind but I didn't say so.

"Could be no link," he added. "And if there's not, we need to know that too. You men need to keep your ears open."

"Yes, sir. I'll mention it to Detective Wright."

"You do that, son. Now what about those proposals you sent?"

And so, side by side at the desk, we went over my improvement ideas: Hire more young, perky waitresses (check), fit out conference rooms on the mezzanine and make them available around the clock (check), set up a stenographer in a lobby office and charge visiting businessmen for secretarial services (check), hire Detective Wright as chief of hotel security...

Asdeck asked how a hotel security guard might have prevented the cross burning the night before. "My parking lot is private property," he said, "not some clearing in the woods. If you and I choose to hire this or that musician, it's strictly our business. If your friend was guarding the place, what would he have done to keep the peace?"

"I'll ask him to brief me, sir."

"But you already think he can handle the job? And that your budget can handle the salary you propose?"

I nodded. "It'll be money well spent."

"Hope you don't mind," Asdeck continued, opening the desk drawer and removing a photocopied file. "I had a friend of mine over at the Pentagon pull up his personnel jacket. Spencer Wright was twice decorated for valor but has no more than a high school education. There's not a single black mark on his record, though one chief put him down as too much of a loner. He got wounded so bad he was recommended for discharge, but he talked his officer and the doc out of it. Must be a hell of a jarhead, all in all."

"He's energetic, willing to work like a dog."

"Yes, there's that. I can only assume you've considered all of this on a personal level. He's a mud-eating jarhead and a cop; you're a wardroom officer and a white-glove gentleman. How's that going to sit between you two? Can you live with him, sleep with him, drink with him, eat breakfast across from him day after day and still give him orders?"

My throat went dry. Did his words even mean what I thought they did? The time was the late 1940s, don't forget. I trusted Asdeck. Back at the New Victory Club we'd occasionally swapped morning-after stories and joked about my taste in scarred-up officers versus his in shameless geishas. But how did he know so much about my relationship with Bud? And did he see it as some kind of conflict? Suddenly, even though I was talking to my mentor and best friend, I felt cornered.

"Tell you the truth, sir, I sure intended to bring that up. Now I'm embarrassed as hell. Figured nobody was aware of it. Thought we'd been pretty careful."

"I expect you were. No doubt in my mind. But, Dan, you can't ever let anybody hold something like that over you. Gives them power. And the laws of this benighted state concerning the so-called crime against nature—not to mention some of the Caloosa's business—need to be changed. But right now we have to live with the cards we're dealt. Which does give me an idea. What we need is trump cards, our own power cards, an ace or two."

"Sir, I figured you had all that taken care of, important people taken care of, before you ever opened for business."

The admiral got up, crossed the room to the desk, selected a Havana cigar from the humidor, clipped the end, struck a match, lit the stogie and blew a cloud of rich smoke toward the window before he answered. "May I suggest that you start Detective Wright part time. Start by paying him to fill us in on the sheriff's private attitudes toward Negroes, cross burnings and mixed-race staffs. Ought to be no trick at all for a man with the detective's inside connections to draft a report on that subject."

I didn't quite follow Asdeck's reasoning. I was getting a headache and I still couldn't figure out how he knew Bud and I were mixing it up. Anyway, I balked, at least at first. "He works for Lee County," I said. "The sheriff's his boss. I'd be asking him to cross a line."

"Working security directly for you would presumably cross that line soon enough."

"After he quits the force is all I mean," I said.

"Mixing business with pleasure takes balls, Dan. You sure he's the right man? Before you decide to take him on, it seems to me you'll want to survey your buddy right down to the keel. What if he refuses our offer? Will you still love him?"

So there it was. My throat closed up. I'd wondered about that. Would Bud and I become some kind of loving couple, complete with matching bowling shirts and a weekend shack in the Everglades? Or were we merely following the conventional barracks-room track of horniness and mindless sex, and going nowhere?

I tried to answer Asdeck's question. Worked my mouth and failed. Finally, I said I was sure about Detective Wright—sure he was the right man for the job, sure that he and I would get along. I said I'd talk to him about buying reports on the sheriff.

Asdeck nodded, then added, surprisingly, "Dr. Kinsey says there's thousands of men you could get along with. But complications on down the line won't gain us anything. So, as long as you're making a choice, I'd want you to be dead sure, as sure as you can be. One way or the other, this could be for keeps."

"It's complicated. He has a girl."

Asdeck smiled and said he understood.

"He's brave," I said. "He saved my life. He's honest with me, in so far as he knows how to be. But the crazy Norris woman could've shot at anybody, and he would have stepped in."

"Good qualities," Asdeck said. "So why the holdout on being sure he's the one? Besides the girl you mentioned."

"Because, sir, he doesn't know why he does most of it."

"Motivations?"

"Exactly, sir. Which means I don't know what's behind it."

Asdeck laughed. "My wife would consider herself a traitor to all womanhood if she let me know even half of what makes her tick. There's this, though, and let me briefly wonder about it out loud. What if your doubts are ringing a warning bell? Maybe somebody tipped him off on how we operate? Maybe giving you blow jobs is his way of getting inside the operation. Maybe he plans to go to a grand jury later. Maybe he'd like to make a name for himself with some kind of trumped-up charges."

I must have blushed when I responded, "It's been a lot more than blow jobs, sir."

I still didn't have the guts to mention Bud's crying jag or his attempts to push me away in order to save me.

I said, "Honestly, sir, we've talked and I know a lot of his history. I can't figure him having any bad intentions."

"You'll have to teach him a lot," Asdeck replied. "Just like I taught you, back in Japan. And, for your own protection, you'll need to level the playing field before you actually hire him."

I shrugged, not liking the sound of that. "Meaning?"

"Meaning? Get him involved in more than just a sightseeing tour. Mix him up in something that might be interpreted as technically outside some statute or other."

"You don't think," I answered, "that two grown men sharing a bed seven or eight times pretty much covers it?"

The boss laughed. "That might be enough if you wanted to hire him as a towel boy or room steward. But not as chief of security. He needs some kind of entangling involvement. As I say, just to level the field."

Asdeck was probably right. "Give me a week, sir," I said. "And I'll get it all shipshape."

"Take all the time necessary," he said. "And, on second thought, forget about having him write up his boss. I know a better way to check on the sheriff's attitudes. I'll look into it myself."

Asdeck settled himself in the chair again and crossed his legs. "I'm confident you'll be discreet with Detective Wright," he said. "Your middle name is discretion. So let's plan for the three of us to have dinner one night. We won't bring up any of this. Now carry on."

Did I have a choice? Hell, no. Each man is lucky to have one mahatma. Asdeck was mine. I saluted.

"Next, let's look at your daily accounts," Asdeck said.

"Hotel-for-Profit operational theory," I answered, "is taking its sweet time getting inside my thick skull."

Aboard the *Indianapolis*, Ensign Rizzo and I went wherever the admirals sent us. Combat washes out fear in many men, and that was mostly true for us. As officers, we were trained to figure the odds, move fast, follow our instincts and avoid second-guessing. Mike requisitioned a set of earplugs and learned to sleep in the noisy upper bunk, part-time anyway. In continuing to lock the cabin door when we both went off watch, he and I took a series of calculated risks. Doors customarily remained unlatched at sea. But if some knucklehead had suddenly busted in without knocking—which never happened—chances were 4 to 1 that we'd have been in separate bunks, reading cowboy novels, writing home or just sleeping. We never used words like homo or pansy. Mike even joked that our occasional lower-bunk coupling took his mind off more serious problems—such as the little yellow men in big gray ships sailing around the ocean trying to kill us.

When the *Indianapolis* was hit, killing Mike and 900 shipmates, I went to the bottom with her, emotionally, I mean. By the time the medics got me calmed down, the war was over, and there was nobody to talk to about it anyway. So I figured those were the breaks. I also figured I had nothing else to lose. And I told myself I wasn't going to play anybody else's get-married game—or even date women as camouflage—because there had to be another Mike out there.

Passing through San Francisco in 1948, three years after Mike's death, I picked up a copy of the controversial Kinsey report, *Sexual Behavior in the Human Male*, and sailed through the good parts overnight. Mike and I were part of a small but scientifically recognized minority group, the Report stated, and thousands of American men behaved more or less the way we did. That such lovemaking was illegal in most of the land of the free and the home of the brave, to say nothing of the U.S. Navy, well, that was a fact of life that could be gotten around. What couldn't be so easily gotten around was the difficulty of finding the other members of our 10% statistical cluster, men who love only men.

I've already explained how I ran through a pack of potential Ensign Rizzos at the New Victory Club. But I never found another Mike, just pieces of the guy—a shoulder, a shapely neck, a low drawl or simply a man with a hungry need to sleep spooned up against my backside. Often, it was scars and healed-over bullet holes, "battle damage," that caught my attention. Unfortunately, mixing it up with such men usually brought on the nightmares. Mike had gone into battle with me, lost his life and now returned only in nightmares. To my mind, Bud's scars were a fair indication of bravery in the face of almost certain death. But he caused me no unhealthy dreams.

There was one main problem. Bud Wright fit all too comfortably into Kinsey's middle column, men who move uneasily from men to women, though with a preference. Bud risked getting naked with me but he never quit worrying about trouble just around the corner. Even after he'd been seeing me for four months, he was still screwing the waitress.

"Folks are gonna talk if I jilt her sudden," he explained as the two of us grilled hot dogs over a campfire out on Sanibel Island. "See, Dan, the lady takes me for some kind of war hero. I figure if I taper off seeing her, she'll gradually lose interest. And I'll be the gentleman and just let her walk away. Instead of me doing the walking, jilting her like some kind of heel."

"Jilting *her*? Thanks a hell of a lot, Sarge."

He just laughed and punched my shoulder. "Anyhow, don't I need a gal to take to the department Christmas party? It don't do no harm for the boss and some of the guys to see me with a good-looker once in a while. And it don't change the situation with me and you."

"No," I said, reaching over and pulling him close. "Except you're giving her my stuff."

"Could be you need a girl yourself," he laughed. "For parties and all. And don't you worry. I got plenty of *stuff* to go 'round."

elliott mackle

Bud Wright, in other words, was a lot more in tune with the moral conventions and evasions of America than I was.

He and I ate lunch together that Tuesday after my talk with Bruce Asdeck. At Bud's suggestion, we met at the Arcade Café on First Street, right in the center of downtown Fort Myers. The Arcade, a local institution, was the special preserve of cops, lawyers, title-search specialists, bail-bond dealers and similarly mid-level courthouse types. They treated the place as a meeting hall and hideout from wives and ground-level staffers. Precinct bosses and election officials sometimes negotiated close races in the coffee shop's windowless back room. Legal briefs were argued informally across the oilcloth-covered tables and opening and closing statements tried out in what amounted to a pay-by-the-day clubhouse.

The exclusivity of the Arcade was practically guaranteed. Clerks, secretaries and hourly office help, by universal agreement, took breakfast, lunch and coffee breaks at Wallace's Drugstore two blocks away. County commissioners, the mayor and business leaders frequented the ultramodern coffee shop at the old Bradford Hotel. The Arcade was therefore almost as private for regular customers as a judge's chambers.

I arrived to find Bud seated alone at a four-top table in the otherwise empty back room, his attention focused on Slim Nichols. Zipped into a nylon waitress uniform that afforded not an inch of breathing space, she was almost glued to his side. *Now why didn't I expect this?* I wondered. *I set out to meet my Clark Gable for lunch and find him two-timing me with Gloria Grahame.*

Glancing my way for half a second, then returning her attention to Bud, Slim said over her shoulder, "How you be, sugar pie? Take a seat over there, if you like. Will that be coffee or ice tea?"

"Coca-Cola," I answered, and slid into the chair facing Bud. Unwilling to give the woman an inch, I added, "With lemon, thanks. And do you want to tell me what the extra-specials are today?"

Slim pulled a folded menu from under her arm and flipped it open to the meat-and-three list. "Try the baked Spanish mackerel with tartar sauce and lemon butter," she advised. "And stewed Ruskin okra. That's what I was just telling Bud here. Be sweet and I'll save you back the best slices of our butterscotch cream pie."

She knew her trade, that's for sure. "Do it," I answered, glancing at the mimeographed menu. "With baby lima beans and green salad."

"Same here," Bud echoed. "Forget the okra. Whatever else you think I can handle."

"Woo, boy. They tell me you can handle about anything," she retorted, then cut her eyes down at me. "Little joke," she said, touching her collar.

"Better put a basket over that pie," Bud said, looking up and grinning. "I might be up to two slices."

A bell rang in the next room. Beaming, Slim turned toward the kitchen. "Be back with bread in two shakes, sweethearts."

"And the Coke," I called after her.

OK, I was a little jealous. Bud bantered with Slim in ways he wouldn't risk with me. Not in public. Still, I wasn't overly worried. Slim had a toothpaste smile and knew how to use it, but she also had at least five years on Bud. And her good looks were essentially dime-store stuff—hair-net, Woolworth's face paint, crimson claws and matching lipstick. Aside from an added inch to my college waistline, I looked a lot less the worse for wear. And my goods were a darn sight better.

Slim was efficient, though, God knows. She could balance a coffee pot, two ice waters and a cream jug in one hand while handing out menus with the other. As housewife material, she had me beat cold. On the other hand, I could offer free room service.

Bud flipped open his menu, then closed it and set it aside. "Goddamn fucking shit, Lieutenant," he whispered, his voice pitched just above a growl. "What are you doing? You danced in here and sat right down like you was my fucking wife."

Mystified, I leaned back and stared. "Huh?"

"You don't show no sense sometimes." His voice was low and shaky, his tone edging toward barely controlled panic.

"You invited me to lunch, right? What's this about getting married?"

"Keep your voice down, goddamn it. You're putting ideas in her head. She's calling us sweethearts. Next thing you know it'll be homos or something."

I lifted a hand to comfort him.

"And don't you go touching my arm neither. People'll start to talk."

"She's a waitress," I said. "She calls everybody 'sugar pie' and 'sweetheart.' It doesn't mean anything."

"You're livin' in a dream world, Lieutenant. This is Fort Myers. Slim's my lady friend. And now she's calling me…oh, shit, I don't know. Maybe we ought to just get out of here right now."

"Did you get any sleep?" I asked. "You sound like a cat that's been lapping up Maxwell House."

"Told you. I can't be too careful. Nor you either. Maybe I'm imagining something."

It should have been obvious that Bud wasn't thinking right. Fat chance some waitress with baked hair was going to imagine her muscular stud-horse as a pansy, much less the steady sexual partner of another reasonably well-developed, hard-working man. It wasn't possible, not with Bud fucking her as well and as often as he implied he was. For all Slim knew, Bud might have been keeping her as happy as a well-fed clam while taking on the entire Ethiopian Army twice a week.

"What about I pinch her ass when she comes back?" I said. "Or we could all get in bed together sometime. You can have your cheesecake and eat it too."

"Show some respect, Lieutenant. She's not that kind of girl."

"Me neither," I answered, winking at him. "Do you think?"

Relaxing a little, Bud sugared his tea. "You sleep OK?" he asked, stirring the tea with the spoon from the sugar bowl. "The Klan party send any of your Yankee guests packing?"

"All quiet so far. I've still got 20 rooms empty, same as yesterday. And this is winter season. Over in Miami Beach, I hear they're full up."

"What are you doing about it? Hiring Alexander's Ragtime Band?"

"Empty beds don't worry me," I said. "But that cross-burning sure does."

Slim returned, set down my Coke, a basket of corn bread and crackers and four pats of butter, then she turned on her high heels and marched away.

I waited two beats before whispering, "Wish you could have stayed over last night. What about if I come by your place after supper? We could wrestle a little."

Bud's previously jocular voice sank again. "Keep it down. Christ knows what kind of bird dog might be waving his ears around here. I can't afford people talking. Nor you, if you think about it. So don't kid, OK?"

The room was still empty except for the two of us. Slim was out front loading a tray at the kitchen's pass-through window. But I knew Bud was partly right. We couldn't get in the habit of talking like bedmates in public. His defensive panic made me mad, though. Maybe this was what Asdeck seemed to be warning against. I shot back a smartass answer and I didn't keep my voice down.

"How's this, Sarge? How about you stick to beer instead of Bacardi next time? Watching you puke your guts up is nobody's dream come true."

The man's hurt surprise crackled back at me. He swallowed and shook his head.

Quick as radar, I regretted what I'd said, and started to sputter out an apology.

Bud took a quick, deep breath and cut me off. "You must be really worried, Dan. I can understand that. We're both working like goddamn field hands and under a lot of pressure."

He paused, leaned closer and dropped his voice. "So I'm not gonna deck you for mouthing off. Not this time." He leaned back, suddenly barked a laugh and swiped his open hand across my face, missing my nose by an inch, playful once more. "Never gonna touch that rotgut rum again," he said, snapping his fingers. "Let me put your mind at rest about that too. OK? OK, mister?"

I tried to grab his hand but he was too fast for me. Relieved that my tense mood and nasty mouth hadn't made him angry, I looked up and winked. "If anybody's gonna be decked, it's gonna be Coach's little Buddy. You got that?"

Bud laughed again, and nodded.

I finished my apology, keeping my voice down. "I'm worried as hell. I didn't sleep much last night. Those Klan bastards could go crazy and set fire to the hotel next time. And I'm sorry about what I said a minute ago. I'm just lonely and, you...know."

"Right. Yes. I do," Bud answered, nodding again. "Hell of a weekend all around. Hasn't quit yet," he said, picking up a wedge of corn bread and downing it in two bites.

He washed the bread down with tea. "It ought to get better. I squeezed my snitch this morning. Courthouse clerk name of Featherstone."

"First name Leon? I remember you pointed him out."

"Took the ratty little shithead aside for a cup of java first thing. He like to pissed himself when I mentioned seeing through his Sunday-go-to-meeting dis-guise at the march Saturday and again last night. Sort of tried to deny it at first."

"He's not got what you might call Stonewall Jackson's backbone?"

"Nor supposed to be engaging in political activities either," Bud answered primly. "So long as he's a public employee."

"So why did the bastards burn a cross outside my hotel?"

Bud buttered another wedge of corn bread. "Remember the name Willene Norris?"

"Sure. I never forgot the people who shoot at me."

"Well, she's the reason. Her county commissioner daddy was a Klanner. And she knows 'em all. Once she got home Sunday afternoon, her friends all started coming by to give her aid and comfort. And once the thing was in the paper yesterday, more of 'em came over. I guess once they got together they decided something ought to be done. And she convinced 'em all her husband's killing was just part of the rack and ruin that's going on in Lee County generally. And they ought to take a stand."

"Rack and ruin. As in?"

"As in there's immoral, un-Christian behavior going on, latest example being the mixed-race drinking and carousing at the Caloosa."

"And that's why they marched? Because I employ a colored pianist? Hell, we're all but white. Most of the old colored waiters were let go. We're replacing them with young women—white, so far, though I hadn't thought about it."

"You might better think on it, seems to me."

"It's supposed to be gradual and confidential anyway. No reason for Mrs. Norris to know my backstage business. And plenty of places have mixed staffs."

"Leon Featherstone seemed to think it was something more than that."

I thought so too. But before I explained, I quietly asked about possible connections between the riverside cross burning and last Saturday's march on the African Methodist Episcopal church.

"Squeezed him on that too," Bud answered. "Fucker looked like a rat with his tail in a pencil sharpener. So I quizzed him hard. He swore there wasn't any link. Said the Saturday operation was what I already knew about, some white race-mixer down from up North, man named Bridge, just stirring up trouble. They marched as a warning."

"So you think there is a connection?"

"Hard to tell."

Bud was about to open a package of saltine crackers. Setting it down, he leaned back. "You didn't have any Mr. Bridge from Philadelphia registered at the Caloosa last weekend, did you?"

Laughing, I said I was pretty sure we didn't, but I'd check. Then I filled Bud in on the connection I saw.

I told him I'd just talked to Brian Rooney, the club room bouncer, and club manager Cabildo Morales, a.k.a. Carmen Veranda. They'd confirmed my sketchy memory of Hillard Norris's final solitary visit to the Caloosa Club. The incident happened one afternoon back in December. Norris had pressured both employees to rent him a hotel room for a colored woman. When Norris made it clear he'd be sharing the room, first one and then the other had put him off and consulted me. After checking a list of hypotheticals provided by Admiral Asdeck, I'd told them to say the hotel was full. Norris, a regular card player though not a dues-paying member, had cursed them both and left. He hadn't returned to the hotel since.

Bud suddenly glanced over my shoulder and I shut up.

Tap-tapping across the terrazzo floor, Slim set down bowls of Cole slaw and tartar sauce, checked our drinks and went away.

Bud grinned, forked a load of slaw onto his butter plate and whistled. "I don't guess you know the colored woman's name?"

When I said no, he answered that it didn't matter. "This might be easier than I thought," he continued. "Because it just so happens that the dead colored boy in the room with Hillard Norris was married to Mrs. Norris's former house-maid. Don't know her name yet either. Funny if it was the same gal."

"Not funny for her husband," I said. "Or her fancy man, if that's what Norris was."

"Well, I mean to find out," Bud said quietly, slapping the table with his open hand.

"Something wrong, sweethearts?" Slim said, setting a loaded tray on the service stand near our table. She rapidly set down the fish platters, vegetables and a fresh basket of bread and crackers.

"Mean to find out how good this tastes," Bud answered. "How's that, Miss Nichols?"

"You still have our pie under wraps?" I chimed in.

"Don't you worry, lamb. Be back with more tea in two shakes."

"That's another Coke," I called after her.

Chopping up baked mackerel with his fork, Bud shoved several bites into his mouth, chewed and swallowed. Evidently finding the fish acceptable, he started talking again. "Officer Hurston's report says there was only the one gun found in the room with Norris and the colored boy. Gun was in Norris's hand. Mrs. Jenkins says she didn't touch a thing. Says she heard three shots and called the cops. Nobody but her and Hurston went in the room before Doc and I got there, as far as anybody knows."

I bit into the fish. It was so fresh and sweet it didn't need tartar sauce. I'd finished half the fillet before I tossed an idea back at Bud. "Easy call. He shot his mistress's husband to keep the field free for plowing by himself."

Bud stuffed several pats of butter into a baked potato. "We still ain't sure who shot who. Doc did manage to salvage a plate showing how the weapon was found—in Norris's hand. Only Norris's wrist was already blown to bits. He couldn't of held on to the piece."

"Or aimed it?"

Bud salted and peppered the spud. "Or aimed it. Be next to impossible to ding a man right through the ear like that, way he was wounded. And there was blood all over the weapon, the rug and the lady's jacket."

When I looked up, Bud had a bearish grin on his face. "Maybe you want a rare steak instead of that fish?" he said.

"Maybe I'll skip right to the blood-erscotch pie," I answered.

"Just funning with you," he said. "Sorry. Don't mean to turn your stomach. What about a little Bacardi sauce instead of that lemon butter?"

Mock-gagging, I went back to work on the mackerel. When I looked up again, Doc Shepherd was standing two feet behind Bud's chair. No telling how long he'd been there listening. I replayed the last few sentences in my mind. We sounded goofy, like teenagers, but not queer teenagers.

Shepherd had a tall glass of iced tea in one hand, a sheaf of files in the other. "Detective Wright, Mr. E-e-wing," he said, bowing slightly. "May I join you? I had an appointment with a colleague. He must be unavoidably detained. Ha ha." Easing his black-suited bulk onto the chair next to Bud, he picked up Bud's gag line and ran with it. "Don't tell me our esteemed Arcade has graduated from sawmill gravy to whiskey sauces? Very continental. Next thing you know we'll be drinking wine with lunch. I had nothing more in mind than a little cup of soup."

Setting down the files, he picked up a menu and quickly scanned it. "No pheasant under glass, alas. So I will have the vegetable soup after all. At my place of business, we have actually had a pet parrot on ice since August. He's being held as evidence in an aggravated rape-homicide. Detective Wright, you may know more about this than I do. The powers that be decided to bury the old lady who owned him. She and Polly-Want-a-Cracker were beaten to death with the same fireplace poker."

"Case been continued twice," Bud said. "How long you figure you can keep the bird fresh?"

"He was pretty old to begin with," Doc answered, pausing to order soup and salad when Slim arrived, then picking up his joking patter again. "But I expect Polly is good for another six months, ha ha."

Glancing owlishly at Bud, Doc asked, "Or should I go into any of that before you boys have your dessert? Doesn't bother me, of course."

Bud answered that we'd been discussing Doc's skill in saving the photographic evidence of the gun's original position. And that we were saving room for blood-erscotch pie.

"There was indeed blood all over the place," Doc said, digging an investigative hand into the bread basket. He selected a package of saltines and unzipped the cellophane wrapper before he continued. "Including a goodly amount soaked into the woman's jacket we found on the floor."

Doc popped a cracker into his mouth and chewed once. "Both victims had had something to drink. More than something. Did I tell you that, Bud? And it was a Sunday too. We did establish that they died well after midnight."

Finished with the okra, beans, slaw and fish, I pushed my plate away. "Don't tell me they were drinking on Sunday," I said, hoping Bud and Doc would appreciate the joke. "Thought this town was officially dry on Sunday."

"Dry as...ha ha, Dutch gin," Shepherd answered. "Dry as the courthouse." Then he paused, glanced around the still empty room, picked up his glass of tea and drank off about half the contents. Reaching into an inside coat pocket, he drew out a half-empty pint of whiskey, uncapped the bottle and filled the tumbler to the brim.

"Dry as a Navy ship," I said, noting Doc's little secret.

"Dry as the Protestant church," Bud put in. "Pastor Pucklet once told my grandma that Catholic priests are all sinners because they indulge in altar wine. And Grandma says back to him, 'Milton, in that case they are sinning with Jesus and the 12 Apostles. Who are you sinning with?'"

"Your grandmama sounds like a pistol," I said.

Doc swigged his spiked tea, then said, "Our two dead men weren't legally intoxicated, no, no. Just having a little fun."

"Fun with bullets is a little too much," I said. "I'll stick with Regal and be-bop music on the radio."

Picking up a fork, Doc dug into the remains of the cole slaw. "That was very spirited dancing you demonstrated last night, by the way. Nice entertainment for the ladies. The jigaboo pianist you employ...ha ha! He's very talented. But I wasn't talking about man-woman fun. What I meant was this: Two men alone in a room, bits of women's clothing on hand, sufficient alcohol consumed for one or both of them to let his behavior get out of hand. One of them does in point of fact get highly and perhaps criminally aroused. What does that sound like to you?"

Though my gut and balls turned cold, that didn't make me wise enough to keep quiet. "Any blood on the lampshade?" I asked. "That's how them homos act, isn't it? Wearing lampshades like a woman's hat? Either man wearing a bra or panties under his clothes?"

Doc put down his fork. "My, my," he sniffed. "You are indeed well informed on social deviance."

He wasn't going to catch me there. "Not really," I said. "It just seems like one bloody jacket is hauling a lot of freight."

Doc looked right and left and sipped more tea. "In a situation like this, one of the homos nearly always plays the woman, the she-male, it's sometimes called. And with this pair of dead men, ha ha, well, the possibility of sexual high jinks has been bandied about since Sunday afternoon. By people higher up than ourselves. The deviance angle is not my idea, son."

"Both of those men was married, Doc," Bud said. "Sounds to me like the higher-ups is bandying up the wrong tree."

"Remains to be seen," Doc said. "But it's disgusting any way you look at it."

Bud set his fork down. "We identified the laundry mark on the jacket this morning. Manager over at Brooks Dry Cleaning Service looked it up for me. The coat belonged to Mrs. Hillard Norris."

"Probably too small for Hillard to fit into," I said. "What size was what's his name, the colored guy?"

"Here you go, Doctor," Slim said, setting a bowl of vegetable soup, a plate of mixed salad and a bottle of Milani's 1890 French Dressing in front of him. She picked up Bud's empty dishes. "Will there be anything else, gents?"

"Piece of that, ah, pie," Doc replied without looking up.

Slim nodded and went away.

"Keep talking," Bud prodded. "Only you want to keep your voice down."

Doc held up his spoon and wiggled it back and forth over his soup as if deciding how much to say. Then he picked up a second cracker in his free hand and punched it hard with the spoon. Crumbs from the shattered saltine showered down into the soup.

"This is in strict confidence," he began after a glance at me. "You heard me say none of this. You could be called as a witness." When I shrugged, he continued. "In the best of all possible worlds, I'd have had the time required to perform my duties on both of these unfortunate men. But that wasn't the case. Still"—he spooned up several bites of soup—"we can be definite about more than one or two highly interesting facts."

Most of what he said was predictable. Norris's body was that of a healthy white male of middle years. Examination revealed no particular abnormalities aside from gross trauma to the jaw area and a compound wound with multiple fracturing of the right wrist. Both were consistent with the time of death. The head wound would have been fatal in any case. The injury to the extremity may have resulted from the victim throwing up his arm in surprise or to shield himself or someone else. The victim had not suffered a stroke or heart attack; no blade or other object had entered his body; he had not been poisoned with cyanide or electrocuted; there was no evidence of advanced disease, organic failure or debilitation.

Doc took another swig of tea, winked, then added, "The tree our masters have been bandying up does have some considerable basis in fact, however."

My balls went cold again. I asked what he meant.

"Norris got plenty overheated just before he died, ha ha."

Bud stirred his tea without looking at the coroner.

"My examination of the victim's undergarments and genitalia showed that he engaged in a certain amount of—ha ha—sensual activity shortly before death."

Keeping a straight face before the coroner's delicacy of language wasn't easy. "You think he died in the saddle?" I asked.

Doc crushed a wedge of buttered corn bread into his soup. "Hard to tell about that, precisely. But I'm willing to speculate he rode a darn long way."

I could feel the blush on Bud's cheek bloom without even looking his way. "Appears to Doc that Norris was upset for a considerable period of time."

"Sexually excited? Aroused?"

"Right. Yes. You said it."

"I read somewhere," I said, "that hell is a combination of every agonizing about-to-do feeling you can think of—about to eat, about to burp, about to yawn, about to piss, about to fart, about to shoot off. But not doing it."

Bud exhaled as if he'd suddenly tasted something foul.

"Imagine dying in that condition," Doc said. "Pure hell,

you're right. But that's not what I believe happened. No, according to the secretions I found, and what I believe the girls in the lab are going to tell me, our Mr. Norris finished his work before some person or persons unknown finished him." Doc spooned up more soup. "You know there was a rubber in the john. It had definitely been used."

Slim collected dishes. She then set down forks and three slices of pie. Refilling my Coke and the iced teas, she said there was plenty more pie. Half turning, she greeted a pair of businessmen who were just entering the room. "Take a table anywhere, gents."

We ate a while in silence. Then Bud leaned back, a smile glinting. "You don't think," he whispered, "the colored boy had a hand in this?"

I couldn't help laughing.

Doc put his spoon down. "Bad, bad joke. But no, I don't think so. There was no suggestion of any such thing on his body or linen, which were immaculate, I'll have to say. Speaking of hands, you probably won't be surprised that I found not a trace of powder on Hillard Norris's hands. Conversely, there were powder burns on the Negro's right hand."

Bud glanced at the table of newcomers. "May want to keep the volume down, Doc."

"Even though Officer Hurston found Norris with the gun in his hand?" I said. "And you photographed it?"

"Even though he had been shot through his right wrist," Doc agreed. "I would stipulate that it was resting in his hand. I can't say for sure that he ever gripped it. What with the Mrs. disturbing the weapon as she did. But I don't believe Norris fired a weapon Sunday morning. A very unusual situation, in my opinion, whatever tree you bandy it up."

Slim had returned with checks. Stopping behind Bud and leaning down, she said, just low enough for us to hear, "Your switchboard called, sugar pie. They want you back at the office, pronto. Whyn't you give me a call later?"

Bud nodded once, picked up all three checks, dropped three

$1 bills on the table and rose to his feet. "This is mine. I got to get on back and I thank you kindly for the company."

As he swung around, he almost collided with a late-arriving businessman. When Bud stepped back, waving the man forward, the gent ignored him and stuck his hand out toward Doc. "Lem, Lem," he called. "So good to see you."

The man's cadaverous breath fouled the air between Doc and me. He had a red, overheated face, low forehead and thick, mouse-brown hair swept back over his ears like a coonskin cap.

Doc stood up, stepped back and introduced us, pronouncing all three names slowly and carefully. The man, Coleman Bucklew, grinned and gave Bud a man-to-man handshake. His yellow-brown teeth looked false; his tongue and lower lip were stained from smoke and nicotine.

"Work for the sheriff, do you, son? I been a supporter of your boss for many, many years. I count Gene Hollipaugh among my real close personal friends. So lemme know if I can ever do anything for you."

It was another story when Bucklew realized who I was. Instead of shaking my outstretched hand, he took a step back and pursed his mouth. "Sorry to say I can't, in all good conscience, welcome you to our little town of Myers. Perhaps if we met under different circumstances? But I have to object to the cesspool of mongreloid carnality and sin you've come here to run. May you drown in it."

Here was a man I really wanted to deck. In the Navy, no matter how many new assholes an angry superior may bite in a subordinate's butt, decorum dictates that the chewing-out be delivered with at least a minimum of respect. Officers are trained to consider the human being as well as the fuck-up. So I didn't say anything at first, which was OK because Bucklew wasn't finished.

"The honest, churchgoing Christians of Lee County," he continued, "of which I hope I may be included as a believer, do not appreciate the kind of visitors your kind of place attracts. They are not good for business. And we hear that unsavory entertainment is presented."

By that time, having caught my breath, I asked Mr. Bucklew if he'd had an opportunity to visit the Caloosa lately.

"Wouldn't dream of it," he answered.

In that case, I thought, *perhaps you might like to satisfy yourself that the hotel is no Sodom and Gomorrah.* "Hearsay and gossip are no substitute for first-hand information," I answered, my tone perhaps a little too sharp. "You would honor me," I concluded, smiling as best I could, "if you'd come for lunch or dinner, as my guest, and bring your wife and family. Any time. Tell them to bring swimsuits if they like."

Bucklew looked as if he wanted to spit on my shoes. "Such an arrangement isn't possible," he said. "I wouldn't see them dead there. And good day to you."

scu_{tt}le_bu_Tt ————————————

Bud and I met in a booth at the Legion Hall bar late that afternoon. He'd sounded frustrated and angry when he called from a gas-station pay phone 30 minutes earlier. So I bought him a beer and let him talk.

The boss had hauled him on the carpet just as soon as he returned from lunch. He'd been asked, point-blank, what connections he'd turned up between the Ku Klux Klan and the killings at the Royal Plaza Motor Lodge.

"Hell," Bud said. "There's connections from here to Punta Gorda. But nothing to take to a grand jury. Not yet, anyhow."

I dug into a bowl of peanuts. "And you don't want to share your snitch with him?"

"Last thing I'd do. You know me better'n that. Hell, I keep my word."

"So you ate your boss's shit rather than tell him what we both know—that Willene Norris sent the Klan over to my hotel last night? That she's your only suspect in her husband's death? That she fucked up prime evidence in a homicide case? And that she aimed a piece of that evidence at me and fired. Hell, man, she could've killed me and you both, not to mention Doc's trusties."

"Mose and Drackett? Hell, those boys been dodgin' bullets since they was in diapers."

"You came onto the firing line late, Sarge. You weren't out there minding your own business like a sitting duck. You weren't looking down the barrel of a fucking loaded pistol when a crazed, bloodthirsty bitch started firing in all directions."

Bud scooped up a handful of nuts and began feeding them into his mouth. "Wasn't any more blood spilled. You didn't get much more'n a scratch."

"Maybe your boss needs to eat a plate of shit himself. You gonna go easy on the bitch just because she's rich and owns half the town? Hell, man, I had to qualify with a sidearm. I could'a put the bitch down if I'd had a weapon. Hell, I might take on the Klan next time. I mean, I admit you did keep me from getting hit, and…"

Halfway through my prissy blowout, Bud started shaking his head and grinning. "You're going in three directions. It's hearsay is all it is. You want to know what else the boss said? Or do you want to do all the talking? Lieutenant?"

"Sound off, Sarge. Don't let me interrupt."

"What the boss told me, point-blank, is that there is positively no connection between the Klan and the dead men. And not to waste time looking for one. And that if I'm having trouble handling two important assignments without confusing the one with the other, he'll give me all the help he can."

When I let the air stay empty, Bud added, "Like a kick in the butt, is what he meant. And a one-way ticket back home to La Belle if I don't hear him loud and clear."

elliott mackle

"Simmer down," I said, suddenly worried. "You're not going anywhere."

"Not right now, I guess. But I am gonna chat some more with Leon Featherstone."

"Thought maybe you should've collared Mr. Snitch again this afternoon—while he's still willing to talk."

"Too busy. Spent my time readin' files on the Klan and the Norris family. Not much there."

"When you gonna chat with Willene?"

"I'd rather line up my other ducks first. She ain't gonna want to talk to me anyhow, wouldn't think."

"No," I said, "I wouldn't think so either. Guess you could drag her in front of a grand jury." Then, remembering Asdeck's instructions, I added that, besides Willene Norris, there might be some other connection between the shooting and the cross-burning, something we'd catch if we sifted through the whole thing again. "My boss wants us to keep our ears open for him," I said.

Now it was Bud's turn to turn silent. After about 10 seconds he said gently, "You and the admiral been talking about this? And he wants me reporting to you? And you gonna feed it all to him? About my official duties? Huh."

I was about to mouth off again, say something like "Fuck you, Sarge." But then I got it. Bud was ready to cross over. He'd called from a pay phone and not his office. He was telling me everything he knew. And I was about to throw it back in his face. Asdeck had suggested that I entangle my buddy in a compromising way. Well, here he was, as nippy and submissive as a puppy. We might as well have been lying chest to chest on a beach somewhere, wrestling like heavy-eyed teenagers.

So I kept my answer slow and off-hand. "The admiral says it sounds to him like the sheriff may be covering for the Klan. Could be some good reason for it."

Bud said, "Yeah?"

"And it sounds to me like that's what you're saying too."

it takes two

"Right. Yes."

"The admiral first said he wondered if you'd give us a back-ground report on Sheriff Hollipaugh's deep-down racial atti-tudes, what he says and thinks in private—you know, about Negroes, integrated hotel staffs, the white-sheet brigade, things like that."

"Hell," Bud answered, "I bet even the man's wife don't know. He's a politician. He'll say whatever he needs to to get reelected."

"Anyway," I said, "I nixed that. The admiral said he had another way of checking."

"You think maybe your boss is Klan?"

"The opposite. But I figure he wouldn't set up a business without buying whatever kind of insurance was required."

"And he'd need a local agent to write the policy?"

My balls went cold for the first time in the conversation. I sucked down two long swallows of beer before I spoke. "You're thinking maybe our bosses already know all they need to about each other?"

"They could be checking up on us. Or on each other. To them, we're just ground level grunts. Between 'em, they could be running a two-reel lawn mower. With our asses as grass."

"No," I said. "I trust the boss. He knows me inside out."

"Not your, ah... You don't mean your private stuff?"

That stopped me. But Asdeck didn't have many secrets from me either. Not sexual secrets, anyway.

So I said, "Yeah, sure. He knows what I like. I told you, he's liberal."

"You're shittin' me," Bud said, followed by, "He knows you're a...that? And he don't mind?"

No, I said. Not as far as I could tell.

Maybe I should have told Bud about my plan to hire him right then. Maybe it would have saved us a lot of trouble.

But instead I just said that I wanted to spend another night with him and we could talk about it then. And he said yeah, we'd get together. And we left it at that.

Back at the office, I phoned Wanda Limber to discuss a

"special" surprise party for the boss. No doubt I was overcompensating a bit.

"Good to see you last night," I said.

"Same here. Didn't know you were such a high stepper."

"You busy this evening?" I said, getting right to the point. "You and your friend Betty?"

"Never too busy for you, Dan."

"This is for the boss, Wanda. Special favor, OK? Meet us in the club around 7:30. Let me know the charges later."

"You mean Bruce Asdeck?" she said. "You know I know him? He and my husband Butch were at Ford Island together. And we've seen each other a time or two since then. What do you have in mind?"

They'd seen each other a time or two. Wanda had a nice way of letting me know things. She was a lady, no doubt about it, right down to her matched pearls and closed-mouth discretion. She also had a wicked sense of humor. She told me once that men consort with women partly because their own hairy hands and thick fingers never whisper, "More, more, more, big boy."

She and I understood each other. "What about Betty?" I asked. "Bruce ever seen her?"

Wanda said Betty was new in town and she didn't think so.

"OK, Betty just might let it slip to the admiral," I said, "that she's been reading the Kinsey report. She could wonder out loud how anybody, even a scientist, could watch a man and woman actually doing it. She'd have to sound pretty embarrassed about the subject. Probably she could say that no good woman would even want to witness such an act. Bruce can take it from there. There's a room-service pantry with peepholes next to his suite. He'll expect us to take a look after they get started."

Wanda laughed silkily. "I like it. Let me talk to Betty. I don't see any problem. She can dress like the president of the Boston Junior League, and flutter those big, dark eyelashes."

Wanda knew her trade. All of this was fairly standard. I was about to say goodbye when she added, using the little-boy diminutive I didn't like, "Danny, what about you and Betty mixing it up sometime soon? Or I could bring another girl with us tonight. You're too shy. You ought to loosen up and have fun once in a while yourself. What do you do? Bottle it?"

"Bottle it, that's right. And ship it home. Seriously, Wanda, I've been busy. OK, and tell Betty that Bruce is the athletic type. He doesn't require anything special. Just keep a light on. She should stick around as long as he likes. Use her judgment. Good time to be had by all."

"We all like a good time," Wanda purred, her voice measured and confidential but light. "Do whatever you want. But you might take that policeman friend of yours up to Margo O'Hara's place in Sarasota. Margo's a very artistic person. She knows how to toss a salad—mixes up the men and the women so nobody feels uncomfortable. And everything stays under cover, so to speak. I could make a call to introduce you."

I didn't want to discuss my sexuality, or Bud's, with Wanda. "So to speak, right. But you've got it wrong. Detective Wright is a friend of mine. We go fishing."

"Don't pay any attention to me, then. But I did hear you were seeing somebody. And I thought…" She laughed. "It's all the same to me, Dan."

"I'd have to go rent an oyster farm if I was getting as much shack-time as people say. Where'd you hear that one?"

She thought over her answer quickly. My position of economic power—I could keep her out of the hotel if I wanted to—probably made the difference. "Carmen Veranda's a singer with big lungs. But, you know, people always gossip about their honchos."

She was right. Emma Mae had made essentially the same observation over breakfast. And hadn't Bud and I just finished speculating on our own bosses' secrets?

"You want to gossip," I said. "Tell me about Hillard Norris. You ever see him?"

Wanda would probably have broken confidence about the

dead man if I'd demanded it. But her answer sounded honest enough. "He wasn't interested in girls like me," she said. "And I don't mean that like it might sound."

"According to what I read in the paper," I said, "he had a wife, daughter, family business, civic responsibilities, blah, blah, blah. Happiest frog in the pond. He also spent a lot of time in my club last November and December. But he was no big gambler and didn't drink much. So what was he interested in?"

"He married the boss's daughter," Wanda answered. "You know how it goes. They say he had a dark-skinned honey on the side."

That tallied with what I already knew. "Norris tried to reserve a hotel room for himself and a colored woman last December," I said. "When we weren't able to accommodate him, he got nasty. Far as I know, he hasn't been back since."

A series of dull clicks suddenly hit my ear. I wondered if the line might be tapped. I was about to ask Wanda if she could hear anything when she laughed. "That's me," she said. "I was counting back the weeks to December on my fingers. And I probably shouldn't repeat this. But they also say that Mr. Hillard and Sheriff Gene Hollipaugh drove over to the East Coast for a couple of days between Christmas and New Years. You did know they were friends?"

When I whistled, Wanda laid out the story she'd heard in the country club locker room. Norris and Hollipaugh had stayed at the luxurious Breakers Hotel in Palm Beach. They'd played golf with the sheriff of Palm Beach County, gambled at Bradley's casino and attended the horse races at Tropical Park.

Wanda's nails click-clicked the telephone again. "The talk at the club is that our friend Mr. Hillard planned to set up a gaming operation in Lee County. On his own account. With strippers on weekends." At this point, she dropped her voice. "With Gene Hollipaugh protecting his back."

"For a share of the take?"

"You didn't hear it from me. But everybody says things are getting too hot over on the East Coast."

"Actually," I said, "we've been trying to get up a mixed doubles game."

"And Bruce Asdeck and Betty Harris sound like the perfect twosome."

"Thanks, honey. You sure 7:30's OK? I'll introduce Miss Harris to the admiral."

Wanda made kissing noises into the phone. "Till then."

OK, I wondered. *Who's double-crossing who? Would Asdeck sell me out? Did Hollipaugh cut a deal with Asdeck, then look for better terms when the Caloosa take came up short? Or did he merely go for a Palm Beach joyride and then tell Norris, quite literally, no dice? And how would Hollipaugh react if Bud implicated him and the Klan in the killing at the Royal Plaza Motor Lodge?*

None of it added up. Willene, the heir of a Klan leader, would hardly have welcomed her husband's affair with a black woman. In that sense, her shooting spree was understandable. And yet it wasn't. She might have killed her husband in a fit of rage. But why kill the husband of his honey? And in so public a mixed-race place? But then again, if she wasn't the killer, why had her jacket been found in the room with the bodies?

Since returning to Florida, I'd read the *News-Press, Miami Herald* and *Tampa Tribune* whenever I could get them. I knew that Miami war veteran George Smathers and a band of crusading prosecutors and editors had begun a campaign to drive illegal gambling and strippers out of Dade, Broward and Palm Beach counties on the state's east coast. Assorted sheriffs, mayors and county commissioners—many with ties to both the Klan and the Mafia—were being indicted for protecting casinos, horse race wires, nightclubs and numbers games. Times were changing. And the changes made some people nervous.

Jamie and Barbara Mayson, for example, checked out of the hotel the next morning, four days ahead of schedule. The desk clerk called before breakfast, informing me they'd just rung for the bill. I was ready with a smile and a discreetly folded statement when Barbara stepped off the elevator wearing a linen suit and alligator pumps.

"Danny," she said. "It's all been so grand. But Jamie has to see some people over in Miami. This came up out of the blue."

"I don't blame you," I said. "The Klan's brand of Southern hospitality isn't for everybody."

"Don't even think about it," she answered, patting my hand.

"But I do. We have the sheriff's office checking into it. What happened is probably all a mistake. You know the white-sheeters didn't come any closer than the parking lot? You sure you can't change Jamie's mind?"

She pulled a gold compact out of her alligator handbag. "Listen, we had a great time. And with all the hospitality you arranged for us—the boat trip, the picnic, the people we met. Well, then, what happy memories we'll enjoy later, up north in the snow."

After inspecting her makeup, she added in a sympathetic voice, "Lou can be a lot of fun. No complaints in that department. But can I tell you, just between us, that he gets above himself, puts on airs?" She repaired an invisible flaw in her lipstick. "He's got to learn how to behave around a higher class of people. He doesn't like to take orders from a woman. Especially when he's a little worked up. You know what I mean?"

"He was a torpedo greaser," I said. "In the Navy. Waiting tables may even be beyond his capabilities. Should I get rid of him?"

She touched her hair, then put her mirror away. "Women probably spoil him a lot. What about you find somebody to give him etiquette lessons? Clean him up."

I laughed. "You ever tried to train an alley cat?"

A sable eyebrow arched upward. "Every tom can't be a Persian, can he?" She pursed her lips and threw me a kiss. "I had you figured for a sis, Dan. But you arranged everything perfectly. You're quite a guy. Sorry you're not into party games. She must be a lucky girl."

The usual chill cut through my gut and balls. This time, I ignored it.

"Forget about the nights you and Mr. Mayson reserved," I said, accentuating my Tampa drawl. "There'll be no charge. We got empty rooms so it's no loss. After the disturbance the local yokels put you through, I'm not surprised you're leaving early."

She waved away any suggestion of inconvenience. "Too kind," she answered airily. "But like I said, this is strictly because of Jamie being called away, on account of business."

"It's fine." I smiled. "What else?"

She set her handbag on the counter. "You know," she said. "I called down for Lou this morning when I was packing. To give him a little something for his time, and for being a good sport and all. He never showed."

Reaching into the open handbag, she drew out a $50 bill and handed it to me. "Give him this after we're gone," she said. "Just so there's no hard feelings. About us leaving early, I mean."

I thought: *This is class.* What I said was: "If you're happy, I'm happy." I slipped the note into another envelope and wrote Salmi's name on it.

She signed the bill without reading it. "It's been swell, Dan," she said, handing back the fountain pen and the typed sheet. "And you're doing a swell job." She reached across the desk and rumpled my hair. "It's real tough what happened last night. But you'll get things fixed up. And Jamie and I, we'll be back next winter."

Barbara closed the handbag and slung it over her arm. "Half of Jamie's employees back in Michigan are Negroes. We have different laws up there and that puts a real lid on this kind of bullshit, if you know what I mean. Maybe guards and a night watchman—a little more security? With Lou's military background, maybe he could help you out?"

We both laughed.

"Security is right at the top of my list," I said. "Discussed it with the admiral yesterday. Gonna be the rock of Gibraltar next time you stay with us. And Lou will be wearing a collar and a bell."

"You're way ahead of me then," she said, laughing. Then she blew me another kiss and headed back upstairs to collect her furs and train case.

Ta P s

BY FIVE MINUTES TO 2 THAT AFTERNOON, the limestone steps of the
First Methodist Church were three-deep in late-arriving mourners. A Cadillac hearse and two limousines were parked out front,
flanked by three black-suited undertakers, eight pallbearers and
a cigar-chewing *News-Press* photographer.

Hillard Norris was definitely traveling first class.

The pallbearers looked self-conscious and vaguely official,
like county commissioners running for reelection. Bowing to
ladies and children and occasionally touching the white carna-
tion boutonnieres pinned to their lapels, they greeted other
men with handshakes and shoulder-pats. The undertakers muttered to each other without moving their lips. The photographer kept glancing around, clearly waiting for something that
hadn't happened yet.

Two dozen Klansmen, some in robes, others in wash pants

and flannel shirts—or whatever else constituted Sunday best—
were assembled to the right of the church door. Their womenfolk
had been sent inside. The few blacks present, all Norris family
employees, I guessed, and all dressed in strict black and white
mourning, slipped quickly past the white knights, their eyes
searching the ground for nickels.

Bud didn't like me attending the funeral. "You can't find anything better to do?" he'd complained the day before. "You some
kind of ghoul?"

"If it's gonna fuck up your investigation real bad," I had
answered, "I can skip it. But you can't blame a guy for wanting a
better look at the bitch who tried to kill him."

"Don't sit near me," he'd replied, scowling. "I'll be in the
back. And I'll be working."

Entering the sanctuary, I scanned the crowd. Bud wasn't there.

Ralph Nype, the city-desk reporter for the *News-Press*, was
one of the few people I recognized. He was seated about halfway
up the center aisle. Back in December, he'd written a feature
story on the hotel's new menus and waitresses. He'd also done
the whitewash job for the Hillard Norris obituary.

Nype favored Sears-Roebuck suits, suede shoes and flower-
pattern neckties. Today's shoes were dusty black, the suit a
nubby green raw-silk model with not enough shoulder padding.
The tie was stormy-weather gray with coconut-brown orchids.
Nype had a narrow face, birdcage torso and long stork's legs.
Journalism had clearly not made a man of him.

Firmly ignoring an usher's peremptory push toward an
empty space behind a column, I walked forward, tapped Nype
on the shoulder and stepped around his knees. Glancing over
the top of his glasses, he made room in the pew and stuck out
his right hand.

"Glad to see you," I whispered, shaking his hand with both
of mine. "You working or a friend of the family?"

"Little of both," he answered, returning the handshake and
adding his left hand on top. A gold wedding band gleamed dully.
"You know them well too?"

"Just him," I said. "He was a valued friend of the house. We like to honor our patrons in any way we can."

Nype cocked an eyebrow but didn't inquire about the nature of Norris's business at the Caloosa. His eyes stayed busy, checking off each soul who entered the church.

"What's this gonna be like?" I inquired as if innocently, wanting to keep the information flowing. "Bell, book and candle? Hellfire and brimstone?"

"The Norrises being Methodists," he answered, "it could be anything from trumpet solos to a two-hour sermon on free will versus predestination. Give me a good Christian evangelical funeral any time. That's what we had up Ohio way."

"In Tampa," I countered, "we always tip back a few in honor of the dearly departed."

Nype smacked his lips primly. "Not in church, I hope."

"Oh, yeah," I said. "Before the service, during and after. My family is Episcopalian. Altar wine for everybody."

"Roman Catholics use the same ritual," Nype said somewhat snidely.

"I'm also sightseeing," I admitted. "Trying to get to know Lee County a little better. You're probably friends with everybody in town. Everybody that's anybody."

Nype rolled his shoulders inside his jacket. "Just part of the job," he answered, clearly pleased with the compliment.

"Want to tell me who's who? The officer in the Air Corps uniform, third row, for instance."

"Captain Fay. Commander at the National Guard detachment out at Page Field."

"Wow. What about in front of him?"

"First and second pew, you have your county officials and their wives. The mayor of Myers—he's a widower now. All three county judges and their wives. Pretty fair turnout."

"Political crowd, huh?"

"Yes, and you also have Gene Faircloth, former state representative from Lee, next to the mayor. Then Faircloth's wife. After her, with the short white hair, you got an old codger, Philip

Winston. He's some kind of Indiana millionaire, has a winter home over on Boca Grand Island."

The organist, who'd been noodling along Bach-like, suddenly picked up the pace and the volume. The new melody sounded operatic—Wagner, Verdi, something like that. I can never tell them apart. Then she shifted into a slow march. The crowd began to rustle.

Nype smiled and looked over his shoulder. "Here they come. Jeez, would ya look at those flowers."

A bronze casket covered with yellow roses, ferns and white ribbon had been trundled into the vestibule at the front of the church. An undertaker and an elderly black-suited cleric guided the procession. Norris's pallbearers gathered behind the box and then fell into two lines, moving up the wide aisle on either side of the coffin. Self-conscious as freshman football players under lights for the first time, all but the undertaker noted the presence of friends here and there as they passed, ostentatiously avoiding anything more than slight nods of greeting. A second undertaker pushed the casket from behind. The third directed traffic through the pair of Gothic doors that led from the vestibule into the main aisle.

Nype was seated on the left side of the aisle. A moment after passing his right elbow, the casket swerved slightly to port, startling an elderly woman in a feathered hat. Moving quickly, the lead undertaker righted it and pointed it toward the crossing at the front of the church.

"Bet you know all those men," I whispered. "The pallbearers, I mean. They big shots or what?"

"Mostly your leading citizens doing the honorary heavy lifting, yes," Nype whispered back, his tone a mix of playfulness and awe. "My boss is the second man on the far side. Behind him, Bill Nugette, he owns the First National Bank; then Armer Gray, runs the local FHA office. This side you got Ridley Boldt, the lawyer, and Gene Hollipaugh, he's the sheriff."

"Heard of him," I said.

Sheriff Hollipaugh's face was turned away. All I could see

was a burly back, a bald head, a western-style suit and what looked to be a size 18 neck. He might as easily have been a chief warrant officer or a butcher. As he passed, I ticked off a string tie, high-heeled cowboy boots a and thick right hand gripping a Stetson. *Great*, I thought. *Not only a sheriff with a taste for East Coast high life, but a cowboy sheriff.*

"He a valued friend of your hotel too?" Nype inquired.

"Not that I know of," I said. "We're still looking forward to his first visit."

The music ebbed and rose again, the organist setting a surging, heartbeat rhythm, uh-*bah*, uh-*bah*, uh-*bah*-bah-*bah*.

A red-faced clergyman roughly my age, marching backward like a drill sergeant, signaled the last of the procession forward into the lighted church. The widow entered on the arm of a thin, ordinary-looking young man in a blue suit.

"Who's that?" I whispered.

"Beats me," Nype muttered, busying himself with the printed program. "Probably, uh, David J. Norris, nephew. I'll have to check that for my story." Pulling a mechanical pencil from inside his coat, he scribbled a note on the program.

Mrs. Norris's weeds included a shoulder-length veil, black kid gloves and a black skirt that stopped just short of her ankles. The hand not gripping the nephew's arm clutched a bouquet of spider lilies and yellow roses. The flowers shook like pine branches in a November breeze. Moving up the aisle, she glanced around the church—a singer counting empty seats at a matinee. Nearing the casket, she reined in her shaking hand and pressed the palm against the edge of her veil, over her heart.

A younger, thinner version of herself, in black dress, hat, veil and low-heeled shoes, trudged along behind her, followed by 15 or 20 white people. A pair of elderly black servants, both in uniform, brought up the rear.

"Miss Hillary, the girl there by herself," Nype whispered. "First time I've seen her in anything but riding clothes."

"Pretty little thing," I said.

Hillary Norris, like most of the female relatives behind her, carried a spray of tropical flowers: Turk's cap, lantana, ixora and coral vine. Each bouquet resembled the next, as if a single pair of hands had fashioned all of them.

The family settled themselves in the front pews on the left side of the church. The elder minister opened the altar rail gate, stepped forward, almost tripped on the steps leading up to the altar, recovered himself, turned, cocked his hands and called out, "Please rise for the singing of 'A Mighty Fortress Is Our God,' the favorite hymn of our dear departed friend, Hillard Norris."

Dutifully, we all rose.

Twenty minutes later, as the ceremony wound down, a middle-aged wraith wearing a fur neck-piece, black suit and veiled cocktail hat rushed up the aisle. She stopped next to Ralph Nype, tapped the narrow shoulder of his cheap green suit, then quickly slipped around his knees to wedge herself between us. I recognized her immediately. She was Mildred Goodwill Boldt, Willene Norris's first cousin.

"Family didn't leave an inch for me up there," she whispered. "So I thank you boys, thank you. Didn't mean to be this late. Never happens when it isn't important. What have I missed?"

A portrait painter, local art teacher and the wife of Hillard Norris's gambling buddy and pallbearer Ridley Boldt, Mildred Boldt was an occasional visitor to the Caloosa Club. She'd caught my attention the first time we met by comparing the club room to Harry's Bar, a famous watering hole in Venice where she claimed to have had drinks with Ernest Hemingway, Peggy Guggenheim and assorted European nobles. (She also once dropped the name of Salvador Dali, the great surrealist who—she coquettishly intimated—admired not only her talent but her looks. "As a student touring Europe on a strict budget back in the '30s, I posed for him several times wearing little more than Chanel No. 5.")

Mildred patted my arm to get my attention. "Dan, I'm so glad you're here. Do you see Ridley?"

I pointed to the pallbearers lined up in front of us and to the

left. She leaned forward, nodded and sat back. "Guess he could-
n't save me a seat."

"How's Miss Willene taking this?" Nype whispered, leaning
close to Mildred. "Must be a terrible shock."

"You can just imagine," Mildred replied. "Such a strain on
everybody. Terrible shock. Yes."

"You'll let me know if there's anything I can do?"

"That would be so helpful. Yes, of course."

Outside the church a few minutes later, Mildred fished a
handkerchief and a pack of Chesterfields out of her purse.
"Who'd have thought it could come to anything like this?"

Nype struck a match before she could raise her veil. "Umm,
oh, dear, that's good," she said, lighting up. "Thanks, that's very,
very good. And so many thanks for letting me share your pew."

Nype looked past her, catching my eye as if to demonstrate
his own connection to one of the town's most powerful families.
"Do either of you need a ride to the cemetery?" he whispered. "I
have the *News-Press* car."

Mildred stood a little taller. "We walk," she said.

"It's over a mile to the graveyard," Nype answered.

"A family tradition," Mildred replied. "You can drive if you
want to, but I can't. Back before we had cars and hearses, it used
to be the grown men in the family who pulled the casket on a
wagon. Didn't use horses or mules or anything."

Without thinking, I said I'd like a picture of that. She looked
at me sharply, then nodded. "Interesting," she said. "Yes. That's
an idea. Thank you, Dan."

Nype was about to ask her something else. But by the time
he stowed the lighter and looked up, she'd sighed, said ta-ta and
started to move toward her relatives.

"Shit," Nype said beneath his breath. But he quickly recovered himself. "No doubt," he added, "she's consumed by grief."

"Over here," the *News-Press* photographer called. When
Mildred didn't look up, he snapped her picture anyway.
Undeterred, he followed at a distance as she crossed the side-
walk and greeted Hillary. Even in the soft afternoon sun, the

flashbulbs caught and magnified the streaky tears running down the girl's cheeks. When the photographer held up his camera and asked the young woman for just one more, Mildred shooed him away.

A thin smile hovered around the corner of Nype's mouth.

"You do nice work," I said.

"Doubt we'd run anything like that," he answered. "Not the day after a funeral. My editor just likes to keep files on local big shots. You never know what'll come up."

The hearse lead the way to the cemetery followed by groups of Norrises, Boldts, Turnipblossoms and their connections and dependents, all on foot. The pallbearers and a flower car followed, with the Klan contingent crowding in behind. Friends, officials, busybodies such as myself and the grave undertakers followed. A dozen sober-faced blacks formed the rear guard.

The photographer snapped more pictures as the procession snaked across town and into the old city cemetery. The hearse stopped at a large plot enclosed by a coral rock wall two feet high. The Turnipblossom parcel was punctuated with tall, severe headstones. The freshly mown grass looked parched, the ground hard, the spirit of the place even harder. All the usual comforting symbols of death were absent—no cedar trees, no marble angels, no stone lambs, none of the devices that provide an affecting aura of tradition and easeful rest. A long cut in the ground loomed open, shaded by a green awning and surrounded by woven grass mats and rows of metal folding chairs.

The undertakers, assisted by the three youngest pallbearers, lifted the casket onto their shoulders and carried it into the plot. Using a set of stout ropes and pulleys, they quickly and carefully lowered the box into the pit.

Only the grieving widow, her daughter and one very old woman took seats. The extended family gathered at Hillard Norris's feet. The rest of us, mourners and gawkers alike, arranged ourselves as best we could. I was lucky to get a spot with a splendid view, just above Norris's head. Looking around, I caught sight of Nype. He was standing beyond the crowd, near the hearse, chatting with Officer Walter Hurston and taking notes.

I made a mental note myself. Bud needed to know that these two men had talked.

The graveside service was simple. The younger, sunburned minister stood up, led the crowd in the Lord's Prayer, opened his prayer book, intoned, "Praise God, from whom all blessings flow," read a few other calls on heaven then shut the book and looked around.

"We are gathered together," he continued, "to remember our fellow believer and friend, uh, Hillard Norris. It is the custom of his family to offer tributes herewith, and to remain while the final labor is done."

With that, the preacher turned toward Willene and Hillary Norris and bowed his head. Both women rose and looked down into the grave. The widow then dropped her bouquet onto the flower-topped coffin as if consigning a magazine to the trash basket.

"Prepare the way, dear husband of my heart," she called down. "Be with me always."

There was momentary silence. Then the daughter coughed, glanced down at the casket, dropped her bouquet as if it was on fire, choked out, "Daddy, don't go!" and sat back down. Grandmother Turnipblossom, seated beside her, circled her fat arms about the girl and pulled her close. As an afterthought, the woman tossed her own bunch of ferns and bougainvillea into the hole, then began smoothing the girl's hair.

The rest of the family moved quickly, each depositing a floral offering on Norris's casket. Few added anything to the chief mourners' sentiments. Only Mildred Boldt went for a grand gesture. Elevating two sprays of gladiolus above her head, she crossed and held them aloft like a pagan priestess greeting the dawn. Looking west toward the Gulf of Mexico and the afternoon sun, she called, "Fond cousin, from all of us, until we meet on that other, brighter shore: Keep well, remember us to the God of Gods, and know that you truly live forever in our grieving hearts."

Mrs. Norris's hands, now controlled and unmoving,

remained firmly folded in her lap. Hillary's small form, all lumps and twists, shook painfully back and fourth.

I looked around, putting names to faces: banker Nugette, millionaire Philip Winston, sheriff Hollipaugh.

Bud still hadn't shown up. I was starting to worry. Despite the crowd, I felt bone lonely and anxious. Shutting my eyes, choking up, I knew why. It had nothing to do with Hillard Norris.

The faces of the men I'd known on the *Indianapolis* were with me again—officers, chief mates, firemen, gunners, my cooks and supply men, dozens and then hundreds of men, one after the other, each flashing me a snappy salute and then marching through that goddamn door inside my head, the one marked Davey Jones. I blinked and rubbed my eyes, fighting the sight of what was always the last, most painful salute, the jaunty "See you" thrown by Ensign Rizzo.

My eyes overflowed. Turning away from the yawning hole that was Hillard Norris's grave, I bumped into an older man, stepped on his foot, cursed, begged his pardon and stumbled around him.

Nearby, a woman screamed, "Bastard!" She took a breath, then repeated it, "Ba-a-stard!" followed by, "Lemme tell you all something."

I turned toward her, half afraid she was speaking to me. Instead, I saw a thin brown woman with wild almond eyes and a wrenched-open mouth. The crowd parted in polite confusion as she fought her way over to the grave. The lapel of her green striped suit was unbuttoned, revealing a white cotton blouse. She was wearing a pair of maid's or nurse's shoes, powdered snow white. She looked to be my age or a little older, no more than 30. She had full lips and strong hands.

"You burn in hell, Mr. Hillard Norris," she cried, hurling what looked like a rhinestone bracelet into the flowers heaped on Norris's casket. "My husband is dead on me—my Wash, my life, my brave soldier—and you killed him, Mr. Hillard Norris. You killed him dead just like you killed yourself. You killed him and them gambling people at that hotel killed him. You called them yo friends, and you drank poison with them, didn't you?"

At first, nobody moved. And Willene didn't even look up.

"My Wash was a decorated hero," the woman shouted, running her fingers through her sleek hair wildly. "He served in the Army, came out clean. You! Miss Willene," she cried, her voice rising to a shrill edge, her hand pointing. "You killed both our men sure as shooting 'em. You killed Wash and Mr. Hillard. You and them gambling people at that fancy hotel."

By now, Hillary and her grandmother were on their feet. "Mary," the old woman demanded. "Stop it. Stop it now."

Hillary wailed, "Mary, Mary."

Moving quickly, Willene did what under ordinary circumstances might have been most effective. Pushing past Mildred, she put her hands on Mary's shoulders and tried to pull her into a comforting embrace. "Here," she crooned. "Come sit by me, Mary. You're upset."

Instead, Mary almost knocked Willene into Hillard's grave. Hysterical, she pushed back against Willene's raised arms. There was a momentary struggle for balance, with hands grabbing hands and arms, before first one white shoe and then the other slipped on the grass matting. Clumsily breaking free, Willene scrambled safely away, clutching at her cousin Mildred for support. Mary landed in a sitting position on the casket, sobbing pitifully, smack dab in a heap of flowers.

The eldest of the undertakers was suddenly beside her. "My dear," he said as he scrambled down, keeping his voice low, evidently practiced at handling such scenes. "My lamb, let me help you up." Shielding the weeping woman's face with one arm, he gestured toward his assistants with the other.

Sheriff Hollipaugh stepped in behind them, followed by Officer Hurston and the *News-Press* photographer. Hurston and one of the assistant undertakers pulled Mary up, and Hurston led her quickly away. The sheriff turned toward Willene, his arms extended, shielding her from the camera with his shoulders and Stetson hat. The family quickly surrounded them both and moved toward the street.

it takes two

Four cemetery employees with shovels stepped forward immediately, removing the folding chairs and mats. Within 30 seconds, they'd begun showering the flowers and casket with dirt. We had to step back as they bent to their work.

The crowd had thinned to almost nothing before they finished. Nype, looking hot in his Sears suit, waited by the *News-Press* car as I headed for the cemetery gate.

"These people sure know how to throw a party," I said. "Never seen a wrestling match at a funeral before."

Nype, sarcastic himself, looked stunned. "Nobody expected it, not at all. I'd have thought our friend Mildred's dramatic leave-taking would be the outside edge."

"Whole thing just about beats the Gasparilla parade up in Tampa," I said. "You gonna report it?"

"I'll have to confer with my editor," Nype answered, his composure regained, his lifeless grin restored. "In any case, I'm certainly glad you had a memorable sightseeing trip. If you've seen enough, I can offer you a lift. I have to get back to the office and write this up." His death's-head smile didn't budge when he added, "Where's your pal Spencer Wright?"

It was easy to turn my back on Nype as I slid into his Chevy's passenger seat. "Guess the crime wave keeps Bud pretty busy," I answered, not knowing what else to say. "Did you expect him to be here?"

"He's certainly too busy to return phone calls. Perhaps you could jog his memory? We called him twice this morning. My editor wants to give him a little more ink."

"Speaking of that," I said, "How come your paper didn't mention the name of the motor hotel? Or that the dead colored man's widow worked for the Norris family?"

Nype started the motor, shifted gears into reverse, backed up and shifted into first. "You're very well informed," he answered before pulling into traffic. "We didn't print that, no. That's true. Now perhaps you can tell me what Mary Davis has against your hotel? Couldn't be the excellent food or the beauteous waitresses you've been hiring."

"Beats me," I replied, unwilling to even play at speculation. Norris's unsuccessful attempt to reserve a hotel room for himself and a colored woman was none of Nype's business. "Is that her name?" I said, hoping to sound uninterested. "Far as I know, she's never been inside the door." The latter statement was perfectly true.

"But you've been here only—what—since September? Perhaps she slipped in last winter."

"As a guest? No, we observe state law. And she couldn't have worked at the Caloosa and been Mrs. Norris's full-time maid at the same time."

"It's a mystery, then. I'll have to check it out."

I still figured I could trade information with Nype. "Going back to the Norris obituary," I said. "You listed everything about Hillard and Willene except their blood types. But you left out the link to the Klan. And you left out another detail—that the grieving Mrs. Norris shot up the Royal Plaza on Sunday morning and narrowly missed hitting three innocent bystanders."

"We don't ever report on Klan doings," Nype answered primly. "Tends to stir up trouble. We did report that the body of a Negro was found on the scene. I had to convince my editor to include that fact. He isn't in favor of covering Negro strife at all—because the *News-Press*, as a good public citizen, does not want to inflame passions. A killing, by definition, is strife. We report the news. We try not to make it. My editor is very careful about the niceties of our racial situation."

"So you just ignore the fact that the colored man, whose wife worked for the family of the dead white man, had a bullet in his head?"

Nype stopped at another corner, turned, turned again and halted in front of the Caloosa Hotel. "Thank you. I was going to check just that very point with your pal Wright. But, in case he doesn't call me back before my deadline, did you see the bodies close up? Did you have an opportunity to inspect the wounds?"

"All I saw," I said, "was Willene Norris shooting at me. Bud knocked her aim off, or you'd have had another funeral to cover."

Nype slipped the car into neutral. "Mrs. Norris was temporarily deranged due to excessive grief. That's what the family physician told my editor, speaking strictly off the record. And thank you. I wasn't sure you were there. Now you've confirmed it for me."

I stepped out onto the sunny sidewalk in front of the Caloosa. Leaning down to face him through the car window, I tried again. "You gonna report that there were innocent bystanders but not that the woman shot at us? Anybody could see this is some kind of double murder. Your editor gonna ignore the fact that Mary Davis is out of her mind with grief too?"

Nype nodded. "To report on these women's troubles would cause even more grief—not only to Mrs. Hillard Norris, a highly respected citizen, but to her daughter and her aged mother, who are both still living. I'm sure you can understand our position."

"FUCKING REDNECK MECHANIC SWORE THE JEEP would be ready by noon," Bud growled, looking up at me. He was stretched out in my office easy chair when I returned from Norris's funeral. His shoelaces were untied and his feet propped up on a metal waste can. His slouched position caused his shoulder-holstered revolver to peep out from under his arm.

"You asleep on the job, Sarge?" I'd said when I found him there dozing. "Thought the last thing you'd miss was Hillard Norris's decommissioning."

"Hitched a ride over to the so-called garage at 1:30," Bud answered edgily. "Whole goddamn place was secured, with a note stuck to the door saying he'd gone to get glass cut and wouldn't be back till after lunch."

"Maybe he's got a girl," I said, sinking into the chair behind the desk. "Could have been taking a nooner."

"He's too fucking old. Too fat and ugly to cut it. Too married."

"Married guys never screw around in this town? That right, Sarge?"

"Not if they don't want to get shot dead, looks like."

Telling him he'd missed a good show, I ran through the funeral's highlights, emphasizing the push-and-shout finale.

He whistled and leaned forward. "Mary Davis, huh? Sounds like a calf-roping in August. You know she worked as Mrs. Hillard Norris's house-maid till two, three months ago. Regular part of the family is what I heard."

"And the dead colored man at the Royal Plaza was Wash Davis, short for Washington, I guess?"

"Right. Yes. Thing's getting crazy, isn't it? Hey, I got the Jeep outside. You want to go somewhere?"

I said, no but that we could both use a drink. The club room was just down the corridor. Or we could drive over to the Legion Hall.

Bud smiled wanly. "Long as I'm buying."

"Champagne for me," I answered, rising and coming around the desk.

"I'll give you champagne," he said, smirking suggestively. "From my hose."

I dropped down beside him, slapped his flat gut with my open hand and then pushed past his belt buckle. "Lemme uncork that thing," I said. "I've been wanting some La Belle bubbly."

Glancing at the open door and pushing me gently aside, he got to his feet and began to tuck loose shirttails into his pants. Then he reached inside his coat to pat his gun. "You want me to stash this weapon?" he said. "Like the Hollywood cowboys when they visit the dance-hall girls?"

"Your boss was riding herd on the gun-toting widow today," I said, gesturing for him to leave the holster buckled. "Looked like to me, anyway. How married is he?"

Bud said he'd never heard any gossip connecting the boss with other women. "They're probably just good friends," he said.

"Real good friends," I joked, bowing him out the door. "Like some others I could name."

"Stow that," he said. "Let's see about those beers."

"Beer, hell," I said, pinching his shoulder blade.

For cocktail time on a weeknight, the Caloosa Club was moderately busy. Betty and the boss plus two other couples danced to Tommy's piano version of "Some Enchanted Evening." A poker game was in full swing in the corner. Carmen was polishing glasses behind the bar and Lou Salmi had just dumped a bucket of ice into the ice chest.

Tommy looked up from the piano when Bud and I entered, shifted into "Anchors Aweigh," then returned to the theatrical South Pacific with "Bali H'ai" and "Happy Talk."

Stopping by on the way to the bar, I asked Tommy to play me a little funeral music—"St. James Infirmary Blues," "When the Saints Go Marching In"—that kind of thing.

Tommy rolled his eyes, nodded and immediately bridged "This Nearly Was Mine" into a bluesy, wordless "Frankie and Johnny." Then, with hardly a break, he shifted again, parodying the blues lyric:

> Well, I went to the sheriff's infirmary,
> I saw my Ford dealer there,
> Stretched out on a long card table,
> So clean, so white, so bare.

Maybe nobody else was listening. Certainly Bud wasn't paying attention to Tommy's biting words. I looked around the room. Nobody looked back except Tommy. I glared at him. Shrugging, he shifted into a popular Caribbean rhythm:

> Stone cold dead in Fort Myers,
> Stone cold dead in Fort Myers,
> Stone dead in Fort Myers,
> I kill nobody but two husbands.

> I left him stone cold dead in the hotel,
> Shot dead in the hotel,
> Shot two men in the hotel,
> I kill nobody but two husbands.

Jesus, I thought, *this is way too sassy for Fort Myers. Tommy should know better*. Which, of course, he did. As I stood up to speak to him, he spotted me coming and shifted again, into a more-or-less straightforward and, for the moment wordless, version of "Saints."

I sat back down. Bud and I were the only people at the bar. Carmen, his eye makeup heavier than usual, had set us up with long-necked Regals and pilsner glasses. Pushing the glass away, Bud swigged deeply from the bottle.

Tommy snapped his fingers, swayed, grimaced like a tormented Louis Armstrong and plowed into an impudent parody of "Saints":

Up where the sun
Refuse to shine,
Up where the sun
Don't never shine,
I cou-ou-ount up my numbers
With a son-of-a-gun
Who ain't mine.

Asdeck waved from the dance floor. He was clearly paying more attention to Betty and her tight dress than to the lyrics. *I must be Nervous Nellie Forbush*, I thought. *The whole town's talking about the killings and the funeral today. Tommy, Carmen, Asdeck and maybe half the rest of the people here tonight know Bud's involved in the case. Maybe I ought to just relax.*

I didn't like it. But, for the moment, I kept my mouth shut.

Ten minutes later, the club room doors opened again and two men entered, both dressed in business suits. Choosing a small table at the far end of the room, they ordered mixed drinks and settled into what looked like a confidential conversation. The younger man, thin and pink faced with dirty-blond hair, kept crossing and uncrossing his legs, touching his knee to make a point. His companion, a broad-shouldered, older, more athletic-looking figure, did most of the talking. He looked entirely relaxed. The younger one nodded a lot and extended his pinkie every time he lifted his glass.

Bud glanced at them several times before asking me if I knew whether the finger-waving guy was queer.

"No idea," I answered. "None of my business what he is."

"Bull-puppies, Lieutenant, I'm damn sure you got some idea. Just look at him. He don't ever stop moving. And he moves like a sissy."

I shrugged, looked at the couple again, and said, "None of your business either. Unless you're interested in him."

I knew who the men were, all right. Or, at least, I'd read their membership applications. I knew their names and where they came from. I knew that they were repeat customers, that their credit was good and that they'd asked for rooms on the same floor.

I didn't tell Bud any of this. Instead, I described the men's situation in the way Admiral Asdeck might have described it to me back in the beginning of my education at the New Victory Club. I told Bud the two men were both traveling salesmen, both married and both out-of-town members of the Caloosa Club. I said they'd rented single rooms and were therefore entitled to a little privacy. More than that, I didn't know, and didn't want to know. "It isn't fair or safe for me to spill other people's secrets," I told Bud. "Not even to you. Any more than you'd want me telling your landlady about the way we mix it up sometimes."

Startled by what must have sounded like a threat, Bud blinked, then looked around. Nobody was within five feet of us, so he asked another question. "You figure they do mix it up? Can't see the string-beanpole putting it to the older gent. You figure the old guy's hoping to get his cock sucked?"

"Why don't you go ask them yourself, if you're so curious? Maybe they're looking for a three-way orgy. Maybe a nosy detective would be right up their alley."

At that, he got my drift, and backed off.

Another man in a business suit entered the club a few minutes later. After pausing at the bar to order a drink, he joined the poker game in progress.

"You might want to aim your curiosity over there instead," I said with a nod. "That's Ridley Boldt, one of Hillard Norris's pallbearers. My guess is that his wife knows plenty about her cousin Willene's personal business."

"You figure she'll talk to me?"

"Crack reporter from the *News-Press* tried to quiz her this afternoon and got nowhere. You're better looking, though. And more polite. But you know, to a lawyer's wife, a flatfoot cop's probably no different than a reporter."

Bud picked up his beer bottle and drained it. "She might not have any choice," he said. "Once the grand jury gets going."

We were both ready for refills. I looked around for Carmen and finally spotted him across the room. The flamboyant club manager was taking orders from the table of poker players. Bending down to collect empty glasses, balancing a cocktail tray in his left hand, Carmen steadied himself on a chair back with his right. Laughing at something Ridley Boldt must have said, he cocked his right foot behind his left knee, revealing a very high-heeled Texas boot.

As Carmen turned away, one of the other card players reached over and pinched his butt cheek—not sexily, or seductively, or even good-naturedly, but hard enough to leave a bruise.

The man was Bobby Jim Carter, a former Army sergeant and currently the assistant manager of a Bradenton moving-van office. Bobby Jim had been playing cards and drinking, Carmen reported later, since mid afternoon.

Every inch a professional, Carmen righted himself, took a step back and quietly asked Bobby Jim to observe the rules of an honest card game and keep his hands above the table. But Bobby Jim threw down his cards and stood up angrily.

"Some men try to bite off more candy than they can chew," Carmen said, dropping a shoulder. "We gonna have to put you on a diet, sir."

Tommy Carpenter stopped playing. Everybody stopped talking. And so everybody in the room heard what Bobby Jim said next. "Fuck your poontang candy, you spick ass. When I'm in a high-class club I wanna be served by real female waitresses— white women, not wetback she-male pogy."

"Ah, hell," Bud muttered. "I knew we should of gone to the Legion Hall."

"I gotta go to work," I answered. "You want to watch my back?"

Glancing toward the door, I saw Brian Rooney and Lou Salmi moving forward into position. Brian's shirtsleeves were rolled up. His elbows and hands flexed and relaxed as he crossed the room. Lou was right behind him, gripping an empty champagne bottle, prepared to bop the daylights out of the offending drunk if his language got any rougher.

"The gentleman is on his way out," I called to Brian. "He's wanted in the lobby. He has a phone call from his office, a wire from President Truman. Tell him anything as long as he moves."

"He'll move, boss. That I do believe," Brian said. "Or else we wash his dirty mouth out with carbolic soap right here."

Faced with Brian's heavily muscled arms, Lou's bottle, my squared shoulders, Bud's shadow and no apparent support from his buddies at the card table, Bobby Jim didn't put up a fight. Hustling him into my office and dumping him in the easy chair was a snap.

When I came around to face him, he was breathing hard and working his jaw like an overweight bulldog.

"Here's the message," I said. "The Caloosa Club is no kindergarten. We like a little variety. We want everybody to have a good time. And that means all parties keep decent tongues in their heads when they're with us. You read me? Sir?"

He stared back, an overmatched boxer dreading round 2. The confused low-level shifting inside his hooded bully's eyes was unmistakable, though. He was trying to psychologize me and hoping it would work.

"What's more," I continued, "gentlemen keep their hands to themselves around here. Guests either treat the staff with respect or lose their privileges. You read me there? Sir?"

"Look, kid," he answered. "I don't know where you come from. Around here, decent white men don't put up with spicks, niggers, queers and other trash in no social situation. What kind of club is this?"

Brian flexed his oversize biceps in a bored sort of way. Bud raised his arm, letting just the suggestion of the holstered pistol under his jacket register on Bobby Jim's addled brain. Standing in the doorway, Asdeck, Carmen and Ridley Boldt wore neutral, seen-it-all-before expressions.

"Well, sir," I answered, leaning forward. "It's a private club. And one you don't happen to belong to. You do happen to have had a little too much to drink. Since your host seems to have departed the premises, I'd like to have Mr. Rooney find you a ride home."

Bobby Jim looked around, evidently seeking support, and tried to stand up. "Fucking Navy faggots," he muttered, wobbling and leaning on the arm of the chair. "Fucking pansy. Drive my own fucking car. Don't you touch me."

I motioned for Brian, Lou and Bud to step back.

"Lemme tell you something, kid," Bobby Jim said over his shoulder as he lurched toward the door. "You'll be sorry for this. Mark it down. You'll be real sorry."

After he left, Asdeck cracked a grin, nodded and said, admiral-like, "Nice work, men. Carry on."

I almost saluted.

Carmen fanned his face with his hand. "I sure hope you know what you're doing, Dan."

"Relax," I told him. "I mean to keep this place clean. That was just a little trash detail."

"Well, I'd have handled it with a Mickey Finn cocktail," Carmen said archly. "On the house. A Mickey just weak enough so his card-playing pals could clean him out of every cent he owns." Here he winked at Ridley as he began dealing an imaginary deck of cards. "Then, when the mark finally went night-night, I'd ask Mr. Rooney and Mr. Salmi deposit him out on the freight dock. And I'm afraid his trousers and BVDs—oh, my goodness, so shocking—would be mysteriously disappeared. That way, the tramps and garbage truck drivers could fuck his dead ass from here to breakfast."

Asdeck and Brian laughed appreciatively. When I said that I was shocked at such language, we all laughed—all except Bud.

Bud took the threat at face value. That was plain from the expression on his face. But I could also see something else—that he was deeply impressed by the scene he'd just witnessed, and not only by my part in it but by Carmen's as well.

I was about to say, "Back to work, all you fucking Navy faggots and pansies," when the night bellboy knocked on the open office door.

"Special delivery for you, Mr. Ewing," he called. "Them two couples from Louisiana just arrived. Say their train was late getting in."

"Couple of matched pairs," Asdeck explained to Bud as we walked up the hall to the reception desk. "Mrs. Rosamonde Peek and Captain Newton Slidel, Mrs. Dewey Broussard and Ray Bonner Flambeaux. Mrs. Peek is a Navy widow and a very handsome woman. The captain was a year behind me at the Academy. He was Lieutenant Peek's wartime buddy from right before Pearl Harbor. Peek lost his life during the battle of Midway. Newt and Mr. Bonner go back to high school in the Delta. All four were here last winter."

When we reached the lobby, Asdeck and the Louisiana delegation broke into a torrent of satisfied shouts, laughs, handshakes and back pounding. Captain Slidel—tall, lean and leathery, dressed in a Stetson hat, boots and a Western-style gabardine suit—looked like a well-to-do rancher, not a career officer on liberty. He sounded Navy enough, however. "Didn't have a club car on the train once we left Tampa," he explained, shaking my hand. "Damnedest situation."

His companion, Rosamonde Peek, greeted me with an excited shriek. "Oh! Lieutenant *Ewing!* I've so looked *forward* to this!"

"Indeed a pleasure!" her friend Mrs. Broussard put in. "I told the boy to take the bags right on upstairs. He's going to find some ice and then unpack the gentlemen's bags." The widow of a Baton Rouge grain dealer, she resembled Mamie Eisenhower with more money—bangs, short hair, pie face, diamond bracelets and bouffant skirts. Having trained as a nurse at Charity Hospital before her marriage, she was now second in command of the Baton Rouge Red Cross chapter. She was used to giving orders and having them obeyed.

Ray Bonner Flambeaux, a jockey-sized man with a red face and twinkling eyes, winked and grinned as we shook hands. "Drinks in the room, hell, my dear. We're ready for a party," he said, glancing up at the woman beside him and then at Asdeck and Slidel. "Big party, loosen things up around here. That right, boys and girls?"

A yellow diamond the size of a postage stamp flashed on and off as Flambeaux's right hand swept back and forth. He'd grown up dirt poor, gotten an early start as an oil-field wildcatter and struck it moderately rich with an oil lease in his home parish. I was holding his personal blank check to cover all expenses for both couples.

Captain Slidel loosened his collar and bolo tie. "Getting relaxed already," he answered, patting his mistress on the velvet curve of her mink-lined shoulder.

"I want to go fishing tomorrow," Mrs. Broussard put in. "Nobody at home has a boat of any size. I want to try for tarpon again. Remember, Admiral, you swore we'd have pretty weather this year."

Asdeck laughed and began herding them toward the club room. "Can't promise weather that will be as pretty as you are, my dear. But if it rains, well, we'll just stay inside and watch home movies. I've got some Cuban films that come highly recommended."

Starting to move off, the Louisiana men put on dour, interested smiles. Mrs. Peek fanned her brow with a delicate lace handkerchief. "My, my…films?"

"Not easy to find," Asdeck added. "Lucky to put my hands on them down in Miami. Just last week."

Glancing over at me, Bud cocked an eyebrow and dropped his voice. "Why's he gonna show home movies? There's a movie theater two blocks away."

"These aren't Hollywood movies," I answered. "And our popcorn is free."

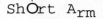

Short Arm

MARY DAVIS'S DENUNCIATION OF GAMBLERS and an unnamed hotel, clearly the Caloosa, worried me all night. But Admiral Asdeck didn't seem remotely bothered by the very public linking of the hotel to the deaths of Hillard Norris and Wash Davis. We discussed the melee at the cemetery during an afternoon meeting. I outlined the possible fallout. Asdeck just laughed. "Mark it down to female hysteria," he advised, "and forget about it." When I explained that there might be something in what Mary charged—that Norris had tried to reserve a room for a dark-skinned honey and been rebuffed—Asdeck replied that at least the philandering Ford dealer hadn't owned a Caloosa Club membership. "We can thank our lucky stars," he added, "that Norris died on the edge of Colored Town and not in a Caloosa love nest."

Bud showed up in my office again that afternoon. Like the day before, I found him stretched out in the easy chair, feet on the trash can, reading the sports page. Surprised and pleased to see him, I almost opened with a jokey "We've got to stop meeting like this" crack. Fortunately I caught myself. A guy like him could mistake irony for truth. And meeting just like this—

in private, at the hotel, on my own ground—suited me fine. So I punched his ear lightly, circled around to the desk chair and threw him a great big smile.

Bud didn't know about my discussion with Asdeck, of course. Dropping the newspaper and smiling back at me like a star student, he reported that he'd put in a full, useful day. He'd interviewed both widows before lunch. He'd squeezed Featherstone the snitch again during the afternoon. And he'd made extensive notes on all of it.

Pulling a small notebook from his jacket pocket, Bud proceeded to fill me in. "Mrs. Norris at first refused to come to the sheriff's department willingly," he read. "She agreed to be questioned only in her dead husband's place of business at the Ford dealership and only in the presence of counsel, a clerk named Stanley Dribble from the Boldt and Hammar law firm. Counsel demanded that her physician and a trained nurse be present, due to the precarious nature of subject's feelings. But Detective Wright agreed only to post the emergency medical team outside the office door. So counsel dropped the request.

"Subject answered most of the detective's questions in a sullen tone of voice. Yes, subject admitted, Mary Davis had been her house-maid for several years. Yes, subject admitted she had met Washington Davis on two occasions: once when Mary became suddenly ill and she'd driven her home, once on a downtown street during a shopping trip.

"'Wash didn't ever work for me,' Subject pointed out.

"Yes, subject had let the woman go late the previous year. No, she hadn't written her a letter of recommendation. No, Mary's work was not the problem. She was a good cook and knew how to keep a clean house. But she'd gotten too familiar. When pressed, Subject claimed she'd discharged Mary Davis after finding her with Hillard, in a, quote, 'disgusting, compromising situation.'"

I agreed, laughing. "Pretty nasty stuff."

"Had she discovered them in Mrs. Norris's own bed, the detective inquired.

"No, the widow answered, it was even worse. She'd found them rooting around on the slip-covered day bed in the maid's room out back."

Bud had clearly enjoyed reading me this detail. "Slip-covered," he said, grinning and slapping the notebook on the arm of the easy chair. "She finds the old man with his pants down fucking her maid and what does she remember? The goddamn upholstery."

Bud continued reading. "After describing the crisis in the maid's room, subject became tearful. Counsel moved to adjourn the meeting until his client was in better control of her emotions. When the detective replied that all three of them might benefit from strong coffee and 15 minutes, subject pulled herself together and rang for a secretary to bring a tray."

Bud threw me a smug grin.

"So did she ever discover old Hillard bare-assed again?" I asked. "Fucking Mary again—like, for instance, at the Royal Plaza Motor Lodge?"

"Denied knowing a thing about it till she saw the bodies," Bud said. "Claimed he promised he'd quit seeing her. Swore it on a stack of Bibles. She says she believed him. Says she was a fool, just a poor betrayed woman, the wife is always the last to know—you get the drill, Lieutenant."

"No possibility that she did the Smith & Wesson job on Hillard and Wash?"

Bud glanced up. "Wasn't a Smith & Wesson. But no, she looks to be covered on that score. Says she stayed with her cousin Mildred at a fishing camp out on Pine Island over Saturday night."

I snapped my fingers. "That's the wife of Ridley Boldt. Remember? He's the card-playing lawyer I pointed out to you last night, the one who was buddies with Hillard. So he sends his clerk to try to rope you off. Pretty tight little circle, huh?"

"Right. Yes. But this is a small town. They all do each other's laundry."

I asked what put Willene on the road to the Royal Plaza Motor Lodge.

"Lady wouldn't say much," Bud answered. "Claimed she got an anonymous phone call."

"At a fishing camp? Where she's staying with a cousin who's her lawyer's wife?"

"That's what she said. Right. Yes. Said the call woke both of 'em up. Said they played cards late with two other biddies from down the road. And then went to bed. Slept sound all night."

I asked what her reasons were for disturbing the crime scene—moving the pistol, stomping on evidence, all the rest of it. And why did she need to demonstrate her sorrow by taking pot shots at one innocent civilian and two county prisoners?"

"Plum out of her mind with grief, that's what the lady will testify. Don't remember a thing about it, she says. Turned completely crazy once she saw her husband lying in a pool of blood."

"Was it a pool?"

"More like big spots. And he was on a dark rug."

"With his jaw blown off."

Bud shrugged. "There was the woman's coat with at least a pint of blood on it too. Which she kicked around some. It was on the floor when Norris went down."

"Two males in a room, both dead," I said. "With a used rubber in the toilet. You don't suppose they were mixing it up?"

Bud glanced at the door. When he turned toward me again, his lips were open but his teeth were clamped shut. He shook his head. "Naw. I never heard of a man using a scumbag to fuck ass."

"Norris was Klan. Wash Davis's ass was black."

"So is Mary Davis's whatchamacallit."

"Maybe he put on a raincoat whenever he took a shower. Maybe he was scared of disease."

"Ain't even sure it was Norris that filled that bag. Doc Shepherd ain't finished doing tests."

"Yeah, but Doc's examination showed Norris got all heated up the night he died. Remember he said that over lunch?"

"The one thing don't necessarily lead to the other," Bud said, grinning. "Investigator has to handle questions like *that* mighty careful."

elliott mackle

"Coach can handle anything you throw," I said. "What about Mary? You sure Mrs. Norris is telling the truth—about Mary bending over for Mr. Hillard? In the maid's room? Maybe Mary killed both men."

"Mary says no."

"What else is she gonna say?"

"Well, I mean, she says no, that Willene never caught them naked together."

"Naked on the slip covers. In the maid's room."

"Right. Yes. Never caught them together period. But yes, she says she and Hillard did have an affair. Which was pretty much over by the night he was shot."

"So she was there? And he filled a rubber in her just for old times' sake? Did her husband watch through the window? Or come inside and hold a gun to the boss's jaw? 'Shoot, Mr. Hillard. Or I'll shoot.'"

"Jesus, Dan, you got a mouth on you. Be serious."

"I wouldn't be able to shoot off for a week."

Bud laughed. "Probably do you good to save some up. But Mary did say something that caught my attention and it didn't have nothing to do with shooting—or shooting off. She said there was bad blood between Hillard and her husband. Seems that ex-sergeant Davis came back from overseas with big ideas. He wanted to be treated like he'd been treated in the Army—with some respect, like a white man. Wanted to manage something. You know he was in an all-coloreds unit that fought in Italy? Got a battlefield promotion. Upshot was that he couldn't keep a peacetime job. Finally, Mr. Hillard offered him part-time pay as a driver at the Ford service department. Wash turned him down, told his wife it wasn't nothin' but a nigger job. She says she told him niggers can't be choosers—claims that that was what Mr. Hillard had told her. And that was the one time Wash hit her. She stopped seeing Mr. Hillard a month or two later."

I whistled. "So dancing on Hillard's grave made some sense. But what about the gambling? Why did she curse the gamblers and the drinkers?" I figured this was information I needed on a number of fronts.

"Speaking of drinks," Bud answered. "You gettin' dry?"

I told him I'd water him down as soon as he finished with Mary. But not to skip any details.

So he finished. According to Mary, Hillard Norris had planned to open a competing card parlor somewhere in Lee County. He was going to use Ku Klux Klanners as his muscle and the Ford agency as his bank account. Free-flowing whisky and Miami strippers would serve as draws. He originally expected to start operations before the winter season was over. But then something happened—Mary didn't know what. When Bud pressed her, she speculated that Norris had formed some kind of grudge against his friend, Sheriff Hollipaugh.

"Why, because the sheriff didn't want to go along with his plan?"

"Don't know," said Bud. "I'd like to, though."

"Christ," I said, not bothering to censor my reaction. "My club is barely breaking even. How'd he think a second club could make out? I don't care if he brought in Margaret Truman to do a striptease."

Bud laughed. Then he blasted another homer right over my head. "Mary Davis admits to being at the Royal Plaza Motor Lodge on Saturday night," he said quietly. "The laundry-marked jacket is hers. Says Miss Willene gave it to her more than a year ago. She admits that her husband did surprise her with Hillard that night, but she doesn't know how he found them. Was only the second time they used the place. Says she agreed to see Hillard one more time, just to tell him what she thought of him."

"So maybe she ends up lying down for one of her studs and then shooting them both?"

"Would stand to reason, in a way," Bud answered. "Only that's not what she says happened. She claims that when Wash busted in, she tried to stop him from shooting Hillard. Only Wash grabbed her arm. He shoved her outside half dressed and slammed the door. So she was sitting on her ass on the pavement when she heard the two shots that killed Norris."

"And she rushed back in?"

"And she rushed back in. You want to tell this, Lieutenant? Says she tried to reason with her husband, argued with him, cried and carried on, but he shot himself right in front of her eyes."

"You sure she didn't see this in a movie someplace? With Lena Horne playing the dancehall girl, maybe?"

Bud leaned forward in his chair, patted the holster under his jacket, then leaned back. "Pushed his wife away, jammed the pistol to his ear, Whammo! Brain salad."

"OK," I said. "So now she's batting 0 for 2. She leaves, right?"

"Wrong. She says she looked at both of 'em dead and turned into an ice cube. Said that all she could hope to save out of the mess was her husband's reputation. Said she knew the rich, white Norris family would come out OK no matter what. So she did a little rearranging before she left. Tried to make it look like Hillard shot himself after killing Wash."

"Thereby hoping to suggest that what she wished had happened might actually be true."

"She didn't put it quite that way, Shakespeare. The girl don't talk near so fancy. Took the better part of an hour, this is over at her rent property in Colored Town, to pull the story out of her. Then, after she spilled it all out, she laid her ears back, said she wouldn't sign no statement. So I may have to start all over. Anyhow, she messed up my crime scene by moving the pistol, dropping it in Hillard's hand. I respectfully asked her to tell me why only Wash's hand had powder burns on it. That's according to Doc Shepherd's tests. Asked her to explain to me how Mr. Hillard could have killed himself with shots to both the jaw and the wrist."

"I want a beer, now," I said, changing my mind. "Are you almost finished? Mary sounds like a better liar than General MacArthur's publicity man."

Bud stood up. "Mary started getting confused at that point. Tried to claim there must of been powder on Hillard's hand, only it got brushed off in the struggle with Wash. Tried to claim the powder got transferred someway from Hillard's hand to Wash's hand. Claims as evidence that Hillard was known as a fast shot."

"Fast with a shot of whisky, maybe."

"Look who's talking."

"Beer, Sarge. Set you up a Bacardi and Coke this evening?"

"Shut up, Dan," he answered, genially. "Buy me a beer and I'll tell you how I squeezed my snitch."

Which I did, and he did, at a two-top table in the club room.

When Bud caught the clerk Leon Featherstone alone during his afternoon break, the snitch also coughed up a tale worth hearing. Sheriff Hollipaugh, according to one of Featherstone's associates, returned to Myers before dawn Sunday morning and spent about an hour in his office before leaving for home.

Bud subsequently checked with the weekend-duty operator on the county switchboard. Being no fan of the sheriff, she initially refused to gossip with one of his underlings. Once Bud sweet-talked the lady into seeing that he wasn't setting her up, she consulted her records. The sheriff, according to rough notes she'd made Sunday morning, put in call to a number on Pine Island. He also called several residence numbers in Myers.

"Bingo," I said when he finished. "Presume your boss has witnesses to his whereabouts after Saturday midnight?"

Bud looked worried. "Well, if he don't, he can get some."

"Would figure to get somebody to do his dirty work, come to that."

Bud sucked his beer, hunched his shoulders forward and said, "Whole thing don't stand to reason."

"No? How's this: Norris got his dick out of whack when my people refused to break the law and let him bring a colored girl upstairs. He must have figured—wrongly—that this place is practically printing money. So he decides to get back at us and fill his own pockets at the same time. He takes his buddy—your boss—on a tour of fancy dives and gambling dens over in Miami and Palm Beach, then explains his plans and asks Hollipaugh to look the other way for a cut of the take. For whatever reason, Hollipaugh leads him on for a while and then shifts course and turns him down. So Hillard goes to the Klan, and gets his muscle there."

Bud shook his head. "Norris didn't need to open no gambling hall. He was rich."

"It's his wife's money. Her daddy left her the car dealership. Turnipblossom Ford paid the bills. Far as we know, Norris never made a dime on his own."

"And got big ideas?"

"And maybe knew a little bit too much about how your boss operates?" I said.

"And the boss figured Norris couldn't be trusted? Which would go double with the Klan at his back?"

"Yeah, and don't you suppose the sheriff might have known about Wash? Norris must've bragged about his honey. Wash could've shot Norris in a jealous rage. He knew how to handle a weapon. Norris borrowed his wife and then offered him a pissant job to buy him off and keep him quiet," I said.

"So we got two mad dogs and one howling bitch and one hotel room."

"And your boss," I said, tipping up my beer and draining it. "Or somebody around him. Somebody tipped off Wash that his wife was at the Royal Plaza Motor Lodge with Hillard. Both men wound up dead. That rids your boss and Fort Myers of an in-the-know, too-big-for-his-britches white man as well as a potential colored troublemaker."

Bud rubbed his eyes with his hands. "You don't really think Gene arranged all that, do you?"

"Sure does fit your boss's movements on Sunday morning. See, there are shots at the Royal Plaza early Sunday. The neighbors call the police. Officer Hurston arrives on the scene and checks back with the switchboard. Wouldn't a double murder bounce around the police forces pretty fast? Even on a Sunday

morning? Which would make it possible for the sheriff or somebody else to then call Willene at the fishing camp?"

Bud shrugged. "Well, the next-of-kin is usually called anyway."

"Did Hurston identify Norris when he called in? Nobody
phoned Mary."

Bud shook his head. "Don't think so. Let me check again."

"But you get what I mean? What you told me Sunday
morning at your rooming house was that you'd been called
about two dead bodies in a tourist court. That it was too
much for the rookie on the scene to handle. You didn't mention anything about a rich businessman or that his next-of-kin
was being called."

"No," Bud admitted. "Switchboard gal didn't say nothin'
like that."

Carmen appeared at my side, set down two frosty Regals and
whispered that Mr. and Mrs. Boldt had entered the club room. I
looked around. This wasn't Ridley Boldt's regular poker night.

Nonetheless, he walked directly to the card table and was
immediately dealt in. Mildred settled herself at the bar, ordered
a drink, sipped it and then crossed the room to our table.

"You gentlemen want an old woman's company?" she said,
sitting down as soon as we rose to greet her.

She'd never met Bud, so I introduced her. But she knew who
he was—that was soon made clear—and she wanted to talk to
him as much as to me.

Before getting to the point, she rambled for three or four
minutes about the extraordinary weather, memories of drinking
with Hemingway and the art show she was organizing at the
women's club. Then she turned to the funeral.

"A sad occasion," she remarked, glancing at Bud. "Yes. And
one made infinitely more unbearable by that wretch of a colored
girl, Mary."

When Bud merely nodded respectfully, Mildred Boldt presented her case. "Willene pulled her out of an orange grove. Yes.
She was just a pickaninny and Willene brought her up from
nothing. Taught her how to clean house and polish silver and

nurse Hillary. Gave her things. Paid her when she was sick and that buck of a husband she had was off in the war."

Bud and I looked at each other, then back at Mrs. Boldt.

"Mary had herself a kind-hearted mistress who'd given her everything," Mildred continued. "Who had made her part of the family. And what did that Mary do? Well, sir, she put herself right in Hillard's way. Wore uniforms that were worse than skin-tight. And Hillard, well, a man doesn't always have good sense about that. Certain kinds of men are like a bull with a red flag when a bad girl shakes her you-know-what at him. Don't you think that's so, gentlemen? Don't you think that's so?"

I could think of nothing to do but nod and murmur, "Yes, ma'am. You may be right."

Bud smiled charmingly. "Man has to control himself," he said, pitching his voice low, "against his animal urges. Most of the time."

It looked as if Mildred Boldt might shiver seductively. Instead, she cast her eyes down and said, "It was common knowledge among our friends that Hillard had a roving eye. Mary must have started going after him a couple of years ago. I told Willene the first time she found them at it that she ought to file for divorce. And—"

Bud put his hand up, interrupting her. "First time?" he asked, letting the words hang there.

Mildred Boldt didn't seem remotely embarrassed by the question. She'd probably cleaned up after her cousin before.

"Once he even took Mary out on his boat," she hissed. "And ran out of gas and they had to be rescued by the Coast Guard. And one time last month Mary telephoned him at work. Only Nana—old Mrs. Turnipblossom—was there in the office. She picked up the receiver and recognized the girl's voice."

"Have to keep that in mind," Bud said neutrally. "It's a lot of aspects to it."

Mildred wasn't finished. "But it was still a shock for dear Willene," she said, glancing toward the card players, "to have someone call her out at our fish camp way out on Pine Island last Sunday morning."

Ridley Boldt was bent over his hand, choosing a discard. True or not, Willene's alibi had been carefully crafted and was likely to stick.

"Our whole family loves getting away to Pine Island. It's so quiet compared to Myers. My children hate it, of course. No movie theater." She laughed. "You know, I almost feel like this is a Broadway play, with some man calling to inform Willene that Hillard is lying dead in a hotel room in Colored Town. It just didn't, but of course it did, ring true."

"Who answered the phone, Ma'am?" Bud asked, choosing his words carefully.

"Well, I did, of course. And the man's voice sounded familiar, though I didn't think much about it, not much at all, no. Not at first because when he asked for Willene I must have thought it had something to do with a broken-down Ford in a ditch someplace. And that he was just a regular family customer. So I called her, then turned over and went back to sleep. Yes."

"And you still don't know who it was?"

Mildred finished her cocktail and looked around. "I've thought and thought," she said, putting on a sorrowful expression. "But it just won't come. No."

Tommy Carpenter entered the room through the service door, stopped briefly to pick up a glass of water from Carmen, then crossed to the piano. After opening the lid, he reached beneath the keyboard and flipped a switch. Suddenly the baby grand, dance floor and pianist were washed in white light.

Tommy's flashy black suit with zebra-striped lapels wasn't quite a tuxedo but it wasn't informal either. The bow tie was also striped, the shoes white patent leather, the cufflinks and shirt studs cats-eye red.

The room was about half full. Cocktail hour was in full swing, and when Tommy opened with a medley of fox-trots, several couples got up to dance. Asdeck and the Louisiana party, who had been out fishing all day, drifted in two by two after showering and settled at a big table at Tommy's right hand.

After 15 minutes of bouncy dance music, Tommy paused, riffed a set of scales that became a fanfare, then turned to the audience and rose to his feet.

"Ladies and gentlemen," he announced, "It is with *extreme* pleasure that we introduce a little lady who is making her *debut* as a singer on this *very* occasion." He reached down and struck a rising progression of jazz chords. "The little lady is no big name, no Dinah Shore or Jo Stafford. But we *guarantee* that you honored guests will not be disappointed. And we predict"—he struck two more chords—"that the whole *wide* world will soon be hearing about the *star* of tonight's *tea dansante* extravaganza...in the glamorous Caloosa Club...direct from Milwaukee, Wisconsin...the fabulous...the accomplished...*Sarah Shaw!*"

Flipping the lights down and then up again, he led the applause before swinging into a lively introduction to "Zing! Went the Strings of My Heart."

Asdeck looked across at me and grinned. Spreading my hands and shrugging, I gestured back that I had no idea where this Tommy-and-Sarah show had come from.

Sarah Shaw was small, round, auburn-headed and white. She wore silver glasses. A large rock weighted her left hand. The sleeves of her pale blue cocktail dress bunched along her arms when she spread them out to sing.

And she could sing. OK, she was no Judy Garland, no Jo Stafford for that matter. Nervous at first, she missed notes here and there. Toward the end of the song she got behind Tommy's rhythm and he had to slow down to let her catch up.

But we listened. Everybody in the room stopped talking until she finished. And when, after a burst of applause and whistles at the end of the first number, she moved confidently into a slow, aching rendition of "Come Rain or Come Shine," it was clear that she and Tommy had put together a rousing set of tunes.

She sang four more songs, gaining confidence with every note. After applause and prompting from Tommy, there was an encore—"Bill" from *Show Boat*. Then she bowed again, threw us a kiss and headed for the exit.

Moving quickly, I crossed the room, introduced myself as the hotel manager and asked her to my table for a drink. Glancing around, she looked unsure whether to agree or not, but when Carmen came over and kissed her hand, whispering "Judy, Judy," she recovered herself and accepted.

Tommy followed her to the table but didn't sit down. "Surprise for you, boss," he said, standing behind the singer. "She's good, isn't she?"

Carmen arrived with hot tea and lemon. "We have to protect this angel's throat," he said. "She had a little help with her hair and makeup."

Sarah Shaw seemed about to explode with happy energy. "My throat never felt better. If we'd rehearsed more numbers, I could've sung for another two hours."

"And you will," Tommy whispered over her shoulder. "If you want to."

She put her hand to her mouth and didn't say anything.

"We want her to, don't we, boss?" Tommy asked me, withdrawing his hand without a fuss. "At least one set a night?"

"What is this?" I said. "Broadway Melodies on the Gulf Coast?"

"I've never had so much fun," the singer exclaimed. "My husband's going to kill me."

Tommy beamed. "This lady sang in her glee club, sang during her summer abroad. Then bang, got married, had two children, show's over."

"My daughter takes piano lessons. Her teacher also coaches voice. We live in Milwaukee, you see. I took a few song sheets home one day, some Cole Porter, *Oklahoma!* Until a year or two ago, I only sang in church."

"Sang solos," Tommy put in. But now little Sarah is gonna sing before the *public* with all her might, not just the Lord."

"Jack, that's my husband, and I decided we could afford a winter holiday this year. But something came up in the business and

Jack had to stay at home for a few more days. And my sister had already come over from Chicago to stay with the children. So I just got on the train like I planned. Jack won't be able to join me before the end of next week."

"And she heard me play in the lobby a couple of nights ago," Tommy added. "So we put a few numbers together. Whatcha think, boss-man?"

"I think you two ought to be on the radio," I said. "Meanwhile, we definitely want you to continue the gig here."

The diamond flashed on her hand as she gestured a little bow of thanks. "If you think it would be all right, Mr. Ewing."

"Call me Dan," I said. "We can't pay you much."

"But something?" She was, after all, a businessman's wife.

Though I could have paid her pin money, the look of her country club gown suggested a better solution.

"Lucky for us," I said, "your husband's stuck in Wisconsin. You sing two sets a night from now until he gets here and I'll set you up with a credit for evening dresses at Flossie Hill's Department Store."

The singer laughed and clapped her hands. "I don't have a second set ready tonight," she said.

"Can you work with me a couple of hours later?" Tommy asked, grinning. "Late?"

"We'll go to Flossie Hill's tomorrow," Carmen said, bending down to collect the empties. "We can also look into a champagne rinse for that hair."

The three of them went away laughing. Bud took off for the men's room. While he was gone, Admiral Asdeck came over with an invitation that was essentially a command.

"Why don't you join us for dinner," he said. "You and your buddy. My Louisiana friends are looking for a good time. Betty Harris—your party girl, Wanda's new friend—she's joining us too. So, why don't you have Carmen set a table for eight in, say, half an hour?"

When I told him that sounded OK, he added something that didn't sound quite as OK. "I thought I'd break out the blue movies after dinner. Carmen's going to set up a projector in the Edison Room. Your buddy will get a kick out of it, I'll bet." Asdeck's face was as serious as if he was talking business. Which, of course, he was.

Tommy Carpenter was playing again. I sucked my Regal down to the foam. The thought of Bud, me and stag films in a room full of other people sent a confusing, slightly agreeable shiver down my spine and around my balls.

I couldn't say yes, I couldn't say no. So I nodded, meaning that I understood.

Asdeck went away. Bud returned. "Huh," he said when I delivered Asdeck's invitation. But in the end he agreed to stay, though he didn't sound happy about it.

I guess dinner went well enough. I remember nothing about what we ate. For all I know, the menu consisted of breaded and deep-fried Mae West life jackets served with cocktail sauce.

Carmen kept the alcohol flowing. Ray Bonner Flambeaux, the Louisiana oilman who was footing the bill for everything, drank Haig and Haig Pinch "with a good splash of branch" (I do remember that), one highball after the other, and never slurred a word. Bud put down two or three Bacardi and Cokes.

After dessert, Carmen led us to the private room on the mezzanine. Sofas and easy chairs were lined up facing a portable screen. Lou was stationed behind a bar stocked with liqueurs, whiskey, coffee, cigars and two big bowls of popcorn. Carmen took his post in the rear behind the looming green metallic projector and switched it on as soon as we were seated.

Bud and I were in back row, the darkest part of the room. The admiral and Betty Harris, Mrs. Broussard and the jockey-sized Flambeau sat down front. Captain Slidel and Mrs. Peek occupied a sofa in the middle.

Most of the black-and-white Cuban action was routine dog-and-pony show. The first movie featured two women in abbreviated maid's uniforms and extremely high heels. Busily feather-dusting what must have been the reception room of a Havana whorehouse, one woman acted as if aroused by the act of cleaning the torso, legs and private parts of a nude statue of Bacchus. Her associate, dusting the breasts of a reproduction Venus de Milo, was similarly affected.

Behind an oriental vase, the young master of the house peeped hornily at the maids, hands busily exploring his pants pockets.

Quickly stripping each other of everything but their lace caps, garter belts, stockings and shoes, the maids retired to a Louis XIV-style settee and began to lick and explore each other. After five or six minutes of variety kisses, the darker and taller of the women went to a cabinet and removed two large dildos fitted with belts and straps.

The young master's pants having now hit the floor, he began to stroke his flaccid equipment while leering at the camera.

"Little fella," Carmen called out. "Don't you bet he grows up."

Lou, meanwhile, was none-too-subtly rubbing the front of his pants. When one of the Cuban maids inserted her dildo into the vagina of the other, I heard him groan. Soon, he was breathing like a horse and had both hands in his own pockets.

A few minutes later, as the young master demonstrated how to fuck one maid while kissing the breasts of the other, someone in the Edison Room slid down a zipper. Then somebody else gasped. I'm not sure who either person was.

"Hi yo, Silver," Carmen called. "Ride 'em, cowboy."

Once the young master had proved his manly satisfaction, Carmen deftly changed reels without switching on the overhead lights. Lou refilled drinks during the short interval. Bud sank a little deeper into the sofa, sticking his legs straight out in front of him, carefully not touching me. When I looked over at him, he threw me back a sloppy grin. "Not so bad," he said, rubbing his chest. "Saw a live show like that in the Philippines one time."

"Saw it? I thought you starred in it."

"Won't let me forget that, will ya?"

The second film featured a middle-aged black man with a phallus the size of Ray Bonner Flambeau's forearm. His scrotum resembled a sunburned cantaloupe. Sweating under studio lights, and looking none too clean, the man kneaded himself vigorously without ever becoming entirely erect. Just when he seemed about give up, a mulatto woman wearing a garter belt and mules entered the scene, fellated the man as if enjoying her work, then squeezed his testicles roughly.

"Look at her handle those peaches," Carmen called.

Asdeck's head and shoulders had disappeared from the front row. Betty's head, meanwhile, rolled and bobbed from side to side.

Trying to get in the spirit of things, I moved a little closer to Bud. His eyes stayed on the screen. His arms were crossed on his chest. When I put my hand on his thigh I felt the muscles tense, relax and tense again, as if he was arguing with himself.

Maybe he was. Anyway, he let my hand stay where it was. When I slowly began to move it higher, he covered it with one of his hands but didn't stop me until I touched the cloth over his hard cock. Then he laughed.

"That Santiago cane-cutter isn't laughing," Carmen cooed. "Anybody want to get in line?"

In the next shot, the Cuban stud had shifted positions and was kneeling over the body of what appeared to be a frightened teenage girl—she'd arrived while I was working on Bud. The Cuban leaned back lazily and beat his chest like King Kong. Pushing into the girl like a bull on a cow, he humped her slowly with a glazed expression on his face. When the garter-belted mulatto woman stuck a finger into his ass, he smiled like a monkey.

"Jesus fuck," Bud whispered, reaching over to grope me roughly.

Though I wasn't hard, I was certainly horny. Using both hands, I unbuttoned Bud's pants and reached inside. He was wet and a lot harder than the Cuban. Gently slipping a finger under his skin, I brushed the moisture around the tip. Bud held his breath, stiff all over.

Moving carefully, I gathered the loose cotton fabric of his boxer shorts into one hand. Wrapping it around the unprotected helmet at the end of his cock, I twisted gently.

He folded up, almost breaking my fingers. "Hey, Coach," he said, taking short little breaths. "Better...hold off on...that."

I leaned into him. "My hand," I whispered. "Jesus, you're gonna break my hand."

Still breathing fast, he sat back. "Just—it feels pretty late to be messing around," he whispered back. "On a school night. Cold showers would be the thing this time."

By then I was as hard and wet as he was. A cold shower probably wasn't going to do it for me. I thought about asking him to stay, but I didn't. He wouldn't have agreed anyway, and there was no point in putting him on the spot.

Bud reached over, touched the tent of my pants and lightly shook my tent pole. "Nice bat, Coach," he said. "All the same."

I felt him again but he gently pushed my hand away, picking it up with two fingers, like a fish, and placing it firmly on top of my own erection.

"Cold showers," he said, rebuttoning his pants. "With all these people around."

He left just after the third film started—an epic variation on the Cinderella tale in which a horny prince tries to insert his phallus into the "slippers" of a dozen women and girls.

Though I hadn't jerked off in months, I took matters in hand as soon as I got upstairs. Even before I got all my clothes off, I was on top of the ghost of Mike Rizzo, pushing him against the tan blanket, breathing in his ear, talking dirty, telling him what I intended to do. Mike was a rough-and-tumble lover that night. He made jokes, laughed, kissed my cock and balls, roughly pushed and sweated against me in the narrow bunk. I gently brought him off with my mouth and hands.

And then, because I hadn't yet climaxed, we started all over again, this time just after a battle at sea, when we were both wound tight as steel spools. We made it standing up, fighting for balance against the rolling motion of the old ship. I unbuttoned Mike's uniform quickly, and he mine. He hurt me when he pulled me close, but we couldn't get close enough. We pushed against each other, filthy dirty and sweating like deck apes, grabbing for air, muttering, "Fuck, yes, fuck, yes," him quickly spilling on my heaving stomach like a desperate school kid after a winning game.

Then, in the sweaty, dead-real split second just before I started to shoot, I was kneeling over Bud out in the fishing boat. He was lying there, flat on the deck, and about to release his load. I sucked him and sucked him. And he was someplace else, eyes closed, passive, fearful, waiting for me to get us where we were going.

But I couldn't do it. My cock misfired and started going numb. An ache throbbed somewhere behind my balls. Bud and the boat disappeared. I looked for Mike again and couldn't find him. Searching for dependable fantasies, I revisited the Australian colonel with the shot-up knee, the one who wanted me to dwell with him in Queensland. I grabbed at him briefly, but couldn't get his pants off.

And then nothing, nothing except my own cold hands and soft, unfinished wetness and a chilly breeze on my heaving gut.

A window facing the river was open a crack. Out on the water, I could hear a passing marine engine. Summoning up an *Indianapolis* full of horny sailors, a New Victory Club weekend with a dozen horny officers and Bud on the fishing boat, I tried again, but with no success.

Cursing tiredly, I crawled under the sheet and rolled myself around the pillow. As I drifted off to sleep, I made a firm resolution: *Hit the swimming pool tomorrow, Lieutenant. Do at least 50 laps. You've got to get the pressure off. That'll be a start.*

If I dreamed at all that night I don't remember a bit of it.

DₖₐfT BOₐᵣd

"YOU SAY YOUR MAN'S BEEN WITH PHILIPPINE WHORES," Asdeck cheerily observed the next morning. "But I noticed he skedaddled on home halfway through my Cuban vaudeville show."

"Too many civilians around, must've spooked him," I answered. "Can't blame a cop for caution."

The morning was bright and cloudless, the crisp February air as bracing as a splash of Old Spice. We were stretched out in lounge chairs by the hotel swimming pool, enveloped in fuzzy terry-cloth robes, feeling tired but self-satisfied. I'd just finished 30 up-and-back laps, with Asdeck matching me stroke for stroke.

He left the water game but breathing hard, laughing at the unaccustomed effort. I felt relaxed and alert, happy that some of the previous days' frustrations lay in my wake.

Homer Meadows approached and set down a tray containing coffee, cream, sugar and a breadbasket. Asdeck turned his attention to the sweet rolls and hummed a little tune.

"Marine grunts stick with their buddies," Asdeck continued after Homer went away. "They go on liberty together, drink too much hooch and egg each other on. Whole platoon will hit a whorehouse at one time. Wear the girls out. Exec has to pour the men back aboard ship before he can sail. Next day the doc lines up the whole platoon for short-arm treatments. And you think he was embarrassed?"

"Admiral, you know this isn't some whorehouse in Manila. Those weren't his buddies upstairs."

"Except for you."

"I gave it a try."

"He still seeing that woman, the waitress?" Asdeck's lip stiffened almost imperceptibly when he pronounced the last word.

I sugared my coffee. Asdeck's probing compounded my doubts about Bud and set me on edge. "Yes, sir, he sees her," I answered, "Don't know how often, though."

"Appearances count," Asdeck said. "Not disputing that, Dan. Even if you and your buddy do hook up for good, it can't hurt for him to have an occasional woman on his arm. At the Legion hall, community events, that sort of thing."

"Yes, sir," I said again, knowing well enough—and knowing Asdeck knew it too—that Slim was more than just a beard. "Except, well, if he's going to work for me here, as house detective, that'll keep him pretty busy."

"Have you finished your background check on him, son?" Asdeck asked. "I know I said to take your time. But you take my advice and you'll lay your cards on the table soon. Talk to him flat out."

I swabbed my face with a towel. I swigged half my coffee before I answered. "Admiral," I said finally, "You trained me and made a man of me, and I appreciate that. I was drowning and you pulled me onto dry land. But you didn't just throw me in bed with some horny palooka the first night, and show me dirty movies, and shout that you knew all my secrets."

Reaching into the breadbasket again, Asdeck held up a banana Danish for inspection. "You were drowning. But you already knew how to swim. All I did was give you a hand so you could get moving again and feel better about wherever you got to, whether you used a backstroke or the crawl."

I nodded. He was right.

"Your buddy," he went on. "We don't know whether he can swim or not. He's hardly gotten his feet wet. He'll drown unless you quit being his water wings."

"I need to train him," I replied. "According to my plan, sir. Not yours."

Asdeck remarked that we were already in deep water and explained that the unlucky Ford dealer had hoped to open a rival card room in Myers. The local official he'd turned to for protection, however, refused to cooperate.

"In other words," I answered, "Sheriff Hollipaugh decided to honor the bargain he'd already made?"

"I'm not at all sure how your buddy would react to hearing *that*," Asdeck answered. In any case, he added, we'd have to put off making a decision. He had a finance meeting to attend in New York and an overnight train to catch.

I told him I'd stay in close touch. I didn't say I'd decided to invite Bud to supper for a powwow.

Needing more, and better looking, waitresses, I'd run a want-ad in that week's *News-Press*:

TOP PAY FOR LADIES
Dining Room. Uniforms supplied. All shifts. Interviews on Tuesdays and Thursdays before lunch. Only experienced servers need apply to Manager, Caloosa Hotel, Fort Myers.

it takes two

Four candidates showed up that morning, their appointments set up by Carmen Veranda during the previous few days. The first combined grandmotherly appearance with prewar experience at all-night diners in Norfolk. The second, 30 years younger, wore a cross on a chain around her neck, and spoke extensively of arranging church suppers and after-service coffee socials at the United Tabernacle Church of the Blessed Redeemer. Both were white. Neither was what I was looking for. I told each woman I'd keep her paperwork on file.

The third applicant was a thin brown woman about my age. I'd seen her only two days before in a very different setting. Carmen hadn't recognized her name when she telephoned, nor did he have any particular reason to.

Did Mary know how much I knew about her? I wasn't sure.

She appeared in my office wearing a green maid's uniform, white oxfords, a plain gold wedding ring and a nurse's cap neatly pinned to her pomaded hair. Yes, she said, she'd been a housemaid at one time. But she needed work now and the prospect of better pay in a hotel led her to apply. She'd worked as a waitress in a colored hotel in Tampa, waited tables at a roadhouse in Pinellas County and then at a lunch counter in Ybor City. Although she'd never worked in a white hotel, she knew food and how to write up an order.

References? No, they'd been lost when her house was broken into.

Given her barely disguised charges about the Caloosa two days earlier, it crossed my mind that she might be here to do her own investigation. On the other hand, I felt sorry for the woman, figuring her to be a friendless double widow, down on her luck and, as she said, out of a job.

So, instead of showing her the door, I played her story back to her as gently as I could.

A defeated woman might have raged or collapsed in tears. A stupid woman might have tried a transparent lie. Mary Davis was neither. She listened coolly, covered her face, took a breath, and stood up once I'd finished. "Guess you don't want to talk to me no more," she said, gathering up her purse and smoothing her skirt. "Thank you kindly all the same."

"But I do want to talk to you," I exclaimed, also rising. "About a lot of things, including a job."

So she sat back down. I was feeling generous. I figured she had about as much to lose as I had in late 1945, the day Asdeck plucked my personnel file out of a Pacific Command fuck-ups pile and pulled me off that troop ship in Japan.

"What things would that be?" she said. "Aside from a job?"

"You've worked all your life, all the time you were married?"

"Yes, sir. We always needed the money."

"Even when your husband was in the Army?"

She sat up a little straighter. "Mrs. Roosevelt, she couldn't do much about raising benefits for the wives of colored enlisteds."

"Your husband came home safe, though?"

"Yes, sir, came home from Italy as a sergeant and wearing all kind of decorations. Proudly served in the all-Negro 92nd Division for over three years."

"But had trouble keeping a job back home?"

"Had trouble finding a good job, sir. Finding anything to fit his experience."

"So you had to keep working as a maid?"

"Yes, sir, that's how it was. Like they say, my Wash, he didn't adjust too well to peacetime."

"Or to the politics down here?"

"You mean, in the…South? The war didn't change much. Southern people been like this a long time."

"So why did you choose to apply to this hotel?" I asked. "Given what you said over Hillard Norris's grave?"

Covering her face again, she shook her head, then said, "You was there, then? Huh! Well, you know, not too many other places in this town would be likely to hire me."

When I asked if she couldn't get another house-maid's job, she answered dully, "Not after what I been through."

When I said I knew something of her history with the Norris family, and that I'd heard how her husband had refused Hillard's job offer, she scowled, then spat back an answer: "That was Wash's low point, Mr. Ewing. And mine, up to *that* point. Only I didn't know it."

I started to say something else but she cut me off.

"He tried to do what they taught him in the Army: to lead men. He tried to do some organizing here. You know what I mean? Getting colored folks to vote. Going door to door. He even tried to start an NAACP chapter. Wrote off for a charter application, started calling meetings. Only nobody came. And the preachers pushed him aside, said it wasn't the right time, said he wasn't the right man for the job, that he was goin' too fast."

"Excuse my asking," I said. "But did Hillard know all that?"

"Mr. Hillard, he knew some of it. So did Miss Willene."

"Some guy told me her old daddy was a big-time Klan leader."

Mary shook her head. "The colonel didn't believe all that. Was just politics is all. Course I never knew him. And Mr. Hillard, he wasn't like that at all."

Just politics. Bud had used the same phrase in characterizing Sheriff Hollipaugh's links to the Klan. On the one hand, I was shocked at what sounded like willful innocence on both their parts. On the other hand, thinking back, I'd grown up in the same racially segregated society they had. Our assumptions were much the same: There was never a right time for reform. Politicians didn't really believe the poison they fed to the public. Only other people, never one's family or close associates, knowingly did evil or joined evil groups.

How much different from her innocence was mine concerning the prospects for men who loved men? *Maybe*, I thought, *Bud is the only level-headed one here.*

Like I say, though, I was cocky and full of fight. Having read Kinsey, I knew Bud and I weren't alone in the world. Being young, I nonetheless hoped that social reform, like the latest movie, was coming soon.

And job or no job, it was not my business to ask how or why she became Hillard Norris's mistress. But, having come this far in the conversation, I wanted to know a little more of what she knew about him.

"The Klan marched at his funeral," I said.

"That was for the old woman," Mary said. "The colonel's wife, the old—" Catching herself, she finished, "Old Nana Turnipblossom."

"How long did you work for them?"

"Too long. Close to five years. Wash was thinking of reenlisting. And if he'd gone in, I'd 'a gone with him."

"Might have been better."

She laughed silently, without smiling. "Wash was a good man, and I was a whore for Mr. Hillard. But that was over and done with. I'd told them both so. I was breaking it off for good that night, last Saturday, when Wash come in and…and everything changed."

Breaking it off for good… And yet, Hillard had been sexually aroused before he was killed. Plus the whole condom thing.

I wanted to keep Mary around. But I'd have been stupid to let her handle drinks or enter the club room. "I'm sorry, Mary, all our waitressing jobs are filled, but we might find a place for you as a chamber maid."

Startled, she shook her head slowly, then evidently changed her mind and said that would suit her. I sent her to the house-keeper for a second interview.

Candidate 4 had more, and more recent, waitressing experience. When Slim Nichols entered my office, she took one look at me and her sharp jaw dropped. Then she laughed.

"Seen you with Bud," she said, smoothing her hairdo. "Over at the Arcade."

"And I thought you had the best job in town," I answered, feeling awkward and unready to put her at ease. "I know you're darned good at it."

"Oh, yeah, thanks. It's all mink and pearls, hon. Only a girl-friend of mine pointed out your advert. And I called your Miss Emma Mae, you know? That works for you on the dock? And I asked what is up. And she said you had in mind hiring some younger women. And that there was benefits and paid vacation."

Mentally noting that I needed to have a word with Emma Mae, I smiled welcomingly and answered that everything was negotiable.

"So what are you paying, if you don't mind if I ask, sweetie? And how do the tips get divvied up?"

I countered with a question about references and experience. Slim joked that she could provide as much of those as I could handle.

Ha ha, I thought.

More to the point, I wondered: *How would I like having Bud and his paramour both working for me, even if Slim does become, as I'm planning, his ex?*

The whole thing didn't feel right. On the other hand, she was a pro—not to mention somebody I'd keep running into week after week as long as I stayed in Myers.

"We just hired a lady not 15 minutes ago," I said. "But I definitely want to keep you in mind. So will you let me keep your job application on top of the pile? And we won't say anything about it, natch, while you're still working the mink-and-pearl circuit. Right? Call me Dan, by the way."

"Miss Emma Mae told me you was still a bachelor man, Dan," she answered. "How come a frisky young fella like you don't have a girl yet?"

This question I could handle. "Oh, my fiancée died," I said, dropping my eyes to the desktop and assuming a somber expression. "Drowned. A good while ago."

Slim touched her lips with her fingertips. "Jesus, honey," she whispered. "That's tough."

"Oh," I answered. "I'm trying to get over it."

Sailor Beware

"*BUENOS NOCHES, LADIES AND GENTLEMENS,*" Carmen Veranda chirped, seizing a stack of menus and waving them under Bud's nose. "I reserve for you the most—how you say?—the most secluded-est table on the pool terrace. Very nice and *silencio*, for a little more privacy, yes? And now if you will follow me? *Por favor?*"

Bud looked blank, then closed his mouth. "Oh," he said, glancing my way. "Sure."

I wanted to tell Carmen to knock off the flamenco act. But what the hell? Unless Bud's 20-20 eyesight had suddenly failed, he'd already spotted the rouged cheeks, mascara-lined eyes, Duchess of Alba fingernails and theatrically cocked hip.

Carmen's emphasis on privacy and seclusion seemed almost certainly a reference to our mezzanine make-out session the night before. His post at the projector had given him a ringside view.

Leading the way through the half-filled dining room, across the terrace, past the pool and out to a trio of empty tables lined up beside the diving board, he stopped at a table for two and pulled back the chairs. Once we were seated, he handed us menus and lit the candle in the hurricane-glass shade.

The deuce had been specially set. White linen cloths, yellow napkins, stemware and embossed Syracuse service plates were standard. But the tabletop also contained a RESERVED sign and a pair of red and yellow ginger blossoms in an oriental jar.

The spiky symbolism was unmistakable.

I thought: *Somebody won't quit.* I said: "Pretty. But you went to a lot of trouble."

"Oh, boss-man," Carmen cooed, waving a delicate hand over the flowers. "There is no trouble when I got two such handsome gentlemens on my hands." He sniffed the faraway orange blossoms that perfumed the winter air. The scent drifted into town every evening, spilling out of the citrus groves upriver. "Order whatever you like. If we got it in the kitchen, I promise to bring whatever you desire."

"So what's particularly good tonight?" I said, opening the menu. "Anything we shouldn't miss?"

"Coconut cake," Carmen answered immediately. "Cookie made it from our own Lee County coconuts. The cake is as fresh and untouched as a 10-year-old bride."

"You can save a slice for me," Bud said, his voice low. "If you would."

Carmen made a note on his order pad.

Bud picked up his own menu. Then he glanced at me as if to speak. He thought better of it when stud waiter Lou Salmi arrived, showering ice cubes and water into the goblets and drenching the sweet air with Old Spice aftershave.

"Gents," Salmi boomed, puppy friendly. "Welcome back. Pleasure to serve you again."

Bud nodded but didn't say anything.

Salmi wouldn't quit either. "How'd ya like them fuckaroo films the admiral got hold of, huh? Boy, Sarge, I bet there wasn't a virgin safe in Myers today, not with you and Mr. Ewing on the loose."

Bud scowled. Carmen rolled his eyes. Salmi continued, "You know, the old man, he got right down to it. That gal we fixed him up with? He gave her panties a regular tongue bath."

Carmen swatted Salmi with a menu. "Shut your trap, amigo. Go get the gentlemens some bread and butter."

"Maybe you need your Parker House roll buttered, Miss Chili con Carne. Could be the boss-man here ought to rent you out to a donkey farm."

I almost laughed. The foul-mouthed bastard needed another assignment. At the New Victory Club he'd have functioned perfectly as a room steward for female officers. I wondered if Admiral Asdeck would let me take him off table-waiting duties altogether.

I was thinking with my dick, and my next question came out too coarsely. "So that's all the old man was up to? He ate her out and she popped? He didn't get inside?"

Carmen batted his eyes in mock shock. "*Mamasita del Guadeloupe!* You two nasty sailor boys going to embarrass our Lee County official detective here." He slapped at Lou with a menu. "Do as I tell you. The bread."

"With my best butter and cheese on it. Coming up. Hot stuff."

Carmen huffed, turning his attention to us. "You want nice drinks?"

I looked at Bud.

"Beer," he said.

"*Dos?*"

I nodded. "*Dos.*"

Carmen made another note. "We have everythings on the menu for you tonight. Is nothing we are out of. What you want? Fried shrimp? Shrimp good, yes. And we got sea bass and spotted ocean trout catched by Miss Emma Mae, yes? Start with chowder," he said, addressing Bud. "Chowder is very *bueno*. And as a first course, may I suggest"—he leaned down and touched his pencil to the menu's appetizer list—"our *especial* whores douvers that we prepare for you two gentlemens." He winked at me, then leered mildly at Bud.

Carmen's teeth reminded me of white neon in a barroom window. "Estreemly *especial*."

"OK," I said. "Hors d'oeuvres, chowder, fried shrimp platter, skip the French fries." I glanced at Bud. "Take the appetizer and soup."

He nodded manfully. "Same for me. Except T-bone steak for the shrimp. Well-done. Don't forget. Well-done."

"I don't forget nothing you say," answered Carmen. "That's why I escribble it down. Yes?" He removed the menus with a flourish and pranced toward the kitchen door.

A sly smile creased Bud's face. "No forget, *señorita*," he said. "Fried T-bone. Well-done shrimp platter."

He took a sip of ice water, then held the sparkling glass up to the light, twirling the stem slowly back and forth in his fingers, examining the shifting pattern of ice inside the glass.

"This is one damn fine hotel," he said. He took another swallow and set the goblet back on the table. "Damn fine."

I accepted the compliment with a nod, took my own sip of water.

"Looks like you manage it right too," he continued, putting down the glass. "So I have to laugh. I mean, why is the admiral trying to piss it all away? Where do you people find all these shit-buckets to work for you? Your restaurant manager thinks he's a girl. That waiter's a fucking weasel in heat with a mouth like an open sewer. Not to mention some of the other clowns and strays around here. No offense, of course. Don't mean you."

My pulse began the predictable run from idle to full ahead.

Salmi returned, set two chilled mugs and two uncapped Regals in front of us, then silently marched away. I poured both beers, took a long swig of mine, then finally gave Bud the same pep talk the boss had given me.

"I'm as stray as they are," I began. "And I'm here to make a living the only way I know how. That means helping other people get what they want—helping them have a good time, relax and take the pressure off."

Bud said "Huh," then swung his eyes out at the river.

"Sarge," I said, recalling Asdeck's remarks that morning. "You've been in Philippine whorehouses, but have you ever been in the YMCA shower room in 'Frisco? I have. And I ran a club for the admiral in Occupied Japan. We had hot and cold running geishas and card games and Marine studs on call for female officers. You know how many complaints we got? One. From a badly bent preacher the morning after he emptied his nuts into one of our gals."

"It's different overseas," Bud answered. "Soldiers, hell, loneliness. And not everybody goes for that shit. You must of paid somebody off."

"Commander of the shore patrol just so happened to win our Christmas door prize," I replied, grinning because I was a little embarrassed. "Fleet officers from Yokosuka patronized the club pretty heavy. Army officers—on up to bird colonels on Emperor Doug's personal staff—came around a lot. So did the Royal Australians. Did I ever tell you about the time this Aussie fell for me right hard? Wanted to take me home to meet his mom?"

Bud's scowl deepened. Even in the half-light of the terrace I could see that the scar on his neck had turned scarlet.

"You're bragging," he said. "Keep it down."

Looking Bud square in the eye, I said, "I fought the Japs to be free. Not to prop up a bunch of cracker Tojos and Hitlers. If I want to drink beer on Sunday morning—which I do—or wear a dress and fuck black butt—which I don't—it isn't the sheriff's or the Klan's business. People have a right to do what they want, as long as it doesn't hurt anybody else."

"Didn't hurt nobody the other night," Bud countered, "when the Klanners put their dresses on and burned that cross in your parking lot. How'd you like that?"

Bud wasn't hearing me. I was about to reply when he said, "I ain't gonna argue with you about whether colored folks is better off in their own part of town. But you got to admit that most decent people have better things to do on Sunday morning than drink beer, and that the good book forbids one man to treat another like a woman."

I held up two fingers in a Churchillian V-for-Victory sign. "You don't act much like a woman when we're mixing it up."

Bud gave as good as he got. "How would you know, Lieutenant? You told me you'd never been with a woman."

We both laughed. The tension lessened 20 degrees. Bud nudged my shin with his foot. "That right? That right? Never?"

Paraphrasing Asdeck's plan of operations, I explained that the club room, though potentially profitable, was technically outside the laws then on the books. "Laws that are due to be rewritten," I said. "A whole set of forward-looking young veterans are being elected to the legislature and Congress." I had no reason to doubt Asdeck there either.

"I trust the old man with my life," I said. "For whatever that's worth. Ask me are there any risks in running this place? I'll tell you, hell yes. But I don't have anything to lose. When the old man asked me to come home and work for him, I resigned my commission flat. No matter what happens, I believe backing him up is the right thing to do."

Bud leaned forward. "You ever been in jail, Lieutenant? Because, you know, people get arrested for no more than 10% of what you and your Mr. Carmen do every day of the week. Maybe what goes on overseas or even in 'Frisco is different. But running what amounts to a whorehouse and a speakeasy in Myers isn't the same as being some kind of Robin Hood or peacetime hero."

I wanted to shout, *You ever had a ship blown out from under you—had your best buddy and all your men killed? Ever been on a raft on the Pacific day after day?*

But I didn't. Bud Wright had done what he had to do, gone where the generals sent him. So instead, what I said was, "I'm no hero. I'm lucky, that's all. And I believe the old man when he says he knows what he's doing."

Our mugs were empty. Catching Salmi's attention, Bud signaled for refills.

"Guess you feel like you're still wearing a uniform," Bud said gently, turning back to me. "It's natural. Especially working for your old skipper. Took me five, six months of nightmares to get over it."

"I'm not talking about nightmares…and quit changing the subject. Our war ain't over, Sarge," I said. "The battles didn't stop in August of '45. Colored boys still get lynched and women still get raped."

"Then you can't be too careful," he said. "Because sissies like—what's her real name? Cabildo Morales? They give homos a bad name. And I'd say your weaselly waiter Mr. Big Salami doesn't do much for the other side, come to think of it."

"Hell," I said, "I don't live as openly as I want to, but Carmen and Lou do."

"Right. Yes. Your Miss Carmen's as open as a window. But I can't see it gets him nothing. Because no real man, much less a woman, would want to bed down with a pansy like that."

Salmi delivered our refills, checked the untouched bread basket and disappeared again.

"They feel safe working here," I explained. "They act natural as a result. Maybe too natural. But Carmen's my best worker. And I may find the right slot for Salmi yet."

"Right. Yes. Only your Miss Carmen wouldn't act so pansy if she was working some other place."

"No," I said. "He couldn't. He's the tip of an iceberg. There are thousands of others like him. They just blend into the scenery. I bet you didn't see them in the Marine Corps either."

"Weren't any," Bud said, "that I knew about."

"Promise you they were there. Playing possum and under cover. The same way they stay safe everywhere else. Mostly."

"Mostly? Dan, you got to understand that you're…well, not talkin' my language."

"Mostly. Meaning there are lots of snug harbors. Carmen—Cabildo Morales—served his country as a female impersonator in Army soldier shows. He even got decorated for bravery under fire. Claims to have a buddy over in Miami who's still doing drag shows. Hiding absolutely nothing. And getting arrested once in a while. Carmen hides very little here. And stays safe by serving the club. And vice versa. So far."

"He couldn't feel too safe," Bud replied. "Not after that drunk's threats the other night."

I felt the alcohol hit my system. The image of Carmen lying dead in a hotel room, his jaw shot off, the bed soaked with blood, jumped up and stopped my train of thought. "I'm mixing this up," I said. "Excuse me." Reaching across the table, I poured some of my Regal into Bud's mug. The beer foamed up swiftly. "Maybe strays and loners don't ever feel safe," I said. "I don't. Not on land, anyhow." I looked him in the eye. He looked back solidly.

"When I was a kid," I said, holding the glance, "everything seemed OK. Not a worry in the world. I went up and down Tampa Bay in my uncle's boat. Swam at school most mornings and afternoons. Classrooms and home were just shore time. Went fishing and sailing out of Cedar Key when I was at Gainesville. Joined the blue water Navy to see the sea—and keep the world safe for Mrs. Roosevelt and the American way. And it was always safe out there. I had friends."

"And when the *Indianapolis* went down?" Bud asked. "That wasn't so safe. Having her blown out from under you." He saw me blink and swallow hard. "You mentioned it before, Dan. Forget I said anything if…"

I shrugged, took another sip of beer, and another. "It was time for that old lady. By wartime standards, she was ancient—13 years, and a lot of hard work under her keel. Time to go."

"Not like that."

"It was bad," I admitted. "But it taught me something."

Carmen appeared at my elbow. "Gentlemens, gentlemens," he crooned, setting chilled plates in front of us. "*Mucho gusto.*"

"Two more beers," I said. "Fine."

Bud stared down at the food. Each serving was an exquisitely composed erotic phantasmagoria. Oysters had been opened and garnished around the edges with dill weed. Lobster medallions, topped with sliced stuffed olives, resembled nipples. Cold peeled shrimp and poached scallops suggested randy male equipment.

"Somebody's idea of a joke," I muttered.

"Joke food is still food," Bud said, picking up a cocktail fork. "Never had nothing like this. Looks fresh, though." He speared a mock penis and dunked it into a puddle of pearly horseradish mayonnaise. "What did the sinking teach you?"

"Taught me it's luck that counts."

"Your luck? In not drowning?"

"Yeah. But more than that. It was luck that I slept on deck the night the sub found us. Luck that I had a pneumatic life belt with me. Luck that I found a raft within a few hours. Rotten luck for the men who went insane from swallowing seawater. No luck at all for the almost 900 men who...didn't come back."

I ate an oyster and washed it down with Regal.

"Look, man," said Bud. "Don't—if you don't want to talk about this. Do you?"

"No," I said. "Yes. Not much. I got through debriefings at Guam on pills and alcohol."

"You want some of this?" He held up his half full bottle of Regal. I nodded. He poured.

"There was an officer in my raft," I said. "Another lieutenant, who'd gone over the side in the dark with a quart of scotch in his hand."

"You had shipwreck supplies in the raft, didn't you?"

I ate a second oyster. "No, nothing. No food or water. But having the whiskey to sip for the first couple of days kept us from going crazy. Anyway, that's what the Navy doctors decided later."

"My platoon was in Okinawa by then," said Bud. "There were stories about the sinking in *Stars and Stripes*. Got written up again when your captain was court-martialed after the war."

"Can't stomach scotch whisky anymore." I laughed. "I throw it right back up."

Carmen's hand reached out of the darkness, collected empty bottles and set down fresh ones. The pool deck beneath us seemed to move, as if I was on a ship again, only drunk and confused by the wartime blackout.

"Chowder's coming right up," Carmen said.

it takes two

When he was gone, Bud topped off our mugs and smiled. "Maybe beer is your luck now. Not water. Nor scotch."

"I grew up on the water," I said. "Out on Tampa Bay fishing with my uncle. Winning swimming races in high school. Thought I was God's redheaded gift."

Bud leaned back, still smiling. "Water was our good luck anyhow, wasn't it? Out on your fish boat that time?"

I grinned, remembering that second fishing trip. We'd anchored, stripped off our clothes, dived into the water and almost immediately begun messing around. Once we'd gotten too aroused for any face-saving jokes to stop us, I'd kissed Bud's neck, wrapped an arm around him lifeguard style, and started hauling him back to the boat. "We ought to lie down," I whispered, my hard cock cutting the water like a mast. "Stay with me, Buddy."

And he did. We hauled up the metal ladder, moved forward to the cabin, sat down side by side on one of the bunk and quickly worked out patterns of exploring each other all over again.

I kissed the scar on his neck and gently massaged his backbone with my hands. He let me pet him that way for a minute or two, then he leaned back, panting, gently stroking his phallus and balls with both hands, ready to go wherever I decided to take us. I got between his legs and teased his thighs with my fingertips. Then I took his hands in mine and spread them apart, over his head, pressing them against the mattress and raising myself to cover him. Our bats began to nuzzle like inquisitive eels.

When I released his hands, he left them where they were. "You about got me, ah, there, ah, about got me there," he whispered. "Coach, Coach, fucking Coach. You with me? You ready? Teach me, Coach."

Kneeling over him on all fours, I brushed his ears, neck, armpits and chest with my mouth. But as soon as I tried to kiss below his belly button, he twisted frantically, and pulled my face back up to his.

"That ain't the way now, Coach. What we're doing is the best I've ever. Can't get no...you just keep with me, Coach." Rising off the mattress, he took one of my hands and wrapped it around his slugger, doing the same to me with his other hand. He pulled so hard he almost hurt me.

"That's it," he'd said, loosening his grip but then suddenly tightening and tightening again. "I never," he'd said. "I never. Come on with me. Come on, ah, with me. There, there. Oh."

The GOdDamn War

"GO AHEAD AND TALK," Bud said, setting down his fork. "Tell me about your ship." He picked up his beer and sucked down deeply. "Tell me about feeling safe."

I matched him, beer-wise. "You want the whole story?"

He nodded, his smile dead serious.

I began at the real beginning.

"The ship was my home for 15 months. I went aboard right out of supply school. Saw some action in the far Pacific. We carried Admiral Spruance's flag for a while. Then took a kamikaze at Okinawa, ended up back at Mare Island in California for overhaul in the summer of 1945.

"The ship was fast. But old, like I said. And expendable. Which is probably why the War Department assigned her to deliver the Hiroshima A-bomb to Tinian Island. We drove out there like a freight train on a straight track. Went from San Francisco by way of Pearl. The ship even set a record. From Farallon Light to Diamond Head in 74 hours and change. Still stands. Nice trip. Anyhow, we handed over the bomb at Tinian. Not knowing what it was, but speculating to hell and back. Then we continued across the Pacific. We didn't make it all the way, of course. Guam, next port after Tinian, was our last call."

202

The raw oysters were roiling my stomach, making me nauseous. I pushed the plate away.

"Not that I had anything to do with operations," I said. "I heard most of this from my cabin mate, Mike Rizzo. He was an engineer. From Baltimore. Tough little guy."

Lou Salmi noiselessly removed the appetizer plates and set down bowls of chowder. "It was like managing a hotel," I said. "I was in charge of billets, messing, commissary, supply, officers' cooks plus odds and ends like laundry and wardroom cleanup."

I picked up my soup spoon, sipped the chowder, didn't taste anything. "I had 32 stewards, cooks and mess mates assigned to me. Not one came back after the sinking. When the torpedoes hit, I could have been down in the galley drinking coffee. Or refereeing some dumb fight in the cooks' quarters. Or I might have been racked out in our cabin up forward in officers' country. Died with Mike."

Bud was steadily devouring his chowder. "Lucky you didn't sleep in the cabin, huh?"

"I'd be dead if I had. Both tin fish hit forward. Thirty feet of our bow was blown off. Not many officers got out."

"Only your luck was right, and you did." Bud was telling me to go on. "Soup's fine," he added.

"Mike was my best luck, maybe," I answered. "I was minus one roommate at the time he came aboard. I'd just been made billeting officer, so I could have kept the bunk open until Rita Hayworth earned a commission. But other guys were jammed in three and four to a cabin. I took the next junior man aboard."

The beer had flavor, the soup still didn't. I glanced up to gauge Bud's reaction to my story. His eyes were on the chowder. I plunged ahead.

"Found a half I didn't know was missing. And we got...close, fast. Closer than I'd been to anybody else. Sometimes we slept in the same bunk. The door had a lock."

"Lucky for you," Bud grunted, his attention still on the soup. "Lucky nobody got nosy."

elliott mackle

"Lucky as hell," I agreed. "But that late in the war, there was a lot of looking the other way. The exec officer told me about two different incidents of enlisted men found naked together in the blackout. 'Body buddies,' he called them. He didn't do anything except send them to the showers. Maybe he was testing me, wondering if Mike and I were a pair."

"You was lucky to have somebody," Bud said, his voice low. "Even if it was against regs. You know what happened to too many couples during the war—like Sergeant Wash Davis and his wife. He goes off, gets decorated, comes back and finds her whoring."

"You sure Mary didn't shoot both of them?" I asked—my mind making fuzzy connections—then added, "You know, I just hired her as a maid."

Bud looked at me like I was crazy. "Jesus, Dan. You need your head examined."

"Naw, I'm just an old softie. Who else was going to hire her?"

"Better watch your back," he said. "You can push Lady Luck an inch too far."

"Damn right," I agreed, swigging beer. "Anyway, I was sleeping on deck on the Lady *Indy* every night I could. Ventilation in quarters was half of zilch, even with most of the hatches and watertights undone. Below decks didn't ever cool off in the summer Pacific, night or day. And running under wraps like we were—to save fuel!—meant even less air got piped below. So a lot of guys would drag mattresses or blankets out on deck. It was total snafu. We sailed without an escort because the *Indy* had the capability to outrun Jap subs. On paper, that is, at service speed! Ha. We were all alone and moving as slow as a cow on a path. I guess the brass figured there weren't any subs around. They were wrong. Missed it by one."

I shoved the chowder away. "I slept topside, on a ledge port side of the aft stack. It was a spot Mike and I and a few other officers took turns using. My number came up, I was off watch from 8 to 8, right place, right time."

"You weren't hurt when the torpedoes hit?" Bud had emptied his soup plate and begun working on mine. His growly voice seemed unchanged.

"First blast rolled me off the ledge onto a pair of sailors standing watch. We were still in a pile when the second one went off."

"Where was your friend Mike?"

"The fish hit just after midnight. He was scheduled to go off watch in the forward engine room. So he may have been relieved by then, and back in our cabin. Or he could have been still on duty. Or, who knows, wandered somewhere else. But his luck was bad. And so was mine, losing him.

"And, of course, I couldn't do anything. It was pure-hell confusion. My battle station, the wardroom, was burned out by the time I got moving. So I started checking life preservers on sailors. Being sure the strings were tied right. Any fool could see the ship was going to sink. And she did, in 12 minutes flat. Sank like a knife. Rolled over to starboard, went down by the bow. I walked down the port side. It was exactly like wading toward the deep end of a swimming pool. I inflated my belt, found a raft a few hours later and got into it, then pulled one badly burned deck ape aboard and paddled free.

"We drifted all night. My burned sailor was delirious. I heard other yells and screams at first, and whistles. But gradually…nothing. Once, I thought maybe he and I were the only survivors. But the wind had just blown us away from the main group. Toward dawn, we drifted into the lieutenant with the whiskey. He was riding a couple of potato crates, which I lashed alongside. The man was good company, an optimist. I can't ever remember his name.

"My burned sailor died that afternoon, couldn't stand the sun. We tried making a tent out of my blouse but it didn't help. The lieutenant and I put him over the side and watched him sink. The water was clear, just as green and clean as a bottle of 7-Up. He sank and sank, got littler and littler. Then this big old white-bellied shark swam by and tore his legs off."

"Jesus," muttered Bud. He was massaging his forehead and brows with a balled-up fist.

"It was his good luck to be dead by then," I said. "Sharks got plenty of other men right in the water. Men that were still alive. Plenty of bodies, and parts of bodies, floated by us."

I told him about thirst and sunburn; about meeting another two-man raft with oil-soaked gunners aboard; about being taken aboard the destroyer escort USS *Doyle* after four days and nights; about being hospitalized at Peleliu for exposure and returning to Guam for debriefing and recuperation.

While I talked, Lou delivered our platters of shrimp and steak and later brought coffee and slices of cake.

"The worst thing about the sinking," I said at last, pushing away my cup, "was the flat fear. Not of my own death but of Mike's. Being left alone. When he didn't turn up on the *Doyle*, there was the chance some other ship had him. When he wasn't at Peleliu, well, maybe some other island. See, his name didn't appear on either the preliminary survivor lists or the killed-in-action lists. That was because, I found out later, nobody still alive had seen him after Sunday at 10 P.M. I gather he didn't get off the ship. Nobody got out of the engine room. I had to go around pleading for information. I got some funny looks, but also a good deal of sympathy. Lots of men's buddies were lost, so my story didn't ring any different.

"Finally, they listed him 'missing, presumed killed.' I cried for two days. Didn't leave my berth except to go puke every so often. Third day, this psychiatrist came in, had a clipboard with forms on it—a set of questions he wanted to ask me. Asked about the sinking, about my dreams, mostly about Mike. He didn't ask me to betray him—us. Nothing like that. But I got the message. Next day, I straightened up, shaved, put on a clean uniform and started pulling strings to get a ship."

Bud's head kicked back. "You didn't want to come home? War must of been over by then."

"Oh, I did come home," I said. "Was ordered to testify at the kangaroo court-martial the Navy brass set up for our captain.

Shared a four-man cabin from Yokohama to 'Frisco. Had a week's liberty in Tampa. But I'd already figured that if I didn't get right back to sea for real, I never would—that I'd be beached forever."

"Brave man."

"Desperate. Sailing blind. Anyway, I put in for sea duty. Ferried a new troop ship from the yard at Norfolk out to Japan. Then, boom—Bruce Asdeck or somebody picked my name out of some shit-pile hat. When the ship docked at Yokosuka, I got handed a set of orders and put ashore."

"And you never heard anything else?"

"About Mike? He left me his insurance. I wrote his sister in Baltimore to see if she was OK for money. She said she was."

Bud laughed. "Luck," he said lightly. "The brass never caught on to you two horny monkeys. That was your luck."

I stared at him a long time. Finally I said, "Of course they caught on to us. That's how I got a job running a glorified whorehouse in Japan. That's how I got here."

"Jesus," he groaned after what seemed like a minute. "I don't—"

"Sarge," I said, thinking fast now, suddenly sober out of pure desperation. "You don't know how lucky you are. To get hooked up with me. As a team, we don't know lucky we can get."

He looked away and then back at me. "What kind of team? Thought you said—"

"I said business. Here's my proposition. You quit your dead-end Lee County job as quick as you can. You start up a private security business the next day. I already briefed the Admiral. One of his investors will kick in seed money. You'll be on your way."

Bud sipped his coffee. "On my way to digging irrigation ditches for some friggin' tomato farmer after six months."

"Horse shit," I answered. "The Caloosa Hotel will be your first and only client. Long-term contract. Your bravery and honesty, coupled with my fuck-all determination, that ought to be enough to keep this place safe—from the Klan and your boss. Plus which,"—and I took a breath before finishing the sentence—"I'm getting to like being around you, a lot more than I figured would ever happen."

He was grinning. But he had a narrow, quizzical look in his eyes. "You know," he said, "you're the first person since my granny and my old coach to see much in old Buddy-Bud besides shoulders and fists. To see, hell, value and potential? Heart and head? Only that sounds like Boy Scout shit, cheerleading for myself."

I grinned back. Now he was hearing me. "Those officers who cited you for bravery," I said. "They saw something."

He shook his head. "I only did what any man trained to use a rifle would do in the same spot," he muttered. "Platoon leader's different than being Joe Cop or Joe House-Dick."

I asked him to think over my proposition seriously. He said he would, but that his inclination was to say flat-out no. Crossing over from law enforcement to what amounted to the other side wasn't anything he'd ever considered. He didn't see any reason to take such a chance. We were buddies and that didn't need to change.

I shoved back my chair and stood up. "Let's hit the beach."

He rose unsteadily. I took his shoulder and turned him. We were both plastered. "Come on," I said. "Walk."

Heading out toward the Caloosahatchee, we turned east along the riverside path at the far end of the parking lot. There was a soft breeze and intermittent moonlight. We could see each others' faces.

I was tired and disappointed that he hadn't jumped at my offer. Halting beside an old orange tree that overhung the water, shielding us from the hotel's lights, I took a few deep breaths.

Bud rolled on for a dozen paces, then turned and came back. "Cool off, Dan," he said. "Because this thing—this friendship, me being buddies with you, and getting to feel like we, well, you know—this ain't anything I expected."

"Fuck. That's what I just said."

"And you're telling me the admiral thinks we could really do the security detail at arm's length and private?"

Nodding, I took a step closer to him. I didn't care what the admiral thought, not anymore.

"Guess there's ways it might work," he said. "So's not to give anybody ideas." He looked me in the eye and repeated the phrase, trying to soothe me: "It could work, Dan. It's OK. It's OK."

It didn't feel OK. "You want me to stay at arm's length, Bud?"

"Dan, I ain't no pansy. Nor you either. It was just the goddamn war. And you cooped up in that cabin with another man and all."

We didn't move. Then he said, "Arm's length would be better. Safer all around. Luck or no luck."

"Luck or no luck," I said. "OK, OK."

Peeling off my shirt and wadding it up, I added, "Let's get in the water. Clear our heads. Soak the beer out."

Tossing my shirt aside, I reached for Bud's wool jacket. "Skinny dipping," I muttered, pushing the coat down his arms, exposing the holster and pistol. "Cool us off," I said, unbuttoning his shirt.

Cooling either of us off was the last thing on my mind. Getting wet and naked suddenly seemed like the only solution to the muddle.

He put his hands on my bare shoulders. "Too dangerous," he said. "Might get in trouble. Better stay here."

I touched his side lightly, my hand brushing his scar. His hands tightened on me. We stood that way, frozen in moonlit shadows for half a minute. I'd just begun to unfasten his belt buckle when somebody on the hotel dock behind me coughed. I felt Bud's gut stiffen as he looked up.

We sprang apart. His shoe caught on an exposed orange-tree root and he almost went down. I grabbed his arm automatically. He found his balance and looked toward the dock.

Emma Mae, beer bottle in one hand, waved at us with the other. "Tide's running," she called. "We're just checking the lines on the fishing boat."

Slim Nichols, Bud's girlfriend, stood beside Emma Mae, staring.

Given the circumstances and the amount of beer we'd put down, I guess Bud did the only reasonable thing. Shaking free of my arm, he pushed me back a step and, as gently as possible, slugged me in the jaw.

o*dd* Man oUt

THE LIFEBOAT SLID DOWN A BIG PACIFIC roller into a deep trough, taking on water. The stink of scotch whiskey and diesel oil stung my throat and lungs. Painfully pulling upright to empty my guts over the gunwale, I spotted another boat, an empty inflatable. The sun was dropping toward the horizon fast, half blinding me. Rubbing my salt-caked eyes, I tried to keep the buoyant raft in sight. Darting in and out of fog and mist, the raft suddenly became the hotel's fishing boat. She was backing toward me, her reversed propellers kicking up white foam. On the boat's afterdeck, four figures—Bud Wright, Mike Rizzo, Wanda Limber and Slim Nichols—sipped from bottles of beer, threw the empties into the ocean, laughed and chatted. I called out. There was no response. The boat drifted past me, toward the setting sun. As if accidentally glancing back, Slim spotted me, waved almost casually and alerted the others. I held up the bottle of scotch, which was now Bacardi rum. The party of four saluted. A wind kicked up. The boat's diesel engine turned over, caught, roared and settled into forward action. The party moved away.

I bit the pillow and gagged. Beer-shrimp nausea and cold-fuck embarrassment rolled over me. I needed to pee. Hauling myself onto my feet, I glanced out the cracked-open window. The venetian blinds were open. The Florida sun was just up. Birds were cawing and hawking out on the river. Off in the distance a tug slid busily downriver, her diesels singing, the crew headed westward toward the Gulf, perhaps bound for some ship in distress.

After a long piss, hot shower and fast cup of coffee in the hotel kitchen, I filled a Thermos bottle with more coffee and headed over to Bud's rooming house. The front door was locked but the spare key lay where Bud kept it, under the porch steps.

He opened the door to his room wearing only a T-shirt. Prudently, I didn't look down. He tried to shut the door in my face. I blocked it with my foot.

"Get outta here," he said.

"I got coffee," I said.

"Hold the noise down. I can make my own coffee."

"Lemme in."

Turning, he reached for his pants. "Fucking grab-ass game last night's probably gonna cost me my job."

"Bull shit. Two drunks fighting. Probably looked like a couple of bears in a circus. And it was real dark. You got any clean cups?"

"Look in the lavatory sink. Fuck, you know she saw us. That's my girl, in case you forgot."

"Did I tell you your girl applied for a job at the hotel yesterday morning?"

"You fucker. What the hell are you doing to me?"

I poured coffee into the two cleanest cups I could produce. "What's your girl gonna do? Tell the whole town the man she puts out for is turning queer? And so she wants to go work for the man that's queering him? Some babe."

"Watch it, watch your mouth."

"We were stupid, OK? I was stupid. The beer made me stupid. Should've marched you back over here instead of down to the river. Or invited you upstairs."

"Stow that. Could be you hoped to get me fucking disgraced and fired. I'll be damned if I'll work for you. You get me drunk and try to talk me into—"

"You don't understand anything, do you, Sarge? Am I wasting my breath?"

The words turned alternately hot and icy in my throat. I gulped steaming coffee and almost burned my mouth.

Bud turned away, confused and angry, talking to the wall. "Fucking understand one thing, mister. Probably be better for me to stick to women after this." He turned to face me. "I ain't gonna be labeled a queer homo like some fruit-cocktail hairdresser."

"Listen," I said, moving toward him. "You're no fruit. Neither one of us is. I had a lot to learn—about what I want."

"Well, you didn't learn enough." Bud grabbed the desk chair, wrapped a leg around it and leaned his forearms on the back rail. "I know about wanting to touch somebody," he continued. "Wanting to get close to another swinging dick, like my old coach. What you didn't learn is that's all little boy stuff. Grown men have got to learn to bury it. Put their dicks where they naturally belong."

By then, I'd sat too, on the round, padded arm of the sofa. "That's all fine," I said. "If a man's lucky enough to naturally like women."

"You know," he said, glancing up at me, "I think maybe the old *Indianapolis* is where your luck ran out. Because of what you and your—your friend—was doing that you wasn't supposed to."

I wanted to deck him. But he sounded serious. And I realized that he still misunderstood me, and that I needed to teach him better.

"You think me and Ensign Rizzo sharing a bunk sank the ship? You figure it helped that Jap sub captain find us? Jesus, man."

"It's what happened is all I'm saying."

"Tempt fate and go straight to hell? Imagine if Dugout Doug had ever kissed Nimitz's ass. We'd have lost the war."

Bud stood up, walked to the bathroom and returned with a towel, shaving mug and razor in his hands. "Saturday morning," he said, a goodbye look on his face. "But I better go face the music anyhow."

"Assuming there is any music."

"Just listen to me, Dan. Maybe I don't want to learn all you know. Maybe what you learned in the Navy is crazy, tainted. You puttin' your hands on me with other people around, trying to get my shirt off. Crazy. That hotel you run. Crazy. Admirals showing beaver movies to ladies. Men wearing lipstick."

"Redheaded lieutenants who ought to know better," I countered. "Ex-Marines who don't know shit. Never will."

"What?"

"I said: Why the fuck did I give up a regular commission? Florida's not worth shit. Nothing like I expected."

"You mean me, Lieutenant? Fucking jarhead who won't give you all the ass you ask for? Fuck, I never gave it to nobody before. You know that?"

Shrugging, I admitted I did know that. But he wasn't listening.

"Sure," he continued, coming closer, dropping the shaving gear and towel on the chair. "I got off in the showers with somebody else before I ever met you. Played a little barracks grab-ass here and there. But that was it. I-T, period—it. Just women since the day I got discharged. Only you don't care about that score, huh? Only buddy-fucking. Well, that has stopped. Finished. The End."

"Grown men have to make their own luck," I said quietly.

We were glaring at each other, standing close enough to feel each other's excited breath. "The two of us deserve to get lucky together. I mean that."

When he didn't say anything, or even blink, I upped the ante. "Go down and quit your job this morning," I said. "Put in your papers. Forget your double-crossing boss. Take a guaranteed 10% pay raise and start work Monday morning as my hotel security chief. I'll even throw in a room as part of your wages. You can bank the rent you're paying here."

That's when Bud blinked and swallowed hard. But he still didn't say anything.

So I kept spilling my guts. "They want to keep us down," I whispered. "It takes two to fight the bastards."

Bud swallowed again, then said, "You got big ideas, Lieutenant. You want to take on the whole world. But you do give me something to think about. So I'll chew it over. As long as we both understand one thing, that the deal remains strictly business."

I said I understood that. But secretly, I wasn't convinced.

Willene Norris and Mildred Boldt lunched that day at a shaded, poolside table at the Caloosa. Thanks to Carmen's quick thinking, they were served by Homer Meadows, the most reliably conventional waiter on the roster. Willene ordered grilled mackerel, mashed potatoes and iced tea. Her artistic, fun-loving cousin indulged in a chef's salad with shrimp, blue cheese and sliced avocado, tossed in the kitchen and served on a platter. She drank iced tea as well, but told Homer to add a little clubhouse sugar to it. He knew what she meant: a shot of white rum in the glass.

Willene's mourning eyes and face were hidden behind sunglasses and a Panama sun hat. Her dress was conservative cotton—a dark blue liberty pattern with matching gloves, purse and spectator pumps. Mildred wore a pastel sun suit—à la Betty Grable's wartime pinup photos. A sketch pad and a sheaf of colored pencils rested next to her purse.

They were choosing between coconut cake and orange sherbet when I came outside after a three-hour bookkeeping session. I wondered what the two of them, but especially the widow Norris, were doing at the Caloosa together. Neither woman looked very happy. But hell, they were supposed to be in mourning.

By contrast, two younger girls in strapless swimsuits at an adjacent table seemed to be having the time of their lives. A much older man wearing a yellow striped cabana suit was hosting their outing. The girls, tanned and with big boobs, sipped cocktails out of coffee cups and noisily slipped in and out of the water.

Carmen, stuffed into a tight pink sweater and tennis shorts and waving an imaginary microphone, loudly entertained the trio with war stories. "So I said to Bob Hope, who was just wonderful to us when he joined our shows, I said, 'Reach a little farther and you might get your *hand* bitten off!' "

The Louisiana foursome played bridge in a poolside cabana nearby. Overhearing Carmen's punch line, Captain Slidel whooped. "You know what he said to Martha Raye, don't you, young man? When she was supposed to be looking for the keys to the Jeep? And he told her to reach a little deeper into his pants pocket?"

Mildred Boldt rolled her eyes at this, fanning her face and miming outraged virtue. Willene Norris glanced at her and scowled. She wasn't kidding. So I stopped by their table first.

After preliminary pleasantries that included not a word about the gunplay at the Royal Plaza Motor Lodge, Willene got right down to business. She'd had a little talk with her close friend the mayor of Fort Myers the previous night, she said. And she had met with her very close friend the publisher of the *News-Press* that morning. She claimed that she wasn't entirely familiar, and didn't want to be, with the details of illicit liquor sales and high-stakes poker parties and "probably worse things" that went on at the Caloosa. But she did know that the "lurid misconduct" at the hotel had contributed to the death of her dear, dear husband. And so she felt she had to take a stand.

"I must be able to hold up my head, Mr. Ewing. I have a certain position here, and now I have a business to run. And I'm hardly alone in thinking that your kind of business is bad for our little one-horse town."

Filling in the blanks in a script Asdeck and I had perfected in Japan, I nodded and smiled noncommittally. I was certainly sorry about her loss. I added that I took a quite personal interest because Hillard had been such a frequent guest at the hotel, although not, I was sorry to say, during the past two months.

"It goes back much farther than that, Mr. Ewing. As does the deplorable, some say deviant, activity here." She sipped her tea, wiped her lips and continued. "It's certainly my impression that neither the mayor nor the owner of the newspaper had the least, the very least, idea of what's been going on right under their noses."

Not that they'd care, I thought, *unless the liquor, cards and "probably worse things" were paraded before the public in some undeniable, uncontrollable or unprofitable way.*

Willene and I both knew that politicians and newspaper publishers must at least appear responsive to others' concerns. And Turnipblossom Ford was a big *News-Press* advertiser. This daughter of a county commissioner and Klan leader was too well connected to be ignored by the mayor. If she demanded that the newspaper and the politicians shut down the Caloosa, I knew they'd have to pacify her in some way—without radically changing anything.

Cousin Mildred was clearly of two minds in the matter. "Honey," she observed mildly, "People need a safe, friendly place to enjoy a little drink, a nice dinner and a hand of cards."

Willene wasn't buying it. "Decent people," she snapped, "can use the American Legion hall just like they always have."

I didn't bother to tell her I was a Legionnaire in good standing. Or that I'd met the man I was sleeping with at a Legion get-together.

"Now, honey," Mildred drawled, "You always enjoy those limp-wristed artists and dancers I went to school with. Yes, you do. And Miss Carmen is a lot funnier than any of them."

"Funny?" Willene sniffed. "I wouldn't let him wash my hair. The innocent boys of Fort Myers should be protected from such filthy perverts."

"From time to time," Mildred conceded, "just here and there, a few questionable *women* have been admitted to the cabana club, yes. Those two young misses pawing that fat man? They're practically falling out of their bathing suits. Girls like that don't really add much to the Caloosa's atmosphere."

"They're the man's granddaughters," I answered, nodding to emphasize my lying words. "On semester break from Bennington College. Both young ladies made the dean's list, he told me."

"Made the dean," Mildred drawled. "The dean of men. Or do they have men at Bennington?"

Willene leaned forward, peering at the ersatz Benningtonians over her dark glasses. "The dean of monkey business. I've seen that dishwater blond before. She used to work at Woolworth's."

"I could be mistaken," I said pleasantly.

Just then, a man and a woman entered the pool deck from the changing rooms. Both wore robes and beach shoes. Mildred waved her hand and called them over.

"You know Wanda Limber," she explained to her cousin, keeping her voice low. "Plays golf, Navy widow, a real lady."

"Umm," Willene murmured. "Evidently goes for younger men."

Mildred tittered. "Could be the father of your Woolworth jail bait. He's hardly Dan's age!"

"Pretty old," I agreed, keeping it light.

In fact, Francis Bridge had two years on me. When Wanda introduced us, she added only that he lived in Philadelphia.

"We came for a dip," she added, loosening the terry-cloth belt at her waist. "Hope it's no problem, my bringing a guest."

"The only problem," Mildred joked, "is if he doesn't remove his robe and get comfortable."

Wanda and I exchanged a quick look. Francis Bridge was tall and slim, with thick black hair, high cheekbones and a nose like Abraham Lincoln. When he dropped the robe and turned toward the pool, he looked even better. Clearly no stranger to athletics, he had long, firm muscles in his arms and shoulders and flat, pigeon-toed feet. He might have been a middle-distance runner gone to seed or, as I soon found out, a former swimmer. (I'd have figured Bridge for a swimmer sooner if his firm, tight butt hadn't been hidden under tent-like knee-length borrowed trunks.)

Wanda invited me to join them in the water. Having finished a long morning's battle with the books, I decided I might as well enjoy a little exercise, not to mention a nice view. When I got back from changing into trim-cut shorts over a jockstrap, Bridge and Wanda were already in the pool.

"Frank's in town for research purposes," Wanda explained as soon as I joined them.

"Looking into labor conditions," Bridge said, splashing water on his chest and shoulders. "Civic opportunities and so on."

"For the government?" I asked, trying not to stare, just keeping the conversation going.

He laughed. "No, far from it. I work for a private charity. Nothing like that."

"Anybody going to give me a race?" Wanda inquired. "Or are we going to talk all afternoon?"

And so the three of us started swimming laps. Wanda dropped out after 15 minutes. Bridge matched me almost stroke for stroke.

I thought I'd lost him at the end of half a mile. His hands were slapping water and his breath had gotten rough. But the next time I looked, he was right beside me, and he stayed there until we finished 60 lengths.

For me, that was pushing it. But I kept going on adrenaline, testosterone and idealized memories of varsity competition. Of course, it was more than that. Bud and I competed all too often. But when we swam or roughhoused together, there was always the possibility of sex. With a regular guy like Bridge, I just wanted to win.

When I finally hauled out of the water and Bridge followed, we joined Wanda in a cabana. Homer brought us beer and sandwiches.

Wanda had put her robe back on. Bridge didn't bother, which suited me fine. His baggy trunks fit a lot better wet. Because he was so easy to look at, I monitored my eyes, mostly keeping roving glances at chest level or higher.

Bridge was also easy to listen to. His research turned out to be voter registration fieldwork among young blacks.

"It's like the old plantation down here," he observed. "None of your Florida Negroes vote except for a few who hold county or patronage jobs."

"None of us voted in the service either," I answered by way of mild rebuttal. "Except maybe in presidential elections."

"Did someone give you a dollar or a chicken and tell you how to vote?"

I laughed, slightly uncomfortable, yet fascinated. This wasn't anything I'd thought about. On the one hand, I mildly resented Bridge's "old plantation" crack. It was right in line with the WASP complaint that visiting Yankees routinely condemn Deep

South race relations and then return home to the highly segregated North. On the other hand, I didn't care much about how colored people voted—or didn't vote. Bridge was a smart, good-looking Yankee. I was a hotel manager who'd just been threatened by the Klan. So I listened.

"Is that how it is all over the state?" Wanda inquired. "Political bosses and payoffs?"

"That's how it is just about everyplace below Mason-Dixon. You have a few brave souls. There are young people, though not many, who want to stir things up. It's definitely going to take time. Years, possibly."

"Centuries," Wanda replied. "Unless President Truman issues a fresh set of integration orders. And if he does, the Klan'll probably declare war."

"The South will rise again," I said lightly, still playing the genial host. "So save your Confederate money. That's what they say down here."

Bridge smiled back, nodding, his eyes sympathetic but unyielding. "That's not what the Negro young people say, not when the white-sheeters come calling. Not when some of your leading citizens are all but setting the church door on fire."

"You mean here in Myers?"

"Tell him, Frank," Wanda said. "Quit treating Dan like a virgin fresh out of the convent."

"Last weekend," Bridge answered. "I spoke very informally to a youth group at the First African Methodist Episcopal Church. A local contact set things up between my organization and the young people. I don't believe the pastor knew anything about it. Not until afterwards."

Lights flashed and bells rang. "Last Saturday night?" I asked, just to be sure. "That was you the Klan marched on?"

Bridge swiped his face with a towel. "There were three times as many white men outside stamping their feet as there were scared children inside. Still, I was asked to come back."

"Another group asked for him. At the Holiness Temple," Wanda put in. "Isn't that right?"

Bridge rubbed the towel across the damp black tangle on his chest. "This evening," he answered. "Lord willing. And maybe we will double or triple our audience, shoot clear up to a congregation of a dozen or so."

"You're brave," Wanda said. "That doesn't discourage you?"

"I'd be back home in bed if it did," Bridge answered. "It scares me so bad I think I'm going to go jump in the water again. Anybody with me?"

The man's audacity and earnest social conscience were as appealing as his muscular shoulders. But given my political naïveté and Florida upbringing, the idea of organizing young colored people to register and vote offered few attractions. I idly wondered if he was married. He didn't wear a ring.

As Bridge toweled off after his second dip, I invited him to use the hotel pool whenever he liked. "And if you'd like another race," I added, "just send word with one of the staff and I'll put on my bathing suit."

Smiling broadly, he bowed his head. "I'll do that. Thank you. Please call me Frank."

Play It,

Sam

Bud and I crossed paths at Rexall Drugs late Saturday afternoon. We were both buying aspirin.

"You want to go for a walk?" Bud asked. "Take soda bottles with us? It's my treat."

After we paid the clerk, I followed him out onto First Street. We headed east, glancing into shop windows as we strolled.

"Felt like creamed cat shit this morning," Bud said after a while. "Got it under control around noon. Then I ran outta aspirin. You?"

Despite the complaint, he sounded breezy and relaxed, almost impersonal. "Been working all day," he continued before I could answer. "Checked on my girl first thing. She was headed out to Estero Beach with some gal pals, packed a picnic, won't be home till late. So I figured I'd put in extra time at the office, try to wrap up that little shooting match—you know the one."

I said I sure did.

He said he'd cleared off a spare desk and laid out the signed statements from Mary Davis, Willene Norris, motor lodge manager Claudette Marie Jenkins, Officer Walter Hurston and the neighbors on Tamiami Trail. After drawing up a time chart, he'd set up a work table and spread out Doc's medical reports, the on-scene photos, the cellophane evidence bags and his own diagrams of the hotel room.

"Every jot and iota suggests," he said, "that Wash Davis walked in on his wife and Hillard Norris while they was together at the Royal Plaza. Together, but not naked. Doc says he's sure Norris had already been intimate with somebody right soon before he died—counting the condition of his body and his stained shorts and the scumbag in the commode and all. But Norris wasn't dressed funny, like he'd buttoned his pants with a gun to his head. Looks like he and Mary had already mixed it up. They'd gotten mostly dressed when Wash busted in. Which could be why Willene's cast-off jacket ended up underfoot."

I suggested that maybe Mary dropped it while pleading for her lover's life—or for her husband's—before being shoved out the door.

"Wasn't time for much pleading or shoving, far as my witnesses are concerned. Had to put the Lee switchboard log together with the neighbors' statements to see why. Was two shots fired right close together, followed by a third shot within eight to 10 seconds. Three separate accounts confirm that."

I sucked on my Nehi and made the appropriate Holy Christ noises. The meaning was plain: Contrary to what Mary Davis had sworn, no extensive series of between-shots pleas had taken place.

"Could be Mary saw the whole damn thing, and that Wash wanted her to. Wanted to punish her. Maybe it shocked her so bad she forgot what she saw, then made up a version that's easier to live with."

"Could be," I said. "Watching your husband mow down your lover'd be a helluva thing—no matter which side of the hotel door she was on when her husband shot himself."

"Oh, most of the details is like reading the morning paper. Norris must of put his hand up to protect himself—or maybe her—when he spotted Wash coming in with the pistol. First shot caught him in the wrist, that's according to the way Doc says the bones is shattered. Shot to the head killed him, maybe caught him as he turned. That's according to the blood spatters on the wall. He was close to dead when he hit the floor. And Wash put himself down no more than 10 seconds after that."

"And the sight of the whole thing," I said, "turned Mary crazy."

"Right. Yes. But no more than half crazy, I'd say. Looks like she stayed cool enough to try to cut her losses."

I stopped to inspect a display of men's loafers in a shoe store window. "Umm?"

Bud finished his Dr. Pepper. "Gal didn't gain nothing but trouble from Hillard's death, did she? My guess is she was trying to recast the blame a little. Looks to me like she used the jacket to shift the gun from where it fell to Hillard's hand, and do it without gettin' a lot of blood on herself."

"Thus making it appear that Hillard shot Wash?"

"Only it didn't. Not when we look at the powder and smoke marks on Wash's body. And the lack of 'em on Hillard. The colored boy shot himself, no question about it."

"But," I asked, "Can you prove that Mary rearranged the evidence? And how did Wash discover the love nest? Who tipped him?"

"You know my suspicions, Dan. Ain't proved nothing, though. Not yet. Have to talk to Mary again."

"Might find her at the Caloosa," I said. "Remember? She's one of our housekeepers."

"That's right. I was so drunk when you told me—plus what happened after—I forgot. Jesus Christ. Is Mrs. Roosevelt coming down to be your social secretary next?"

That was fair. I laughed, but he didn't. After 15 or 20 seconds, I moved on and he followed. We crossed an intersection, I deposited the empty bottle in a trash can, then I stopped and turned to face him.

"I'm not much good at compliments," I said. But I'd like to praise you some. If I was writing a performance evaluation, I'd cite you for professional care and dedication in working out the facts and for attempting to be fair and honest to all concerned. OK?"

"Well, Lieutenant," he answered. "Since we're bein' honest, isn't that the kind of sweet talk that would tend to get me and you mixing it up again?"

I denied having anything like that in mind. And I wasn't lying. Bud replied, "That's good because we can't let it happen anymore."

We were sparring about where we were going again, what might happen and when. I knew it was important this time.

I said, "Maybe so, maybe we can't, but we aren't finished talking about all this."

Bud agreed. "But no more naked fishing trips," he said.

To which I countered, "And no more sore jaws."

I went to bed early. The phone in my room rang a little after 2 A.M. It was Emma Mae on the house phone, calling from the lobby. "Drop your cock and get your fucking ass in gear," she barked. But her voice shook when she explained why. "Carmen got beat up. The little cocksucker's hurt real bad. Switchboard got a call from the hospital. We got to head over to the emergency room *now*."

I pulled on some clothes and was downstairs in four minutes. We arrived at the hospital in another five.

Emergency rooms are always more fun in the middle of the night. An ambulance blocked the door. A 40-ish white woman and a clerk were negotiating the admittance of a very pregnant adolescent. The tearful girl held her stomach and was muttering, "Oh, Jesus, help me...oh, Jesus...not yet, not yet." Beyond the desk, a policeman attempted to interview a leather-faced Seminole. The Indian was slumped on a gurney, shaking his head. The front of his red striped shirt and blue jeans were bloody. One arm was in a sling. A very old cracker couple had sacked out at the end of a long, battered sofa. Propped against each other, their lined pink faces relaxed, they looked as if they'd been waiting all day.

Carmen lay on a table in one of the cubicles. Snooping, Emma Mae recognized his Texas elevator heels right off. Flinging the white cotton curtains aside, she said, "Fucking fried frogs! Look at this shit farm."

Two nurses were sponging Carmen down with disinfectant.

"You can't come in here, Miss," the younger one called out, pointing back to the entrance hall with her elbow. "It's the rules. Not allowed."

"You his wife?" the other nurse asked. "We need some history on this man. Who's his doctor? We don't even know what shots he's had."

"'Scuse my French, ladies," Emma Mae said, moving in. "But we're close to family as this little spick's got. Can he hear me? His name's Morales, born in south Texas. Smells like a barn in here. Did he piss himself?"

"More like somebody pissed on him," the older nurse answered, nodding. "Bruised and contused from asshole to appetite. No broken bones so far as we can tell. Got some crud on his eyelids. Couldn't be mascara, but that's what it looks like. Doctor's on his way; ought to be here pretty quick. Mr. Morales gonna have to see a dentist too."

Introducing myself as the man's boss, I asked the nurses what happened. They didn't know much. A tramp foraging garbage cans at around 1:30 A.M. had found Mr. Morales in an alley behind a tire-recapping dealership downtown. Whoever'd gotten ahold of him beat the living shit out of him, ripped off half his clothes, tied his hands with his shirt, bound his ankles with his belt, then urinated on him. The Samaritan tramp begged a passerby to call an ambulance, then disappeared, along with Carmen's rings, wristwatch and wallet. The passerby gave a description of the tramp to a policeman who arrived just after the ambulance.

"This here's a Army vet," Emma Mae cautioned the nurses. "Some kind of hero. So you treat him right."

A young man wearing a white coat, mirror and stethoscope arrived. The older nurse moved to shoo us away but neither of us budged. When the doc shone his lamp into Carmen's eye, then gently touched his nose and jaw, Carmen shifted, moaned and tried to look around. "Hurts," he whispered. "Pain my ear, bad. Want Tommy. Where Tommy go?"

The doc and Emma Mae both leaned closer. "We know," the doc answered. "Relax. We're taking care of you." Glancing at the nurses, he added, "He's coming around. Good work."

"What's his name?" the doc asked us.

"Cabildo Morales," Emma Mae responded. "He also answers to Carmen."

"Mexicans sure can be funny," the younger nurse remarked.

"You want Tommy?" Emma Mae asked, bending over Carmen and keeping her voice in neutral.

"Did they kill me?" Carmen whispered. "No want to go die."

"Don't you worry, hon." Emma Mae patted the bed next to Carmen's leg. "Think I know where to find your buddy. We'll have him here in two shakes." Pushing me toward the door, she added, "Let's get outta here, Kimosabe. Fucking time's a-wastin'."

We found Tommy in a juke joint on the river road a couple of miles east of town. The concrete-block building was set a hundred yards back from the pavement in the middle of a dirt and gravel parking lot. The lot contained a dozen elderly cars and pickup trucks, two retired school buses, one flashy gold Cadillac convertible with the top down and a grove of dying orange trees.

Parking her DeSoto sedan near the neon-lined front door, Emma Mae told me the place was called Portia's Paradise. The only sign visible from outside read NO LOITERING. NO FIGHTS.

A large black man wearing an emerald-green suit and fedora lounged behind a table inside the door. He was obliged to charge us a dollar minimum, he said. Each. "Whiskey drinks is 50 cents," he explained. "Beer's 20."

Emma Mae countered that we were just looking for Tommy Trouble and didn't want to drink anything.

"You and who else, Ma'am?" the man answered, curling his upper lip and flashing a jeweled front tooth that matched his suit. "Step right up."

Tommy who? I thought as I paid the man $2, pocketed the drink tickets and followed Emma Mae into the long, shadowy room. The place smelled like sewing machine oil. *Must have been a mill or warehouse*, I figured. There was a bar to the right, about two dozen tables in the center—maybe half of them occupied—and an empty dance floor on the left. We didn't slip in unnoticed. Expressions ranging from open surprise to unmasked hostility followed us across the room. We were the only white people present.

"Do you be seeing a ghost, brother?" one of the men at the bar asked his pal. "Redheaded ghost?"

"Be the ghost that gets in Doc's way," the pal answered. "Follows a cop around so he don't get hisself killed."

I looked around. Mose and Drackett, the coroner's trusty assistants, were either recently paroled or sprung from jail for the weekend. They waved and bowed as if aware that the majority was theirs inside Portia's Paradise.

Tommy Carpenter, a.k.a. Tommy Trouble, was seated at a battered, tinny, upright piano. His back was to the room and at first I didn't recognize him. Two men worked beside him, one plucking a blue guitar, the other massaging a bass fiddle. A kid who looked all of 14 was trying to beat a snare drum to death. All four wore white sharkskin suits with striped lapels, yellow felt hats with turned-down bills, gold-plated watch chains and patent-leather pumps.

Tommy was bridging into a lyric when I started paying attention. His voice was pitched lower than club level. The words were nothing like those of Cole Porter or Noel Coward, the world-weary songwriters he'd assured me he adored. The music sounded like blues, only much faster, more rhythmic, with a heartbeat to match the energetic feet of a bebop dancer. Tommy sang over his dropped left shoulder, eyes hidden behind enormous, white-rimmed shades.

I set fire to my woman,
I set her alight.
She sparked when I touched her
'Cause I heated her up right.

I put my black candle to her tight wick
And we burned through the night.

Hoots and shouts greeted each double meaning. When Tommy Trouble bawled out the phrase "black candle to her tight wick," a woman somewhere behind me shrilled, "Come on home, come on home."

Lemme tell you, I poured gas on my woman
I set her aflame.
It was high-test from my twin tanks
She wasn't to blame.

I put my black candle to her tight wick
Our love won't never be the same.

A barrel-shaped man at a table near us doubled over in appreciative laughter, gasping and pounding the wooden floor with his boots. Drackett whistled and waved his arms. Two women stood up and started swinging their hips and bosoms. "Glory," one of them called out, addressing the ceiling or maybe Jesus. "High test," her companion answered, "in them twin tanks."

Emma Mae didn't have time for such foolishness. She was on Tommy as soon as the song finished, grasping his shoulders, swinging him around and filling his ear with fast, hot words.

The bouncer with the emerald inlay spotted Emma Mae on the bandstand and started across the room. The drummer stood up. "Take five," he squealed, his voice reedy with teenage surprise. "Bar's open. We be rocking and rolling with Tommy Trouble after a short break."

But Tommy Trouble was through for the night. We got him

out of the club and into the car fast. When the bouncer, who was also the club manager, heard what had happened to Carmen, he volunteered to send someone with us. Saying we'd call him with news instead, we headed back up the river road to town.

Emma Mae and Tommy huddled in the back of the car while I drove. Before I could ask Tommy about the gig at the juke joint, he volunteered an explanation. "Now you been to Portia's," he said. "You know my Harlem face. Portia don't pay good as you do. But everybody got to work two jobs," he said, adjusting his zebra-striped tie. "Till they get somewhere. Me, I got two whole careers—because, you know what? I be ambitious." Sounding at once forceful and prissy, he added, "Most ambitious nigger you ever did see."

Jesus, I thought. *I didn't see any of this coming.* "Look," I said. "You're excited. We're all worried about your buddy. I'm just surprised."

"My buddy!" Tommy spat back. "Dan, darling, how would you know? We don't work for you but 5 to midnight. You don't know what we do before or after, what's in our heads or who's in our beds."

"Shush up, now," Emma Mae said, drawing him close. "Both of you. Dan doesn't have any problem with you and Carmen being together. Do you, boss?"

I said I sure didn't. But when I started to repeat how surprised I was, Emma Mae shushed me again.

"Stow it, boss. Pretend this is fucking Noah's Ark. They's matched pairs all over the earth and the water is rising."

By the time we got back to the hospital, the doc had finished stitching up Carmen's split eyebrows, gouged scalp, lip and left ear. He was sleeping when we tiptoed in. The nurse, the younger one, gave Tommy a funny look but said only that somebody in the family needed to check with the credit office before Mr. Morales could be assigned to a ward. I said I'd take care of it.

After 10 minutes or so, Carmen started coming around. He'd been surprised by two young white guys and an older man wielding a tire iron, he said. When I asked if he recognized any of

it takes two

them, he said he was pretty sure the guy with the tire iron was the drunken, foul-mouthed fanny-pincher we'd thrown out of the Caloosa Club on Wednesday night. The young guys smelled bad, he said, and weren't wearing shirts.

"They didn't have no mercy," he said, drawing his hands from beneath the blanket and holding them out for inspection. "But I didn't have no mercy neither. Just look at my nails. See the dried blood under there? Maria! Before they got me down on the ground, I think I scratch one cracker's eyes out."

Tommy started to cry. His pomaded hair had begun curling up, out of control, and he suddenly looked his age, which was three or four years less than mine. "Can I just take you home tonight, honey?" he whispered, leaning over Carmen. "How you feel now? You know you'd sleep better at home. I be taking care of you always, my pretty *señorita*."

Seeing, but probably not hearing, this, the older nurse, who had been waiting beside the curtains, stepped forward, brandishing a cotton swab and a large syringe. "Take off," she said. "All of you boys. Outta here, now. Unless somebody can tell me if this cowboy has had all his shots, I'm gonna stick him with everything from penicillin to horse liniment."

Back at the hotel, I phoned Bud. I wanted him to check on Bobby Jim Carter, the foul-mouthed Bradenton butt-pincher. And to run down the tramp who'd found Carmen.

But the phone in the hall at Bud's rooming house didn't answer. I tried it four different times between 3 A.M. and dawn.

NOw, HeaR THis!

BAD NEWS TRAVELS FAST. The Editor's Notebook column in the
Sunday *News-Press* included two blind items. One was a short
series of upbeat speculations on the years of service, selfless
motives and noble ambitions and of an unnamed county official.
The gentleman was said to be entertaining offers from backers
urging him to make a run for the U.S. Congress.

The second item, buried at the end, reported that highly
placed officials and leading citizens were increasingly concerned
about rumors of gambling, drinking and other unsavory activities
"at an unidentified but highly visible Fort Myers venue."

There was no doubt as to the identity of the official (Sheriff
Hollipaugh), the venue (the Caloosa) or the source of the rumors
(Willene Norris).

I read the piece over coffee in my office. What with calling
Bud and worrying about Carmen, I'd gotten less than two hours
sleep the night before. I'd just started my second reading of the

piece when the desk clerk leaned inside the door. "Long distance," he announced, sounding mournful. "Person to person," he added, "on line three."

Admiral Asdeck had gotten up early too. A Myers friend had woken him up to read the unmistakably linked pair of items over the phone. He wasn't worried, he told me, but he did think it would be a good idea to shut down club operations for a week or two, just to be on the safe side, till the rumors went away.

"Tell members you need to repair a leaky ceiling," he ordered. "Say you're installing a new chandelier and you're sorry as hell about the inconvenience.

"And meanwhile," he added, "ask your cop pal to find out whose loose lips are stuck in that cow-town editor's ear."

"He already nailed that one down," I answered, pleased to offer the boss at least a shred of information. "It's our pistol-packing mama."

After describing Saturday's poolside meeting with Mrs. Norris and her cousin, I told Asdeck that Carmen was in the hospital following a beating. Turns out, I added, that he and Tommy Carpenter are a lot closer friends than I'd thought.

"What a surprise," Asdeck said dryly. "But this unprovoked attack is definitely something for your buddy to look into."

"Yeah," I said sarcastically. "As soon as I can find him."

Emma Mae showed up a few minutes later. She had our new housekeeper in tow, fitted out in starched cotton uniform, apron, matching cap and powdered oxfords.

"Went by and picked up Mary this morning," Emma Mae explained. "Good thing too. People been telling her things over in Colored Town. Folks over there is upset."

Homer Meadows entered the office and set a plate of grilled fish and grits in front of me. After topping off my coffee, he disappeared.

"Could you kindly find us a basket of them fuckin' sweet rolls?" Emma Mae called after him. "It's not like we're invisible."

"Be a lot of talk," Mary confided, a nervous frown on her thin face. "Over in Colored Town. Be rumors, a lot of them.

Saying last night that, that-there, ah, the Klan, well, some folks is sayin' they plannin' to burn more than a cross this time."

Oh, shit, I thought. *Too bad Wash didn't kill Willene instead of her husband. Competition with other men, that I can take. But a powerful, vengeful woman bent on destroying the half of the town she doesn't own?* I had no experience in such matters. Shivering, looking around, I could half imagine the burned shell of the torched Caloosa, with the lynched bodies of Bud, Homer, Emma Mae and Mary hanging from the scorched branches of the oak trees out front.

"Be rumors," Mary continued. "They mean to torch a church, a colored church. Be rumors for some time that they's been outsiders comin' around, stirrin' up folks. Your…ah…Klan people, they don't like it."

"Fuckers don't like anything that's any good for anybody else," Emma Mae remarked. "Bunch a candy-ass spoil-sports with too much time on their hands, if you ask me."

After they left, I phoned Bud at the rooming house. This time I caught him. Careful not to ask where he'd been all night, I detailed the attack on Carmen Veranda, said that he was still in the hospital and that the tramp who'd discovered him was missing. When I mentioned Bobby Jim Carter, Bud said he remembered the gent and would see what could be done to track him down. When I outlined the latest rumors from Colored Town and the *News-Press,* Bud laughed. I asked what was so funny and he answered, "Just another off-duty Sunday shot to hell. See what I mean?"

Still, he said he thought he could find time to check it all out, including the whereabouts of Bobby Jim Carter last night and the possible threat to a church. The whereabouts last weekend of the ambitious but unnamed high official were being checked out again, this time by lower-ranking but skilled associates. Their identities, he said, would also go unnamed.

"One connection did get put together for me by a source I can't mention, but you know who I mean," he said.

"The snitch clerk, you mean?"

"Right. Yes. He does get his nose in a lots of people's business. One thing he told me I figure should interest you and the admiral. You know who the contact is?"

"For what?"

"Contact between the colored youth groups and the Yankee organizers. It's somebody that works in your hotel. A church member."

That I had radical religious elements on my staff was news I didn't want to hear. "Who? Emma Mae?"

"The piano player, Tommy. Didn't surprise me none. My source knows it from the Klan. So I'd say your music man had better watch his step. You tell him not to walk anyplace alone, at night. Give him my phone numbers. Tell him to call me or Officer Hurston if anybody comes after him."

All I could do was swear at the growing complications, and worry a bit more.

Before hanging up, though without much hope, I suggested that Bud and I get together for a swim that afternoon. "No sweet talk," I said. "No fishing trip. We both need the exercise."

Saying he had other plans, Bud hung up without even asking for a rain check.

So I skipped lunch, changed into my suit and swam laps alone. The conversation had made me horny as hell. Kicking through half a mile of chilly water usually took my mind off my other physical needs. It had been more than a week since Bud and I really mixed it up. The bothersome tightness in the front of my trunks didn't begin to dissipate until I'd completed half a dozen laps.

I'd finished my workout when Frank strolled onto the pool deck, a smile on his face, his bathing suit rolled in a towel.

"Hope that invitation was serious," he said, kneeling by the pool and extending his hand. "My shoulders are tight as tweezers today. But I'm back, ready for another workout, if you can stand the company."

I looked up at him, aware of the fine, dark hair on his arms and the small, thin creases on either side of his shining eyes, and wondered, *What would this man look like without his pants and shirt, stark naked, showering beside me, joking and making himself available for a little man-to-man combat?* Taking a breath, I sank back beneath the surface, popped up, cleared my eyes and hauled onto the lip of the pool.

"Absolutely serious," I assured him. "You're welcome to use the pool and locker room any time. Wish I could join you, but I just finished my 40 laps. But another time, absolutely. Maybe if you call first?"

He looked as disappointed as a shut-in puppy. When he flexed the thick muscles of his neck, I hesitated. Rather than pursue the connection, I changed the subject.

"You know about Tommy's friend Cabildo Morales? That he's in the hospital?"

Frank looked at me carefully, then nodded. "Yes, I do," he answered. "Terrible thing to have happen. Is there a flower shop in town? I thought I'd stop by and try to cheer him up."

I gave him directions to Exotic Blossoms on First Street. Then we both stood up, bumping elbows like nervous teenagers.

"Need to check in at the hospital myself," I said.

"Maybe we'll meet up later." Frank looked hopeful.

"Yeah," I said. "Maybe so. Maybe later. That'd be swell."

Night Patrol

While I was at the hospital that Sunday afternoon, all hell (in the form of Gene Hollipaugh) broke loose for Bud Wright.

First off, Sheriff Hollipaugh ordered the county switchboard operator to track down the off-duty detective "wherever the blazes he's hiding out" and to call him into the office "10 minutes from whenever you ketch him."

With Bud on the carpet, and no invitation to sit or report forthcoming, Hollipaugh commanded his junior to mount a close watch on Ku Klux Klan activity at the expense of all other cases in his book. "Stay alert for possible connections to the attack on Cabildo Morales," he'd added, "and keep your big ears peeled for rumors of white-sheet marches and church burnings."

When Bud remarked that everything mentioned so far appeared to be part of the same case, the sheriff threw him a sour look, shook his head as if speaking to a child and replied, "They ain't. So shut your cowboy mouth, if you'd be so kind."

He ordered Bud to complete the report on the motor-hotel killings immediately, and to submit it by noon Monday. Willene Norris's role in the affair was to be minimized, he directed, in return for her expanded statement—which, Hollipaugh explained, he himself had taken that morning and would have his secretary type up in triplicate.

Bud was further ordered to prepare a warrant for the arrest of Mary Davis—who was hardly blameless but no murderess—charging her with evidence tampering and fleeing the scene of a crime.

Officer Hurston picked up Mrs. Davis a few hours later. Still in her housekeeper's uniform, she was booked and jailed on further orders of Sheriff Hollipaugh, pending charges of first-degree homicide, times 2.

While Hurston fetched Mary from her rented house, Hollipaugh sent Bud over to the *News-Press* building with a sealed envelope for reporter Ralph Nype. Once Nype read the enclosed note and alerted his editor that a follow-on story would be slotted for the Monday edition's front page, he let the messenger read the letter. A suspect in the double killing had been identified, Hollipaugh wrote. That suspect was now being questioned about other illegal activities to which said suspect might be able to furnish evidence. Further information might be available later in the day.

Feeling double-crossed and humiliated, Bud charged back to the office and told the sheriff he'd decided to quit the department and start a private security business. The sheriff just rocked back in his chair, took off his hat, swiped his bald, dry head with a handkerchief and asked Bud to come sit awhile and tell him all about the measly 10% raise he was going to get.

Let's give Hollipaugh credit here. Not only was he crafty, self-centered and no dummy, he knew how to listen and how to add things up.

In other words, he was a politician, a skilled operator and a cracker on the take. He knew most of what was going on at the Caloosa—the gambling and party-girl part, the liquor-by-the-drink part, the Cuban movies, Lou Salmi's stud service, even the gist of the plan to hire Bud as director of security.

If he'd known about the Dan-fucking-Bud part, he'd have probably used it, so maybe he didn't know that.

Anyway, after a long discussion in which he probed Bud's loyalty and wavering resolve, Hollipaugh made him a reasonable counter offer. "Accept a promotion," he said. "Stay with me for a year. Work part time. Start yer guard bidness and see how ya' like it. Don't run off half-cocked. Let's us see if ya' really want to quit public suh-viss. Payin' bills without a county paycheck is no Labor Day barbecue, young man, not when you're used to eatin' reg'lar."

Bud told the sheriff he'd always eaten regular in the Marine Corps but had been glad to see his discharge papers just the same.

I returned from the hospital a little after sunset. Carmen was in good spirits and recovering nicely. A dentist would see him on Monday morning.

Bud was waiting in my office. This time, he wasn't lounging in the easy chair. He was standing at the window, staring out at the street, hands clasped stiffly behind him.

"At ease, troop," I called, shutting the door. "About face." As I said it I remembered that neither move can be ordered from parade rest.

He turned on me quick, pointing an imaginary Garand M1 rifle at my midsection. "Pow, whomp, you no-count bastard. Your guts is gravy, Sheriff."

I keeled over onto the sofa, clutching my stomach and moaning.

Growling happily, Bud plunged the make-believe bayonet into the tender area just beneath my sternum, stirring my ripped lungs into confetti and slicing my heart into dog meat.

"Kill the bastard," I cried. "Shove the flame-thrower up his ass. Make him marry Mrs. Norris in the graveyard at high noon."

Bud dropped the imaginary rifle, grabbed my waist with both hands and started to tickle me. "Where you been, Tojo? I hot-footed it over here wanting a cold brew, maybe to wash down some of that Bacardi you keep behind the bar. And come to find your club room locked up tighter'n a schoolteacher's slit. Your club guard's off-duty and that yard dog Salmi said he could get me iced tea but nothing stronger."

I pulled him down on top of me, then rolled us both onto the floor. Riding his heaving chest, tickling him back and mock-fucking him with my hips, I teased, "You want something stronger, Sarge? You know how to ask for it, don't you? Don't you?"

He pushed against me, his smile fading when I got hold of his wrists.

"Relax," I said. "Drop your hands. Gonna have to check you for concealed weapons."

"Quit fucking around," he said, suddenly serious. "What if somebody comes in?"

I thought about it. He was half right. I'd forgotten to lock the door. Somebody who didn't work for me, or who disapproved of horseplay between healthy young men, might just come in and get the wrong—which is to say the right—idea.

And while I pondered, Bud hunched his hips up off the floor, twisted his torso, broke my hold, turned me over and quickly stopped me with a half nelson.

"Could break your arm for you," he said, breathing heavily but keeping his voice just above a whisper. "Only how would that look, with me coming to work for you as security officer right after?"

Relaxing, I dropped my face to the rug and quit struggling. "Did you quit your job? What happened?"

He twisted my arm. "You gonna be good if I let you up?"

"Good enough. Better than you deserve."

He twisted my arm again, hard. "Thought we agreed that kid stuff was all out the window. You got a short memory, huh?"

"Get off me. You're mashing my meat and potatoes."

Rising and stepping back, he ran his hands across his jaw, then reached down to adjust the tented front of his pants. "Wouldn't want to do that," he said. Then he quickly sat down and crossed his legs. "Want you to help me decide something, and not just about coming to work here. If I do, that is."

elliott mackle

"Where to live? What to wear? More than two weeks vacation? What?"

He said it wasn't anything like that, and then he told me that Mary Davis was going to be framed for both deaths and he didn't know what to do about it.

I asked if he and Coroner Shepherd and Officer Hurston were sure about the evidence.

"We got it down cold, Dan. Wash Davis shot Hillard Norris, then himself. Pair of textbook cases. Homicide-suicide. Take it to the grand jury and go out for coffee. What I can't prove," he added, "is that the boss phoned Mrs. Norris out at the fish camp early Sunday morning. Can't prove he alerted Wash to the location of the love nest. But he must have. You know it, I know it. The rest of them ain't talking. Or can't. So he gets off."

Out on the street, a car with a faulty muffler chugged by. A dog barked. The February wind rustled the leaves of the live oaks near the open window. I wanted a beer. This was serious stuff between us, some kind of turning point.

"So you do what you need to do," I said. "You do what's right. Because you're a good, honest law enforcement professional paid to do the best job possible for the people of Lee County."

Leaning back, Bud massaged his jaw with his thumb and forefinger. "I can't fight city hall, Dan."

"We can."

"Right. Yes. You and me and who else?"

"The admiral. His investors. They didn't buy this fleabag and fix it up out of the goodness of their hearts. Like I said before, they must have taken out insurance before setting up this business. What do you want to guess that your boss is either on the payroll or taking orders from somebody else?"

Bud's shoulders sagged a little, then tightened. An angry, questioning look crossed his face. "OK, Lieutenant, let's us assume the sheriff is on your team. Say he helped eliminate Norris to protect your boss's business. If you look at it that way, the blood is also on the admiral's hands. And on yours and maybe mine."

"Two-way stretch," I replied. "If you believe your boss is a killer, even if you can't prove it, can you still work for him?"

"Ask yourself exactly the same question, Lieutenant. Ain't this a fucking helluva mess?"

"Just because I admire somebody, and learned most of what I know from him, that doesn't mean I have to admire everything he does." I was on the spot. And that was putting it politely.

"Didn't Dr. Goebbels and General Tojo use that argument? Didn't get 'em far, though, did it?"

"The boss is no Tojo," I muttered as I picked up the private phone and placed a person-to-person call to Asdeck.

When Asdeck came on the line, I talked fast. I told him that shutting down the club for more than a few of days would give the cracker sheriff and Klan all the wrong signals. I told him I'd find a new chandelier and get it installed in the club room this week. Assuming it was in place by Thursday, I intended to reopen over the weekend, provided that he agreed.

"Who bit you in the butt?" Asdeck asked. "Been waiting for you to take a little more initiative. Can't hold you by the hand forever."

We both laughed.

Bud glanced up, cocking his head.

"My private security service," I answered, "has provided excellent inside information on a certain high official of Lee County. The official may be mixed up in a double murder, and trying to cover it up. And he could be on the take from a particular out-of-state investor. It's rumored he wants to run for Congress. No telling who he might double-cross to get elected."

Asdeck didn't make admiral by treating enterprising underlings like dirt. "Sounds like your source could be onto something," he almost purred. "Tell him good work and we need more of it. But let me look into all this tomorrow, check on a few things. Then we'll talk again."

When I passed on Asdeck's praise, Bud blushed. "You know I ain't on board yet," he said. "We just been talking."

"That's right," I charitably agreed. "It's just talk."

"Here's what I figure," he added. "Wouldn't it seem like to you that no charges can go forward without a signed report from the investigating officer?"

"Sounds right to me," I said.

"Then say I don't go along in framing Mary Davis? What's the worst you figure can happen? That I lose my job and have to start over?"

"A man like you doesn't ever need to worry about getting jobs or moving ahead," I answered. "It also doesn't hurt that you're on the right team."

Bud stood up. The front of his trousers was flat now. "Been some kind of team member all my life," he said, pulling on his jacket. "But my old coach, even my granny, they never said anything like that. Didn't ever tell me they had that kind of confidence in me."

"Maybe I know you better then they did."

"And maybe we can work together better as friends," Bud concluded. "Rather than the other thing."

I didn't stand. I didn't want Bud to notice the forlorn erection inside my pants. After he said goodbye, I thought about getting blind drunk. I kept a bottle of Bacardi in my closet for just such emergencies. But I knew alcohol wouldn't do it. And I didn't have the energy for another 40- or 50-lap swim. Adjusting my pants as best I could, I wandered out to the river's edge to breathe in the orange-blossom perfume and try to get my mental bearings. Walking east into the sweet breeze, I didn't see the man on the dock until I turned around.

The man was smoking a cigarette. He flipped the butt into the stream and said, "Hello, Dan," as I strolled over to him.

"Hope you don't mind me back so soon," Frank added, smiling and shaking my hand. "Swimming laps did the trick this afternoon. Loosened me right up. Had an early meeting with a few student leaders, supper by myself and took a walk. This is where I ended up."

He had on a short-sleeved shirt, dark pants and sandals. I was again aware of the way his neck seemed to flare smoothly from his ears down to his sloping, muscular shoulders. "Gets lonely when you're far away from home," he explained, glancing toward the river but moving a step closer, our elbows momentarily brushing. When he turned to face me, I noticed the whiskey on his breath.

"We all get lonely," I answered. "Horny, frustrated, tired of eating shit, sick and tired of sleeping alone."

He was silent a few seconds. Then he said quietly, "That's me. For years, at least a part of me. Wanda and Tommy both said you'd understand, and might be a good friend for me to make."

Was he saying what I thought he was saying? It was hard to be sure.

"I don't know what to do," he whispered. "Don't know anything. Except, you know, what you mentioned. Frustrated and…stupid and out in the cold by myself."

I leaned toward him. He held his ground, looking sideways into my eyes, not pleading, not defended or puzzled, but open to whatever came next, trusting and ready to learn.

"It is kind of chilly out here," I said, hoping he caught my drift. "Happens once the sun goes down. But I've got a bottle upstairs, if you'd like to come on up to my room and get warmed up."

"I'd like that," he answered, amiably enough. "No sense both of us being cold and lonely. But, ah, you know, what about we, ah, go someplace else?"

I asked him why. Again he didn't beat around the bush.

"I'd feel safer," he said, "in my own place. See, I've got a room over at the Royal Plaza Motor Lodge. It's out on the highway. Not so many people around. Don't want anybody to get the wrong idea."

"Right," I answered. No sense in that. So I asked him to wait two minutes while I went to my room for the rum bottle and a jacket. "We'll take a taxi," I said.

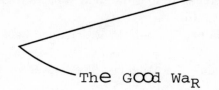

The Good War

We hugged standing up, before he even got the door locked. With his pants, belt and white briefs around his ankles, his shirt unfastened and his cock as hard as a green banana, he dropped his arms to his sides and sobbed.

I held him close. "If you don't want to do this, we can forget it."

He put his hands around me gingerly, as if grasping something fragile. "Show me what to do," he said, glancing down. "Can't you see I want to?"

Kneeling before him, I touched his cock lightly, fingering the smooth, buff-colored ring where some baby butcher had chopped off the protective skin. I thought he'd be wet but he wasn't. Using both hands, I touched his sack, pulling the package down, reaching behind briefly and fingering the hair there. He took a step back. I kissed the head of his cock, licked the ridged underside and then took him in.

"Careful," he said, shifting from one foot to the other. "Mother of God, be careful."

"We'd better get in bed," I said. "Why don't you help me get my clothes off?"

"Is that what I do?" he laughed. "I've never undressed another man."

"Watch the zipper," I answered. "That's all there is to it."

He had some funny quirks. I like to kiss, for instance, but he didn't want to do much more than peck my cheeks in return. When I tried to worm my tongue inside his mouth, he turned away.

He'd touch my cock only when I guided his big hands south. I had to hold them in place and tell him what to do. Under the circumstances, this amounted to fondling myself by proxy and I gave up after a couple of uncomfortable attempts.

And yet I've never met a more enthusiastic first-time fucker. Sure, I was pretty good at warming a man up back there. Good teachers had showed me how to gently rub, prod and tease with hands and tongue until the other man felt empty and frantic.

By the time I inserted a second finger in him, his head was shifting left and right as if he was in some kind of confused pain.

"This OK?" I asked. "You with me, Frank?"

He threw his chest and head forward. "I can do it. Are you going inside me?"

Along with the bottle of Bacardi in my old pea-coat, I'd brought along a jar of Vaseline. Now I smeared greasy wads of it on our cocks and another wad inside him, going slow, stretching as gently as I could. When I explained what might happen, he looked almost startled. But all he said was, "I've never seen another fella's bone before. You're pretty big, aren't you?"

When I entered him, he bit the air like a horse. Then he started crying again. "Hurts," he whispered. "Show me. Is this right?"

I asked if he wanted me to stop. He said no, never, but to go slow and to touch him just a little.

A little was all it took. By the time I tickled his prostate five or six times he might as well have swum another 50 laps. On the verge of hyperventilating, he grabbed my sides and started patting me roughly. Rubbing his cock would have made him blast fast, so I tried to ease off, touching him gently near the base and behind his balls. But when he started fucking my hand, matching the rhythm of our breaths and hip thrusts, I figured time was up and I gripped and released him, tightened and let go, working my palm and fingers like a vibrating jock ring, sure that he was ready.

Frank was a handsome man: smooth skin, thick black hair, thin lips under a prominent nose, eyes you could dive into. His eyes stayed open, locked on mine, when he started to climax. "Yes," he said. "Hurts. Don't stop. Again, again."

Pressing his hands down on the sheet beneath him, thrusting his hips up and down like an old pro, he unloaded three long shots onto his heaving chest and stomach. The first reached to his Adam's apple.

He looked so seriously happy I almost lost control myself, lost touch with what I was trying to do for him. Hell, I was a week's worth of horny, and sad that Bud seemed determined to keep me at arm's length.

But something made me wait, maybe just the prospect of a long night mentoring this sexual neophyte. Or maybe I forgot about myself in the unalloyed delight I was giving Frank.

Anyway, without pulling out, I slowed, delaying my own release until his contractions stopped. As his breathing slowed, I gradually lowered myself onto him.

"That's lesson 1," I said. "You get a gold star."

"I've never…I didn't…nobody told me what—what this was. Was nobody to ask. All I ever heard was, don't do it."

"You heard wrong," I said. "This is dessert. This is what makes up for all the everyday shit men have to eat."

Gently slipping out of him, I rolled off to the side. "Let me go clean up a little," I said. "You want a towel?"

"No," he said. "I don't want a towel. I don't want to change anything about the way I feel right this minute."

"You want to try it the other way?" I said. "Inside me. See how that feels?"

"Can I?"

"You're a natural," I answered. "We'll have you saddled up in record time."

As I got out of bed, he looked up and shook his head as if mystified. "Thank you, Dan," he said, touching my leg. "Bless you."

The glare inside the white-tiled bathroom hit me so hard I almost flipped off the lights. Instead, I squeezed my eyelids into slits, turned the hot water tap, rinsed off, pissed and toweled down. Frank's odor was all over me—musky and slightly sour, a schoolteacher's smell that was entirely different than Bud's familiar combination of fresh sweat, talc and Ivory soap.

Returning to bed, I glanced into the open closet. Sometimes I'm nosy as hell and sometimes I find out secrets that aren't exactly my business. One glance put it all together. I was surprised I hadn't already figured Frank out. He was a voter-registration organizer who met with young people at churches in Colored Town. He'd never had sex with anyone and yet he was bold enough to ask another man, almost a stranger, to show him the ropes.

On wooden hangers just behind two ironed shirts, spillover light from the bathroom set off a Roman Catholic priest's black suit, hard-collared shirt and vestments. A black fedora was perched on the shelf above.

I'd never fucked a priest before, not as far as I knew. So I stood there for a while, not thinking exactly, just taking it in, wondering if this was a step up, or a step down, from some of the mix-it-up sessions I'd sold myself into back in Japan.

When I got back in bed Frank immediately rolled toward me. "I think I'm ready to try that," he said, drawing my hand to his bone. "What took you so long?"

"That your stuff in the closet? You're not sharing a room, are you?"

"Just with you," he said. "I like to travel light. Every bit of it fits in a valise I carry with me."

Though I knew next to nothing about Catholics, I knew a starched-linen dog collar when I saw one, and I said so.

He continued rubbing my hands over his cock for a few

seconds, then fell back on the pillow. "What are you talking about?"

"Your uniform," I said. "The collar, black suit and robes."

I'll give Father Bridge this. The light was still on. His cock didn't wilt or shrink an inch as he answered me.

"I hoped you knew by now," he said. "And didn't mind. I thought you might have guessed that I'm in holy orders. Wanda didn't know at first either. But she caught on to how crazy I've been feeling, how lonely and desperate I get sometimes, doing the work I do. You were the one she and Tommy thought of— who might know how to teach a man with no experience." He reached over and smoothed my shoulder and neck. "Everybody tells me you're a true Southern gentleman."

"And you're really a priest? Didn't you...I thought they...I thought you made some kind of pledge."

"Most of us don't know what we're promising. I went right from the nuns in grade school to Villanova for two years, then the seminary. God help me, I tried. The ideal is a celibate life. But perfection isn't in me." He glanced down at his erection. "I see now how I'm made."

"It's all OK as far as I'm concerned, just a little surprising. But how do you feel about it? Think you'll regret this in the morning?"

"It's a sin, that's for sure. But it's a sin I needed." He pulled my hands to him again and then rose to his knees. "Do you think we should use any more of that Vaseline?"

When I said I thought so, and started applying grease, he moaned, "Holy smoke, yeah, do like that. Tell me what I'm supposed to do. Do you want me here? Or up here? You're going to get a bone too, aren't you?"

Though momentarily deflated, I gave Father Bridge's education my best shot.

When I left the room a few hours later, I found Bud waiting outside in his Jeep. He was parked at the north end of the row of rooms, six or seven doors from the still-sealed room where Wash Davis and Hillard Norris died. He wasn't happy.

"I thought about getting a pass key and going in and breaking your nuts for you," he admitted right off. "But come to find out, just sitting here half the night, I don't really know what to think, or what you are, or why I followed you here, or if I even need the fuck to do anything about it."

He looked so tired and angry and disappointed I couldn't tell whether he wanted to slug me or was about to break into tears.

I touched his shoulder. "Why don't we drive on back to the Caloosa, get some sleep and talk about the whole thing in the morning? We got to talk about what it is we're were doing to each other."

As if he hadn't heard me, he said, "Why the fuck did you have to come over here with that Yankee guy—and go inside with him? Especially here?"

"Because you left. You said you never wanted me to touch you again. And he asked me to be with him and I needed to be with somebody. It didn't mean anything. Didn't matter where it was or who. And now I'm asking you to simmer down and come on home."

Bud hugged the steering wheel for a while and then muttered something I couldn't catch. When I asked him to repeat it he swung his leg over the side of the Jeep, stepped out and yelled, "I'd fucking swim back to fucking Iwo Jima and fight the goddamn Japs a second time before I'd follow you back to your *other* fucking whorehouse, Lieutenant."

And so we swapped salutes and parted company on the sidewalk.

M~o~pping Up

THE CLUB ROOM'S LALIQUE CHANDELIER SPARKLED like a jeweler's daughter. Imported from France by a Tampa wholesaler, it resembled a crystallized banana tree sprouting upside down from the starry-eyed ceiling. Combining long, swooping, clear-glass fronds and rampantly phallic, pastel fruit, the Art Moderne bauble gave me a hard-on the minute I spotted it in the dealer's showroom. Unfortunately, the asking price was double my budget, so I kept on looking. But when the ex-GI salesman saw how much I wanted the thing, and once he learned that he and his secretary could be guests for a free weekend at the Caloosa, he marked the fixture down to cost plus shipping. As a sweetener, he threw in an installation package and stamped the work order ASAP. I was thus able to schedule a reopening party on the Saturday following Carmen's beating.

The winter season was in full swing. Admiral Asdeck was in town briefly on his way to Havana. He and I and Emma Mae

Bellweather stationed ourselves at the bar, telling war stories, greeting customers and speculating on the chances of posting a NO VACANCY sign before Easter.

In fact, the Caloosa was overbooked by four rooms on the following Friday. But I figured we'd work out the tight squeeze someway. If worse came to worst, I could always give up my second-floor single—and set up a dormitory for agreeable bachelors in one of the suites.

While I drifted in and out of raunchy fantasies in which three or four men frolicked in a seventh-floor shower, Emma Mae leaned back against the bar and began another tall tale.

"Well, gentlemen," she said, rubbing her hands together, "There was this here pussy-starved master sergeant from Chicago—excuse my French, Admiral. But this butt-fucking senior trooper with a beer belly and a shirtsleeve full of hash marks, he shows up outside our billet after hours, and three sheets to the wind. Starts beating on the door, howling like a Polack banshee, calling out, 'I need somebody to love!'"

"Love?" Asdeck answered, leaning closer to Emma Mae, his thin, appreciative smile savoring the word. "Imagine that."

"Inspecting waves' bottoms and laying waste to pussy is what was on his mind, Admiral. Not Love. So there was this big Tennessee girl with a mouth on her, Dorothy Ann Claremont, and she hollers down to him, 'Plug yourself into these beauties, Sarge. That's all the loving you'll get here tonight!'" And she threw a big box of stale, leftover doughnuts at him—from the upstairs window."

Couples were dancing and men were playing cards. Tommy was crooning a bittersweet love song:

Like liners passing in the night,
Before the break of morning's light,
We rush apart in desperation
Never knowing that, as lovers,
We could joyfully unite
Forever at our secret destination.

elliott mackle

Gone before dawn, love passing in the night—that about sums it up, I thought. My imaginary, crowded shower room suddenly became the empty bottle in my hand. *Wartime passion*, I thought. *Hell, it's no different than what's served back home. Plug yourself into this or that Navy beauty, Lieutenant. Next, try a Marine stud. Ride him and get off. Rushing, blasting desperation—faster than a Fort Myers' widow's pot shots, faster than Jap torpedoes or a horny priest on his back. Boom, flash, splash and love goes to Davey Jones and your life is changed forever. But the secrets all remain. Doesn't it ever stop?*

I signaled for a refill.

Wearing an aloha-cloth sarong and matching head bandage, Carmen danced toward us from across the room, snaking his hips, undulating his thin, golden arms and snapping his fingers. Following him with his eyes, Tommy quickly bridged through "Anchors Aweigh" before shifting effortlessly into "Little Grass Shack." Catching the cue, Carmen paused at the edge of the dance floor and hula-bumped a quick tale of happy rain, high tides and satisfactory love affairs.

"Aloha, ladies and gentlemens," he cooed as he approached us. "Freshen everybody up, yes?"

Not far behind him, the Caloosa Club's newest waitress worked the room with a plated-silver tray of hors d'oeuvres. Slim had spiffed up one of her nylon waitress uniforms with black fishnet stockings, spike heels, a white lace apron and matching cap. She looked like a middle-aged tart disguised as a French maid.

"How you be, sugar pie?" she said, throwing me a wink before turning her full attention to Asdeck. "Admiral, honey, would you like a delicious canapé?" She pronounced the word "canopy," selling it with a garnishment of upturned tits and the explanation that "these shrimp and cream cheese things are real, real good, sir."

We each took two. She was right. They were indeed real good, seasoned with just enough Tabasco sauce, chopped onion and celery salt.

"Settling in, then, my dear?" Asdeck inquired politely. "We're delighted to have you on board."

"Sure hope to stick around longer than that poor little house-maid," she replied, shifting the tray, clearly tickled to be noticed by the Caloosa's real boss.

"This is gotta be better'n serving cold twat to some bull-dagger jailhouse matron," Emma Mae commented charitably.

Asdeck took another shrimp cracker. "Was Mary Davis even jailed long enough for the dragon ladies to actually notice her?"

Emma Mae glanced over at one of the tables of poker-playing men beyond the bar. "Lawyer Ridley Boldt," she said, elbowing Slim. "You know him, right over there behind all them red and blue chips? He bonded Mary out Monday afternoon. But who you figure put up the money? Mary don't have none. And they tell me he don't run no charity ward."

"Poor little thing hardly got home," Slim said, speaking directly to Asdeck, "before she was back on the street. Didn't even get her shoes off and you know who shows up? Them boys in the white sheets. Girlfriend of mind says they were in a mood like General Sherman with a toothache. Told Mary to tote her ass outside on the double because they were fixing to burn the house down. And she answered, 'You'll burn it with me lying in my bed.'"

Asdeck nodded. "And they were as good as their word?"

"One of them sons-a-bitches tossed a pine-knot torch onto the porch," Slim continued. "House was dry as a church picnic. Might's well a-been a wood pile."

"Fire hadn't hardly spread up to the roof," Emma Mae said, "before little Mary was out the back door and down the alley."

"Cracker boys ran faster, though," Slim concluded. "In the opposite direction. Once they heard the fire engines."

"Them gelded, no-account weasels, they don't like nobody seeing their ugly faces," Emma spat. "I'd like to burn one or two of them out myself someday—put a torch up their candy asses, see how they like that."

"And where did Mary go?" Asdeck inquired politely, accepting a second scotch and soda from Carmen.

"Nobody knows," Emma Mae answered. "Left town, most likely."

"If she knows what's good for her," Carmen offered, "then she is catched some kind of jitney to someplace where they never heard of Fort Myers and don't speak Florida cracker."

And that's basically what had happened. After her house burned, Tommy put Mary on a bus to Frank Bridge in Philadelphia. A few days later, a Lee County grand jury indicted her for evidence tampering. On the advice of Ridley Boldt and a visiting Yale-trained barrister sent down by Father Bridge, she turned herself in a month later, quietly pled guilty to leaving the scene of a crime and was sentenced to time served plus a month's probation.

Willene and her cousin Mildred happened to be out of town the day Mary's hearing took place, having embarked on an extended trip to Mexico and the Panama Canal. Not incidentally, they left exactly one day after Carmen swore out assault-and-battery warrants on his assailants, as well as anyone known to have aided or abetted them. In a small town, not much happens by accident. So we toasted Mary, Willene and Mildred with our freshened drinks, and then the subject turned to fishing.

A few minutes later, Brian Rooney, the masseur who doubled as the club's bouncer, appeared at my side. In contrast to Carmen and Slim, he was soberly dressed in black waiter's pants, white shirt, maroon necktie and blue blazer.

"You got a gentleman of the press outside," Brian whispered, leaning close to my ear. "Says he's a real good friend of yours. Says you definitely want to hear what he's got to say."

"Skinny as a cheap golf bag? Face like a starched wash cloth? A Mr. Nype?"

"That's him. From the *News-Press*. You want I should toss him out?"

"No, let him in. Just be sure he's not carrying a camera. No sense scaring the natives."

Reporter Nype did indeed have something to say. Once he got a whiskey sour in his hand and consulted his watch, he informed me that his Sunday edition, on which the presses were just now rolling, would report exclusively that Sheriff Hollipaugh has solved the double killing of Hillard Norris and Washington Jefferson Davis. Hollipaugh expected to present evidence to the grand jury tending to show that the two men shot and killed each other in a misunderstanding over a job offer. Although two guns were used, one weapon had been removed from the scene of the crime by a person or persons unknown and never recovered.

When I remarked that this news ought to make the town sleep better at night, Nype iced the shit-cake the sheriff had handed him. His newspaper would further reveal that Hollipaugh had charged two out-of-work laborers and a Bradenton businessman with the vicious attack on my restaurant manager, Cabildo Morales.

"The laborers," he said, smiling thinly, "are well-known Klan members presently residing in Dade City, miles from Lee County. After arraignment, they failed to post bond, and are jailed pending a hearing in two weeks."

The troublemakers, in other words, were imports, and thus no reflection on law-abiding Lee County.

Nype had drained his drink and was now sucking the cherry in a distracted way. Catching his meaning, I signaled Carmen. Slim quickly delivered the refill. Nype blinked when he recognized the former Arcade Café waitress, but didn't say anything. Instead, he gulped down most of the second whiskey sour, then added that Bobby Jim Carter, the Bradenton van-line manager, had been arrested in the parking lot of Flossie Hill's department store. Given that Carter was being arrested on an aggravated assault-and-battery charge, Nype opined that he certainly didn't help his case by foolishly resisting arrest.

"Must be one tough cookie," I remarked. "Moving furniture for a living."

"Too tough for his own good," Nype replied. "It seems he was unavoidably injured while being taken into custody. The name of the arresting officer, by the way, was not made available. By the sheriff's office, I mean. And I asked twice. I really did. They told me that the record had been sealed."

I said, "I doubt that Carter was hurt as bad as Mr. Cabildo Morales, who is currently scheduled for reconstructive dental surgery."

Nype shrugged. "An eye for a mouthful of teeth, did I make that up? Mr. Carter is a patient in the hospital's lock-up ward. He won't be moving anything anytime soon. Both his arms were broken. And three fingers and a couple of ribs. He's in traction."

"An eye for a mouthful of teeth," I said. "I'll have to remember that."

Slim returned with the canapé tray. Nype ate six or seven shrimp toasts, one by one, while Slim stood there beaming. Then he finished his cocktail and handed her the glass.

"There any limit on these beauties?" he asked.

"Not for you, sweetheart," she answered.

"Yeah," Nype said, the word going soft around the edges. "You bet. No limits for Ralphie. Let's try one of those martini things next time."

Admiral Asdeck, who had been making conversation across the room, drifted over and introduced himself to Nype. "Believe I'll chance another glass of rat poison myself," he said, his smile that of a shark contemplating a grouper. "Anyone care to join me?"

When Nype replied that he had a new model on order, Asdeck took him by the elbow and led him slowly to the far end of the bar where Carmen was just adding gin to a silver shaker.

Glancing down at my Regal, willing the shower fantasy to reappear, I wondered how I was going to get through the summer. Frank Bridge had left town. And Bud had said he'd swim back to Iwo Jima before he'd return to the Caloosa.

In the background, I could hear Wanda Limber's golf-course gush as she was introduced to Nype. "Oh, I read all your articles," she declared. "So well written."

Behind me, someone in Ridley Boldt's party shuffled the cards. The Louisianans were on the dance floor, fox-trotting to "Happy Days Are Here Again." Lou Salmi had exchanged his waiter's coat for a gabardine sports jacket and was dancing with a rich widow from Norfolk. Behind the bar, Carmen inspected his heavily rouged mouth in the mirror.

With the chandelier gleaming overhead and the soft-focus neon outlining the bar and tray ceiling, my little windowless club room seemed to be transforming itself into a Southwest Florida haven of tolerance and sophistication. *This might all work out after all*, I thought. And I felt like hell.

So I hardly noticed the low click-click of the bulletproof door being opened. The newcomer was dressed in a freshly pressed gray suit, electric blue sports shirt, brown and white wing-tip shoes and aviator sunglasses. His broad shoulders and the muscles of his arms and thighs strained lightly against the fabric of the suit. A smile dodged here and there around his wide, just-shaved face. When he caught sight of me, his smile widened out into a grin.

I touched my eyebrow in salute. Detouring around the dance floor, he shot me a V-for-Victory sign.

When he was standing next to me, icy nail-pricks skittered around my scrotum and up and down my spine.

We both spoke at once.

"Lieutenant, I'm damned glad to—"

"I heard somebody rounded up a whole herd of Klanners and—"

We tried again, with no more success, before falling silent. Dropping into a chair and signaling for beer, I patted the empty seat next to me. "Welcome back, Sarge," I said, my throat going a little tight.

He lowered himself jauntily, made fists and pounded softly on the chair arms. Then he grazed my shoulder with his balled-up hand. "Happy to be back," he said, raising the aviator shades and winking at me. His left eye-socket was black and purple. The tan, cat's-tongue cheek below it was badly bruised. "Can't tell you how glad I am to see you."

I could have just smiled and smiled, stayed goofy all night, gotten nowhere. Instead, I leaned forward, inspected the eye briefly, and asked, "A man named Carter do that?"

Bud shook his head. "Was one of his little buddies caught me off guard. Had to take all three of them in. See, once I got a good description from your Mr. Morales there, and asked around a little, it wasn't no trouble finding them two worthless crackers. And Carter I seen once, right here."

"Carmen," I said. "Carmen Veranda. "That's what he goes by around here."

"Right. Yes. Carmen," Bud agreed. "If you say so. Have to say he wasn't looking like no movie star in that hospital bed. But he sure told me enough to round up those bastards. Told me he'd got two of 'em good with his fingernails. Scratched their ugly faces. So there wasn't no trouble about initial identification."

When I said I wouldn't have thought so anyway, Bud glanced in Carmen's direction. "He's tough. He rode in the squad car with me up to Dade City to finger the first two. Had his head bandaged like a busted bowling ball. Same for sighting Carter. The two of us just marched right into the bastard's office, took a look around, rode back and swore out the warrant."

I asked Bud who'd helped bring the Klanners in. He looked surprised. "Wasn't but three of 'em. And the boys from Dade City is just little fellas. Bobby Jim Carter now, he does put on a good show. He's big. And when I come up to him and asked him to go peaceful, he tried to knee me in the nuts and get me in a hammerlock all at the same time. Might of worked if he knew what he was doing, and was half in shape. But he moves slower than a yard dog sniffing a rattlesnake hole."

I mentioned the broken arms, fingers and ribs reported by Ralph Nype. Bud looked delighted. "Traction, huh? Gonna have to find somebody to wipe his butt after he shits, that right? That right?"

"Gentlemens," Carmen cooed, setting down two iced Regals and leaning close to Bud's ear. "Don't let me interrupt nothing." He stepped back, covering his ruined mouth, as if casually, with his hand. "But can I just say only that I express my appreciation, *mucho mucho*, for you catching those bastards who smudged my lipstick so bad."

Looking up, Bud muttered something about the line of duty and no trouble at all, adding that "You was just in the wrong place at the wrong time, Mr. Ca— ah, Carmen."

Carmen waved this away. "Was my fault, truly, Mr. Policeman. I should know better than to run in high heels."

Bud's jaw dropped half an inch. Carmen continued, this time speaking directly to me. "This is one very good cowboy you got here, boss. A real gentleman, like they say. He treated me with such respect when he interview me in the hospital bed. No make fun of me, all strictly business. We don't none of us think you ought to let him off the ranch again."

I heard Bud whisper, "Fuck," under his breath. He didn't look up.

Carmen shifted on his heels and made a joke. "So now tell me, you two big, strong gentlemens, wasn't I right when Carter was first here and tipsy-face and insulting with his hands? When I say he deserve a Mickey Finn and a night on the loading dock with his pants missing?"

"If we can send him to Raiford on aggravated assault-and-battery," Bud answered, finally glancing up, "he might get a dose of that yet."

Carmen tittered and touched his sarong. "Maybe that's what he's wanting when he pinch me in first place."

Bud smiled back. "Could send the bastard up wearing his Klan dress, and get him assigned to a Negro cell block."

Carmen and I both laughed.

"Look," Bud said, rising to his feet. "I owe you an apology"— Carmen's expression turned quizzically neutral at this—"and a debt, I guess, for showing me that even a freak can be brave and ballsy."

Carmen took a step back. Bud caught himself and raised a hand. Carmen spoke first. "No, no," he said, his voice low, his mouth stumbling over the hurt places. "I been called worse since

I was in short pants. It doesn't bother me no more. I'm a sissy, a fruitcake. But you know what? Some men like freaks like me. Only it took me a couple of tours of duty to find that out. Also it took, you pardon the expression, gentlemens, it took balls for us sissies and fruitcakes to wear skirts and wigs in our soldier shows. I guess we was brave to try to dance and sing in high heels in front of five or six hundred horny GI's day after day, night after night. So maybe"—he brightened—"you are right. Brave and ballsy freaks."

Bud worked his mouth, clearly discarded a couple of retorts, then said haltingly, "Like I said. And you have a roommate? That you live with? Tommy over there?"

Carmen answered with a wink, "He plays more than the piano, sí."

"Carmen and Tommy attend church together," I said.

Carmen giggled. "Plays that organ too."

"Tommy leads the youth group, the one involved in the voting campaign."

"Jesus," Bud answered, clearly shocked, but also impressed, and listening.

Carmen daintily pulled the hem of his sarong higher, revealing a shaved, shapely knee and thigh. "Jesus had balls," he said, "under those blue and white skirts."

Carmen picked up his tray, hefted it over his head and sashayed back to the bar, swinging to the lilting beat of Tommy's "Once in Love With Amy."

Bud and I sat back down. He clasped his fists together and began tensing and relaxing the muscles of his arms. At first he wouldn't look at me.

"Offer's still open," I said. "Admiral Asdeck's impressed as hell with you. The details—the private room, you and me in some kind of partnership—those are negotiable."

"You got balls, too," Bud said, looking up, half smiling. "Because what you call details, that's what needs the big discussion. And I guess it's my balls that's in question, maybe. Do I have the balls to quit my county job when I just been promoted?

And when the boss might decide to run for higher office in a year or two? Do I have the balls to work in a racy place like this? Do I have the balls to…negotiate, is that the word? Mixing it up with you one day and asking you for the afternoon off the next?"

I laughed. "How about we keep our clothes on when we're working?"

"Naw. Here's what I mean, Dan. Do I have the balls to do what we're talking about, and then go to church in LaBelle with my aunt or shop for shoes in the men's store or eat lunch at the Arcade and put up a good enough front so's not to worry about what people might be thinking and saying?"

I thought before I answered. "You know, I'm dead sure the admiral took out an insurance policy before he opened this place."

Bud looked at me funny. "Why you changing the subject on me?"

I shook my head. "I'm not. He took out a local policy. And you'd be covered, just like I am, and Carmen and Brian and Lou. I buy shoes where I want to. The Klan can kiss my ass. That little misunderstanding is over."

He cocked his head and threw me a narrow look.

"But you're right," I continued. "The card games, the whiskey, you and me mixing it up, most of that's technically against the law. Nobody's forcing you. You have to be sure you want to go with us."

He leaned close to me. "One thing I'm dead sure about now. I'd rather mix it up with Coach Dan than with Miss Slim Nichols. And I figure you'd rather have a steady thing with your fishing buddy than break in some fucking Yankee snowbird every weekend. That right?"

"That's right," I whispered.

He wiped his mouth with his hand, then removed the shades and peered directly into my eyes. "Thought I'd had the corners knocked off, Dan. You know: been around, seen the world, served in the Corps and walked some rough patrols. Kinda the same as you. Shook the sand out of my shoes and tried things." Then he blinked and looked down. "Maybe I'd even tried a few things with a buddy or two before I met you. More than just grab-assing." His voice was strained and tight. "But if it's only bumping around in the dark or mixing it up in a shower room, and you can't chat and make it mean more than two bulls pawing up a paddock, what's the use?"

"There isn't any use," I answered. "But when it does mean something, then...that's different. When it hits right."

"That's what you made me think about." He took a deep breath. "Only it took a while to penetrate my thick skull."

"Mixing it up isn't a relationship, Sarge. But two people who get together and plan to stay together, however they can do it, and who say they care about each other a lot, maybe even, you know, love each other, that's a relationship. And it takes two—the two of us working at it."

Bud's hands gripped the chair arm. "Working together all the time. Except, like I said, that's the thing that worries me. We got to be careful how we act. Because, see, I spent a bunch of time chewin' over what happened last Sunday night. And what I got to finally admit is my red-eyed jealousy."

"Because I went to bed with Father Bridge?"

"Right. Yes. Some priest he is. But I guess I owe him one too. Because you and him getting together made me remember how I felt when Coach Andy quit treating me special. And how this felt the same way."

"The jealousy, you mean?"

"And the lust—just the pure, blue-balled, shoved-aside lust. And something else too—caring about somebody, like you say. So you and me, we got to check that out. Because I'm not ready to let you go pogy hunting every weekend and take a chance on you getting' away from me. I been too lonely for too long."

"Me too," I said.

"See, I never caught on to the right language, how to talk to a man about this. And growing up, I didn't have a word to say to women." He laughed softly. "Lot of 'em talked to me, though. But it wasn't any good. And when I got back to La Belle after the war, well, lonely doesn't cover it."

it takes two

"And you heard about the Lee County job?"

"Sure. Country goes to town. The work was good. And I met Slim, and we started going out." His hands made fists again. "And that helped some."

My own voice wasn't entirely steady. "You're a damn brave man." I tapped his near fist, nudged it open. "Goddamn life-saver." He turned the hand up and I tapped it again, suppressing the temptation to clasp it in mine.

"I still got a lot to learn, Dan."

"Doing fine." My hand withdrew across the now narrowing gulf. "We both do."

His temporarily orphaned hand slapped the chair arm once more. "You made me see something I couldn't of imagined. Those things you told me—about losing your buddy Mike. About what it meant. How you felt when he turned up missing. Well, I just played that alongside what I felt about Coach Andy and, well, about you going off. Mixed it up, flipped it over, added in Slim and then subtracted her. May get to be a tight little situation, with her working here and all. Not that she isn't a real nice lady. We'll see."

Rising to my feet, I held out my arms. "You want to dance with me, Buddy?"

He looked up, startled, and shook his head. "You kidding? Here? Anyhow, I don't know how to dance with another man."

"You're gonna learn," I said, pulling him upright.

He half embraced me, then turned to face the room. "No, I ain't quite ready for that. Not with so many people around."

After resetting the sunglasses on his nose, he slapped me gently on the butt. "You got a party to attend to. So why don't you go dance with one of your girlfriends. Say we continue this discussion later on, Coach? You want to do that?"

"Yeah, I do," I answered. I was about to ask why we needed to wait. But just then Emma Mae and the admiral began to stroll back across the room in our direction. Slim was right behind them, laughing and hefting a tray of boiled shrimp and cocktail sauce.

Bud moved an inch or two away from me, stood a little taller and, when the trio arrived, asked Emma Mae what was up.

Emma Mae punched his chest with her forefinger, a Raggedy Ann grin on her face. "You boys think you're so smart. But didn't nobody say a word to me about those prick-tease movies the admiral brought over from Miami couple weeks ago. 'Scuse my French, Slim. So we got to have another peep show. Just for laughs. You all with me?"

Slim cocked her eye and said, "Count me in, boys, as long as it's after I get off shift. And didn't somebody say Admiral Bruce ought to be in pictures too? Quite a man, I heard, once he gets his steam up."

Slim and I needed to have a talk, I realized. Personal remarks like that amounted to insubordination. Firing the woman on the spot ran through my mind. I was about to say something sharp when Asdeck caught my eye, raised a glass and toasted gallantly that all present should bow to proven superiority in the stud-horse department, "because Lieutenant Dan Ewing was voted the number 1 swordsman in the Pacific Theater of Operations."

Hooting, Slim jabbed Bud in the ribs. "Is that why you punched your buddy out last weekend down by the river? He hardly got hold of your belt. Is he too much for you to handle? I was kind of looking forward to seeing you two boys going at each other, really mixing it up! And I was thinking, maybe"— she shrugged delicately and dropped her voice—"if the three of us?"

My buddy looked confused and embarrassed. Firing seemed too good for the bitch now. Only strangulation would do. Once she was dead we'd take the fishing boat out to the Gulf and throw her body to the sharks.

Bud recovered quicker than I did. "Only three?"

Asdeck cocked an eyebrow, Emma Mae nodded happily and Slim barked a brassy laugh. When Tommy bridged from "I've Got a Lovely Bunch of Coconuts" to the romantic ballad "So In Love," people got up to dance. Slim, Emma Mae and the admiral drifted away.

Bud's foot nudged mine. "We don't need no stag films, do we Coach? Shower bath's good enough for us, huh?"

When he increased the pressure, I pushed back.

But I didn't want to start like this again. "I'm not Coach Andy," I said finally. "I'm Dan Ewing. And you're not my little jerk-off buddy."

"Huh?" he answered. And then, "Oh, you mean, we're getting serious about this."

"You're not Mike Rizzo either," I said. "He's dead. We're us two."

"Right. Yes," Bud said as his leg gently pressed against mine. "And it's gonna take a lot of discussion. Fact is, I guess you could say we've already started."

"It's kind of loud here," I said. "For serious talk. You figure we ought to go somewhere else?" My heart pounded. This was it.

Bud turned to me. "Your place"—he was smiling broadly now—"or mine?"

"Upstairs is closer," I said. "And quicker."

. Bud threw me a sideways wink. "You got a radio up there? So we could dance a little...first?"